"I think," Lucien began, ve
we deserve. And unfortu 'e-
serves any."

For twenty-two-year-old Noah, the revelation that his biological father is an ex-professional footballer is like tearing the wrapper from a cheap chocolate bar and discovering he's won the elusive golden ticket. Every homeless young man's dream, right?

Wrong. Because his father has also served a lengthy prison sentence. For murder.

With nothing to lose and facing a winter sleeping rough, Noah travels to France to meet him. Despite an angry encounter, Noah reluctantly agrees to stay at the ancestral home of one of his newfound father's friends until he finds his feet.

Twenty-five-year-old Toby loves his village of Rossingley so much he's never left. Working as a manny caring for the children of the eccentric sixteenth earl is his dream job. Sure, he'd like to travel someday and maybe find a boyfriend, one who doesn't treat him like a doormat. But with his deformity denting his confidence, Toby counts his blessings and takes what he can get. That is, until a sullen, handsome misfit comes to stay, flipping Toby's ordered village life upside down.

TO MEND A

BROKEN WING

ROSSINGLEY, BOOK FOUR

FEARNE HILL

A NineStar Press Publication

www.ninestarpress.com

To Mend a Broken Wing

First Edition, January 2023

ISBN: 978-1-64890-613-8

Also available in eBook, ISBN: 978-1-64890-612-1

CONTENT WARNING:

This book contains sexually explicit content, which may only be suitable for mature readers. Depictions of anti-Francophone language. The POV character lives with complications from a birth defect (phocomelia).

CAST OF CHARACTERS

Dr Lucien Duchamps-Avery, sixteenth earl of Rossingley. A reluctant heir to the Rossingley estate. Likes: nightdresses, pearls, his husband's soft hoodies, and using the word 'gosh' unironically. Has a flirtatious alter-ego: Lady Louisa.

Dr Jay Sorrentino. Hunky doctor and devoted husband to Lucien. Likes: DIY, grey sweatpants, and keeping Lucien happy.

Marcel Giresse. Senior French civil servant and Lucien's nerdy, oldest friend. Never very far from his asthma inhalers. Likes: hot chocolate and completing the crossword puzzle before Lucien.

Guillaume Guilbaud. Married to Marcel. Ex-professional footballer and ex-prisoner. Does not suffer fools. Likes: Marcel.

Freddie Duchamps-Avery. Lucien's favourite cousin. Drop-dead gorgeous catwalk model and all-round cinnamon roll. Likes: everyone.

Reuben Costaud. French head gardener at the Rossingley estate and ex-prisoner. Married to Freddie. Likes: mixing his metaphors and his cat, Obélix.

Gandalf. Mysterious pot-loving gardener and bohemian paramour of Uncle Charlie.

Uncle Charlie. Retired politician and father of Freddie Duchamps-Avery. Now a redeemed ex-pompous fool.

Joe and Lee. Gardeners on the Rossingley estate.

CHAPTER ONE

TOBY

"DARLING, WHICH DO you prefer, Moonlit Navy or Magenta Surge?"

The job description had outlined caring for three children, all under the age of five. The wording had been economical with the truth. By my calculations, there were four. Number four had recently celebrated a milestone birthday and was a smidge sensitive about it.

"The navy's good," I hedged, examining the nail polish

on both of the earl's elegant index fingers, pressed side by side. "It complements your...er...outfit."

He sighed in consternation. "Moonlit Navy is my go-to normally, darling, but I'm concerned it's beginning to complement not only this divine outfit but my knobbly blue veins too. Don't you think?"

During my three years of study at childcare college, none of the modules had offered handy tips on how best to sensitively reassure a gay earl dressed in a sky-blue satin nightdress that he could paint his fingernails navy, magenta, or pink with yellow spots, and no one would notice. For the simple reason that the trillion-carat diamond adorning his ring finger, not to mention the other sparkly rock in his ear, and the string of boulder-like pearls around his neck, kind of drew the eye. And did I mention the nightdress?

"Magenta," came a masterful deep growl, accompanied by two strong arms wrapping themselves loosely around the earl's shoulders from behind. "I like you wearing magenta."

Leaning back into his husband's wonderfully secure hold, my boss tipped his face up to meet Dr Sorrentino's and accepted a tenderly loving kiss on the end of his patrician nose. *Thank God.* The cavalry had arrived. I averted my eyes as they shared a swoony moment.

"Magenta Surge it is, then," the earl declared. His voice took on a throaty, sultry tone.

Never taking his eyes off his husband, he addressed me. "Toby, my darling. I do believe Jay and I will sojourn to the west wing for a while. The light is so much better up there for nail painting, wouldn't you agree?"

As sex euphemisms went, this was typically delicate.

"Absolutely." As if I'd ever dare disagree with my boss on such matters. "I'll listen out for the children."

"Thank you," the earl replied graciously. "You are an absolute treasure."

Tell me something I didn't know. Pushing himself back from the table in a single fluid movement, the earl stood and took Dr Sorrentino's waiting muscular arm. Another swoony kiss; anyone would think they'd been married six minutes, not six years.

"I don't know how we'd cope without you, Toby," he added, giving his husband's arm a squeeze.

You'd have a hell of a lot less sex with the delicious Dr Sorrentino, probably. I pushed that thought aside. *I did not envy my boss. I did not envy my boss.*

I watched them dreamily wander out of the kitchen, already oblivious to my presence. The earl's satin nightdress trailed soundlessly along the floor behind him, and I shook my head, smiling to myself as I cleared away the forgotten pots of nail polish.

My phone pinged—a daily text from my mother, checking all was well in my world. And, as usual, it was, as long as I ignored the teeny fact that my knight in shining armour had missed his cue to take centre stage. Despite that, I shouldn't and wouldn't envy the earl. He might have the delectable Dr Sorrentino carting him off to bed at two o'clock on a Thursday afternoon, but how could I ever be envious of a man with his grim family history?

The tragic deaths of the fifteenth earl and his oldest son and heir eight years ago had cut deep into the soul of Rossingley. I'd been fifteen years old, and the shroud of grief that settled over families like mine was a testament to the Duchamps-Avery stewardship of the village. Rents in Rossingley for local families were low, and the Duchamps-Averys had never succumbed to the lure of greedy property developers. The current earl's money kept the village pub alive, provided the school with much needed extras, funded new church bells as required, and repaired holes in the church roof.

The profound impact of the accident on the current earl didn't bear thinking about. While Rossingley mourned,

Lucien Avery vanished, leaving my Uncle Will, the estate manager, to keep the Avery affairs functioning while the reclusive new earl grieved in private.

Stories sprang up about him, of course, almost overnight. The silliest being that he was a vampire. Or a ghost. That he'd died in the helicopter crash along with everyone else. That his continued existence was a fabrication to prevent his wicked uncle getting his hands on the dosh. That he'd been sighted wearing a flowing white dress, dancing in the moonlight down by the still lake. That he swam in the lake at midnight. That he walked on water. That he spent his days wandering the attic rooms calling for his lost brother. That he was crazed and locked in a basement asylum.

Uncle Will debunked all these myths, and more, but people carried on spouting them anyhow. Why let the truth get in the way of a good story?

Like all gossip, two-thirds were total bullshit, but some held a grain of truth. The earl *did* wander the estate dressed in flowing gowns, albeit with the addition of green wellies. I'd seen him with my own eyes, an almost ethereal, waiflike presence, as I helped Uncle Will refence the north fields during the school holidays. I recall I'd stared and stared at him, fascinated, half expecting him to float away on a strong puff of wind, up to the heavens to join his beloved family. When my uncle noticed my staring, he ordered me to let the poor guy grieve in peace. Joe, who worked in the gardens, reported the new earl spent his days sitting on a bench smoking himself to death. Steve—another gardener, now retired, said he'd been ordered to place fresh flowers on the family graves every single day.

And then, a couple of years later, a ray of light burst through the new earl's grief, lifting the thick bank of clouds. Once again, bright sunshine beat down on the lush green fields of the Rossingley estate. By then I was eighteen and working with Uncle Will every spare moment I wasn't in school, saving for college. A mysterious new car appeared in the big house yard, a flashy red Audi, its owner a burly hunk of masculinity, equipped with brawny arms and a mass of black curly hair.

They were spotted together, the stranger and the earl, holding hands by the lake, kissing against the south wall of the old stone chapel. Reuben, the new gardener, told everyone the stranger was another doctor, that the new earl had found his one true love (Reuben was a French romantic), that the man with the Audi would be staying for good. Seemed he was right because a wedding followed not long afterwards. The village celebrated; I drank far too much free champagne, vomited in the walled garden rose bushes, then snogged Rob Langford, the dairy farmer, for the first time. But that's another story.

I busied myself with preparing the children's supper. Five-year-old twins, Eliza and Arthur, were at their weekly riding lesson with Emily from the village. Orlando, the most scrumptious bundle of fifteen-month-old goodness to ever exist on this planet, would soon be awake from his afternoon nap. Mary, the housekeeper, had finished for the day, and the earl and Dr Sorrentino would be indulging in afternoon delight for at least another hour. Which gave me a rare quiet moment all to myself.

The house phone rang, a number known only by a very few—Dr Sorrentino's family, the earl's family, Uncle Will, the children's school, and the earl's closest friend, Marcel. All other calls were routed through the estate office. The chance of interrupting Dr Sorrentino in whatever pleasures he was currently providing, in order to answer a phone call was roughly as likely as my Prince Charming galloping through the kitchen on one of the children's ponies. So I answered it myself.

"Oh, Lucien, you are never going to believe what's

happened. You should probably pour yourself a glass of something orange and vile and sit yourself down."

The voice sounded breathy, flustered, foreign, and familiar.

"Uh, hello, Marcel. Sorry, it's Toby. The manny."

"Oh, my goodness. Toby! So sorry! Is he around? I called his mobile, but he didn't pick up."

Right. First rule of Rossingley: you do not talk about Rossingley.

"Um...yes; he's...um...somewhere, I believe?"

"Thank goodness. I'm having a teeny-tiny, non-asthma-related crisis, and I'd really appreciate his pearls of wisdom right now. Although, obviously, don't ever tell him I admitted that."

"Obviously."

I'd experienced one of Marcel's non-asthma-related crises the last time he came to stay. It involved a tricky sudoku and the French Minister of the Interior. From his urgent and breathless manner, this one sounded more serious. I checked the time. The earl had been gone less than twenty-five minutes.

"Okay." I stalled, rapidly assessing the situation. "I'll... um...shall I...um...ask him to call you as soon as he's...um...

available?"

Second rule of Rossingley: When Dr Sorrentino eye-fucked his husband in that tone of voice, then tugged him purposefully towards the west wing, it was a brave soul who dared interrupt. Or someone who had been best friends with the earl for yonks, like Marcel.

"Toby, my dear?"

Some of the breathiness left Marcel's tone, replaced with a touch of steel. "Lucien is in bed, isn't he? In the middle of the day, with that ravishing hunk of a husband."

"Um...well, I...possibly?"

"Listen. And this is very important. Go upstairs to the west wing, bang on the bedroom door—loudly—and inform Lucien I need to speak to him. I expect he will decline."

"Um...yes...I, yes, you may be right."

Marcel knew my boss exceedingly well.

"When he does, you have my permission to inform him if he doesn't bring his skinny, oversexed, ridiculous aristocratic self to the telephone at once, Marcel will whisper in Jay's ear a little story about a porcupine cactus, a Cuban waiter, and a silver teaspoon. During *that* memorable trip to...aah...*Morocco.*"

Morocco. Third rule of Rossingley: If ever Marcel

dropped the *M* bomb? Fetch the earl at once.

*

"LUCIEN!" I HAMMERED loudly on the bedroom door. "Bloody hell! Lucien!"

Fourth rule of Rossingley: There were no airs and graces at Rossingley. The sixteenth earl was Lucien, Dr Sorrentino was Jay, and if Marcel threatened the Morocco story, nowhere in the house was off limits.

"Toby! Where's your sense of decorum, darling? A little more delicacy, please; you'll put my husband off his stride."

A low rumbling laugh emanated from behind the thick wooden door, followed by a higher pitched breathy giggle. Lady Louisa had come out to play.

"It's Marcel. On the phone. He says it's important."

Jay let out a heavy groan that I preferred to imagine was in response to my words and not because...

"Is he trying to die again?"

"No. At least, I don't think so."

A low growl of contentment from Jay smothered a soft squeal from Lucien. Childcare college never covered this scenario either. I began listing the contents of the fridge under my breath, steering my brain away from images of Jay naked, stretched out over Lucien, the taut muscles of his tanned upper back rippling gloriously as he nailed his pale, slender husband to the mattress, the two perfect tight buns of his arse...

"Then tell him I'll phone him back. I'm in the middle of something terribly important. These fingernails won't paint themselves, you know."

I inhaled deeply. I'd revisit that satisfied growl and Jay's nakedness later, at my leisure. "Er...Lucien? Marcel sounded quite agitated. He...um...and he mentioned something about a type of prickly plant and a...erm...a north African country?"

A pause, a gasp, and a most unseductive yelp. Then, "Oh gosh, oh gosh. Jay, darling—untie my hands at once. Toby? Pour me a tot of neat Campari. I'll be there in two seconds."

CHAPTER TWO

NOAH

I HATED THE French. Principally because they all spoke fucking French. And not the lumbering phrasebook French we learned at school, but a sneering, bastardised version of it, at three times the speed. My hatred thickened the farther south through France I travelled; it extended to the woman behind the ticket counter at Montparnasse station, closing her shutter at two minutes to one, forcing me to queue all over again at an adjacent counter. It extended to the portly ticket collector, scrutinising my valid ticket as though I'd handed him a fake fifty quid note, as his *train à grande vitesse* crawled at a snail's *vitesse* through countryside far too pretty to belong to this arrogant, snooty nation. And it most certainly extended to the skinny *madame* seated opposite me in the carriage between Montparnasse and Poitiers, angrily flicking each page of the latest copy of Vogue as if I was personally responsible for the *interdit de fumeur* sign above her head.

Discovering I was half-French myself was the fucking icing on the cake. Mind you, for as long as I could remember, anger and hatred of pretty much anything and everything had been my default. I'd recently found out why, which made me angrier than ever.

The whole journey was questionable in the first place. More of a fool's errand than a knight's quest. What I labelled a determinedly headstrong personality, teachers had called reckless and disruptive, all traits contributing to why I would see this damned stupid idea through even if it killed me. To call quits now would be to admit I'd made a huge fucking monumental error.

Maybe I had. But what were the alternatives?

Sofa surfing sounded cool until it no longer became a choice, and then it very quickly became exhausting. Permanent impermanence. My daily reality since my mother had kicked me out. No privacy. Nowhere to keep personal stuff. Being asked to move on at any time. A few nights out on the streets.

I couldn't blame her for showing me the door, not really. Entertaining the fuzz in your front room while neighbours ear-wigged over the fence soon got old. Nicking twenty quid from her wallet and smacking her husband round the chops hadn't helped. Mind you, he'd given me a decent smacking back. I still had the bruises on my jaw to prove it.

She'd spat out the name of my real father after so much goading, and I swear if she'd had a knife in her hand, she'd have used it, then wiped the blood off and never looked back. Because I could be a really fucking annoying tosser when I put my mind to it. She'd spelled his foreign name out carefully, almost triumphantly, which should have been my first clue that I'd have been better off not ever knowing. But right now, me and emotional intelligence weren't on speaking terms. I saw obtaining that name as a huge victory; she saw it as a route to getting me out of her hair for good.

Naturally, I justified my downwards spiral of bad behaviour. To myself and to anyone who cared to listen. Shiny new husband, shiny stepkids, shiny new life; finally, my mother had everything she wanted, and the brown-skinned misfit with the hot temper hanging around from her old life made the place look untidy. She'd done her best with me in the early days, but a quick shag on a moonlit beach at seventeen, followed by an unwanted pregnancy wasn't the healthiest start to familial relations. My mum had been a resentful skint kid bringing up another resentful skint kid, and one with a different coloured skin to all the other kids in our backwater town. And with no man in the house to keep him in line. Not exactly a winning recipe for a mutually fulfilling relationship.

From that miserable hand-to-mouth existence to finding out that my biological father was an ex-professional footballer? Like tearing the wrapper from a cheap chocolate bar and discovering the fucking elusive golden ticket. Even if he was French.

Yep, yours truly was the result of a quick shag on a moonlit beach. Times were different back then, I told myself. So, what if this Frenchman about to receive a surprise visit had enjoyed an ungentlemanly one-night stand twenty-two years ago with a girl barely legal? Instantly forgiven and totally understandable. Everyone knew hot young women practically threw themselves at professional footballers, didn't they? He'd have had to maintain the self-control of a Trappist monk not to succumb from time to time.

My son-he'd-never-known-he-had homecoming would be magnificent. I'd pictured our reunion scene: My dad's house would be a dazzling white villa, somewhere very hot, overlooking miles of sandy beach. An azure sea. A sleek yacht moored nearby. The villa would have a kidney-shaped swimming pool, perhaps two of them, one indoors and one outside, and they'd be those fancy designs that created the illusion of merging with the ocean and the brilliant blue sky. My dad—in my head, he was Idris Elba's double and twice as cool—would be patiently sipping an ice beer in the shade of the pool as if he'd been waiting for me his whole life, a missing piece of his perfect jigsaw. We'd exchange a manly embrace, his eyes brimming with tears of joy; his fit ex-model wife would be crying with happiness, too, because after years and years of praying they'd be blessed with a child, their dreams had finally come true. And so on and so on and bloody so on.

That fucking idiotic fantasy had lasted all of thirty seconds.

Because page two of Google painted an entirely different story. A Pandora's box I'd prised open and now would give anything to slam shut again. As the truth screamed at me from my phone screen, in black and white, the red mist descended.

Hatred and contempt for my mother grew even stronger.

Noah Bennett was the bastard spawn of a murderer.

*

THE TRAIN SPAT me out at La Rochelle station, hungry, grubbily weary, and with a growing realisation that I was bewilderingly out of my depth and running on fumes. Righteous indignation had carried me only so far. As if the journey across miles of his godforsaken country hadn't cost me an arm and a leg already, my murdering French sperm donor had chosen to live on the same bloody island where he'd been incarcerated for fifteen years. Which meant negotiating another bloody bus journey. On no money and insufficient sleep, working out which bus to catch felt like an insurmountable obstacle, so most of my remaining euros were swallowed up by an extortionately priced taxi.

Page two of Google was more than merely a place to hide murderous activity; it had also yielded the ex-convict's current employment—bar manager at Le Coin, an establishment providing moderately priced booze and betting, lying a couple of streets back from the port where he lived. I'd imagined staking him out at the bar (he'd be the one dressed in the orange prison jumpsuit) and then accosting him on his way home. I'd confront him, he'd cower, plead with me not to expose his criminal past, and then I'd probably punch him. Or something like that. To be honest, the details became a little hazy, except for the utter certainty that afterwards, I'd feel better about myself.

But it turned out my task was even easier than I'd imagined, and I'd be confronting him on his own doorstep. The guy brazenly hid in plain sight! *Pages Jaunes,* the French online phone directory, listed numbers for two G. Guilbauds with island addresses. The first number I tried was answered by the whispery, petrified voice of elderly Gisele Guilbaud, who sounded ready to choose her coffin handles. She answered my dreadfully accented "*Guillaume, s'il vous plait*" with a longwinded torrent of French, the word *non* in amongst the mix. So I struck her off my list, which only left the other one. The banality of dialling the second number, then disconnecting sharply as a man's deep voice answered hit me as a terribly anticlimactic ending to such a profound moment of personal discovery.

The taxi driver dropped me off at the pedestrianised entrance to the port. I'd pored over images of this place on Google Maps; reality was smaller, quainter. At eleven at night and outside of holiday season, the cobbled streets were empty and unwelcoming, the cafés and bars shuttered. A cool breeze swirled, setting off a clanking chorus of ropes bashing against masts from rows of fishing boats moored a few feet from where I stood.

I walked past the austere grey house at the far end of the port three times before plucking up the courage to climb wide stone steps leading up to the imposing front door. I don't know what kind of home I expected a murderer to deserve. Probably, I imagined him eking out an existence in a pitiful hovel somewhere, not growing blooms of winter pansies in pretty stone pots either side of a smart entrance.

I blew on my hands, wet with perspiration. The journey had rendered me hot and sweaty, which annoyed me. That I even cared about first impressions in front of this man annoyed me even more. Confronting him in travel-creased clothes, with a coffee stain on my sweatshirt from an unwarranted jolt of the train, set me on the back foot. When I coolly hammered on the door, squared up to him, and looked the bastard in the eye, I wanted to see shock, recognition, and above all, shame. Shame that his son knew his past. Shame that he'd passed on his fucked-up genes, already well on the way to creating another monster. And then I'd say... I had no fucking idea what I'd say after that.

The heavy iron knocker set in the middle of the green-painted wooden door resembled a fist. A metaphor for the violent nature hidden behind it. I lifted it twice, the solid *rap* as it dropped reverberating like gunshot, shattering the quiet of the night. I stepped back a pace onto the step below, putting some distance between me and when the killer answered the door, and then stepped up again when I realised it left me at a significant height disadvantage.

Muffled noises reached me from within the walls of the house. I sucked in a deep breath and rolled back my shoulders. To my right, a chink of light appeared around the edges of the closed window shutters. The outside lamp above my head flickered into life, causing me to flinch. Two dull clunks sounded as bolts were drawn; I clenched my fists as the chunky door was dragged open, my whole body coiled tight.

I'd prepared a whole speech in shit schoolboy French for precisely this moment. Five lines of painstaking words designed to cut right into the blackened soul of the evil bastard I had the misfortune to call my father. After printing it out from Google Translate, I'd memorised it, practiced aloud in front of my mate's bathroom mirror, carried it around with me as I taunted my mother, and hatched plans for my trip. I'd recited it under my breath on the train, over and over, hating the way my tongue stumbled around each unfamiliar vowel and softened consonant, but determined to deliver every drop of venom directly to him when the time came. The moment this man opened his green door to face the son he never knew he had and, after tonight, the son he'd never see again.

As the door pulled wide, my carefully honed script flew off into the night breeze, taking every other measly scrap of French vocabulary stored in my head along with it. My grand rendezvous was not going to plan. A scrawny white man, a little shorter than average, dressed in stripy pyjamas and swamped in a grey towelling robe regarded me. I waited for his polite expression to change to fear.

If he hadn't spoken first, I might still be waiting now.

I towered over him, chest out, chin up, and scowling. A pose adopted by young male thugs the world over. Still no fear. Me, a big brown youth in a scruffy black hoodie and jeans, the kind of guy old ladies crossed the road to avoid, a guy security guards trailed in department stores. If this dude had lived on our housing estate, he would have slammed the door shut and phoned the police quicker than I could accuse him of being a *fucking prejudiced bastard.*

He spoke in a jumble of quick French; I caught a *bonsoir*; the rest was a haze of white noise as my mind reeled and my vision blurred. The strain of the journey, of the months prior to the journey caught up with me. I swayed on the step and held out an arm to steady myself against the cold stone wall. Humiliating hot tears of frustration pricked at my eyes. This was all wrong; where was the bastard who screwed young women on dark beaches and saddled them with a kid like me for the rest of their lives? Where was the violent criminal, the killer, my ugly, evil fucker of a sperm donor?

"You're my father," I blurted crazily, stupidly, and (annoyingly) fucking tearfully.

Even as I sobbed the words, I knew them not to be true. I knew how genes worked; white plus white did not equal brown. But my bastard father lived here! He had to live here! I'd spent six months hunting him down; I'd hung up the phone on him when he'd answered my call; I'd spent every fucking penny I had to travel all the way to this fucking doorstep to finally meet the worthless piece of shit who'd given me this worthless life. And now I was having a nervous breakdown, miles from home, on this bewildered, harmless, little Frenchman's doorstep instead.

"My dear."

I looked up. He had a trace of an accent, although he'd said 'my dear' in perfect English. I was no one's dear, never had been, never would be. But just to confound me, he said it again, his voice soft and breathy as if he'd run up a flight of stairs. His tone was kind too. A caring voice that sounded as if it belonged to the sort of man I'd like to have called my father. Behind his wire-rimmed glasses, something else replaced his polite curiosity. Still not fear, probably because even thuggish-looking brown-skinned men like me weren't very scary with tears running down our cheeks. Shock, maybe?

"My dear," he repeated, a slight tremor to his words. "I'm... I think you've made a mistake. I'm...aah... Let me reassure you in no uncertain terms that I'm not your father. With one hundred per cent clarity and without going into my...um...gender preferences, naturally, but no. Not possible, I'm afraid, even if you and I did bear some passing similarities, which we don't, of course. Far from it, in fact. But do come in."

He paused and hitched his glasses up his nose before giving me a hint of a cautious smile.

He was inviting me in? I was being set up, surely. The guy was insane. No one travelled four hundred miles and turned up on a stranger's doorstep at eleven o'clock at night to be welcomed into the fucking house. He should be slamming the door in my face and phoning the police.

"I think...I think the man you might be looking for is...yes, oh my goodness. Yes, I see it now. Yes. You had better come in. I believe the man you are looking for is my husband. Guillaume."

CHAPTER THREE

TOBY

"DADDY?"

"Yes, poppet?"

Eliza twisted in her seat at the kitchen table, treating Jay to the full baby blues. It wasn't only the china doll looks that made her a chip off the old block, she could turn on Lucien's pervasive charm, too, especially with her lovely, generous daddy. More of a clone than a chip. Lucien's diva-ish behaviour, she tended to save especially for me.

"Why don't fish have eyelashes?"

Sometimes it was hard to believe stuff like that didn't come out of kids' mouths with the specific intention of making adults look stupid. Pausing in chopping Orlando's food into tiny pieces, Jay frowned, trying to both simultaneously come up with a sensible answer and not fall about laughing.

Having worked out a satisfactory reply, he cleared his throat. "Because, my sweet, they are aquatic creatures. Eyelashes are an evolutionary phenomenon designed to prevent harmful particles such as dust and moisture from flowing into the eye. Fish live in water; ergo, eyelashes would be superfluous."

He sat back, clearly pleased he'd come up with an appropriate and plausible response.

Early on in this job, I'd realised Lucien and Jay's parenting style included not talking down to their children. Eliza narrowed her eyes as she absorbed his answer, then quietly resumed her colouring. Jay went back to chopping up pieces of sausage into Orlando-sized mouthfuls.

"Papa says it's because they don't have arms, so they can't apply mascara properly."

I snorted, attempting to disguise it as a cough. Eliza eyed me suspiciously.

"Thanks for your support, Toby," Jay murmured, trying to keep a straight face.

"Fish wouldn't wear mascara anyway," Arthur butted in, coming to Jay's rescue. "Even if they did have eyelashes. It would come off in the water, silly."

Jay threw his dependable wingman a look that said he'd earned himself a second helping of ice cream after supper. Lucien's mini-me threw Arthur a look that said he'd earned himself no pudding at all.

"Duh, Arthur. There is such a thing as *waterproof* mascara!" She tutted disapprovingly. "Gosh, don't boys know anything? Papa let me try his blue one on my eyelashes. And he told me that inner beauty is great, but waterproof mascara is even better."

"It's a shame no one ever passed that little gem of knowledge onto the fish," Jay responded placidly, refusing to meet my eye.

Fortunately, Orlando filled the lull in conversation, which would have otherwise been replete with another snort from me, with a noisy belch, followed by a giggle of appreciation at his own joke. His curly dark head bobbed with delight. My goodness, that toddler was adorable. The image of his darkly handsome father and with a temperament to match.

Papa himself, the fount of all mascara wisdom, blew into the kitchen. "Toby, darling?" He swept up Orlando and his plate of food on his way past and then settled the boy onto his lap.

"You are forgiven for interrupting my, ahem, nail painting earlier." He turned to Jay with a look that could only be described as lascivious. "You and I, however, shall most definitely pick up where we left off. We have some outstanding *buffing*."

He nuzzled the back of Orlando's curly head, inhaling deeply, while Orlando busily smeared ketchup over his sleeve.

"Marcel and Guillaume had a rather interesting visitor last night."

"Was it the tooth fairy?" asked Arthur, desperately waiting for his first tooth to drop out.

"No, my sweet. Marcel doesn't have any teeth because he ate far too many sugary treats as a child—he paints white squares on his gums every morning. It's a very sad situation, and we don't talk about it."

Arthur's little mouth fell open in horror. Somebody was going to scrub their teeth exceedingly thoroughly that evening. Lucien tenderly patted Orlando's face with his bib before continuing.

"It would appear that sometime in the dim and distant past, when he gadded around as a young man about town, dashing Guillaume had a—" He raised his eyebrows in the direction of two very interested five-year-olds. "—an exceedingly brief alfresco frolic with an equally youthful tourist of the double X-chromosome variety, the product of which, more than twenty years later, has presented himself at Marcel's residence."

"They're doing that thing, Arthur," observed Eliza disgustedly in the silence that followed as Jay and I translated and then digested that juicy nugget of information. A disadvantage of never talking down to the children was that holding conversations above their heads was increasingly challenging. "Where they use long words so we don't understand. Come on, let's go to the playroom and make up our own secret language."

They scampered off.

I made a move towards the door. "I'll leave you to discuss it."

"Gosh, no, darling. Stay. We don't keep secrets here. All opinions gratefully received."

Jay sat back in his chair and folded his arms. "Did

Guillaume even know he'd fathered a child?"

"No," answered Lucien. "He and Marcel were utterly gobsmacked. This young man literally turned up out of the blue from nowhere—well, from some godforsaken small town up north, and..."

"What? England north?" I interrupted. "He's English?"

"Yes!" Lucien smoothed down Orlando's wayward curls. "It's extraordinary. This boy claims his mother was on holiday with a gaggle of girls in Ibiza when she was still a teen herself. They met some hunky young French footballers in a bar, and she had a whirlwind romance with one of them. By whirlwind, I mean lasting approximately less than four minutes, and by romance, I mean one episode of unprotected drunken sexual intercourse on a dark beach. Anyhow, they did the deed, both went on their merry way, and six weeks later, she found out she was with child. According to the boy, she hid her pregnancy from everybody for as long as she could. By the time her own mother found out, even if she had wanted to end it, it was too late."

Jay frowned. "How is this man so sure Guillaume is his father? How old is he? And why has he chosen to track him down now?"

"I asked Marcel exactly the same questions. He's twenty-two, apparently. This chap—Noah—had a rocky relationship with his mother and essentially prised the information about his father out of her. One can only assume that at some point early on during his life, she found out Guillaume was in prison and thought it in Noah's best interests not to know."

"That must have been quite the shock for him." Jay nodded thoughtfully.

"I should say so. And for Marcel and Guillaume too. Marcel was in a bit of a state."

I left them to it and went to seek out my twin charges, leaving Orlando to be cossetted by his adoring parents. I'd been living and working at Rossingley since they proudly brought him home, and there was never a dull moment. Folding the children's laundry, I listened to Eliza and Arthur twittering on in the playroom next door. Their new secret language pivoted around Arthur trying to teach Eliza to wink.

How must it feel to track down your father only to discover he had such a dreadful criminal conviction? Maybe it was better that this Noah had grown up not knowing, at least until now, and old enough to come to terms with it. I knew everything about my father and his relatives—we'd been fixtures on the Rossingley estate for six generations. Row upon row of my unexciting ancestors were lined up, side by side, in

Rossingley Church graveyard next door to our house. I could sketch our family tree simply by looking out of my old bedroom window. Noah, I mused to myself. A nice name. I wondered what he was like.

*

TONIGHT WAS MY night off. When Lucien offered me the manny job, I'd moved into a room in the east wing, a fabulously palatial room. I could have chosen to stay with my parents in the village, overnighting at the big house only when required—if Lucien and Jay took an evening or a trip away, for example. But at twenty-five, the time to cut the parental ties was long overdue, even if I had only moved a quarter of a mile away. I'd had my reasons for staying at home as long as I had; one of those reasons, dangling uselessly off the end of my elbow, had stopped me venturing further afield for a long time, including training to be a manny. Thank God I'd finally plucked up the courage because I wouldn't swap my job for the world.

My college friends in Bristol teased me rotten for coming back to work in my home village. We'd been trained to be the best, and while they were gadding off to smart London homes and kids' camps in America, I was back in provincial, homespun Rossingley. As I strolled into the Rossingley Arms, its comforting fug of warm beer and countryside smells wrapping around me, I wouldn't have had it any other way.

The usual pub regulars propped up the bar, blokes who'd spent all day tending livestock, driving tractors, and trimming hedgerows. Every face was familiar to me as I was to them. No one stared, pointed, or whispered behind their hand as I made my way to join them. One could almost describe it as another evening in paradise.

Well, aside from wishing Rob Langford would bugger off and find another village pub to haunt.

I spotted the dairy farmer immediately, drinking his usual pint in his usual spot and surrounded by his usual crew. If he'd seen me come in, as always, he pretended not to notice. I gave a cheery wave to my dad and Uncle Will, sat together in their regular corner, received a nod from Gandalf, quietly supping on his own with *The Guardian* crossword for companionship, and took up a position at the bar next to Lee, one of the Rossingley gardeners. Lizzie, the landlady, gave me a welcoming smile.

"Pint of the usual, Toby?"

She'd cracked the same joke a couple of times a week since I'd been old enough to order a drink, and I swiped my card as she parked a very ordinary gin and tonic at my elbow. Anyone craving boutique flavours, with a hint of rhubarb or a sprig of rosemary, would be trekking into Allenmouth. The Rossingley Arms gin menu restricted itself to a lukewarm shot of Gordon's mixed with generic cheap tonic water, and if I was lucky, Lizzie would slice up a lemon. Sometimes, if she'd had a few bevvies herself, she stuck a paper umbrella in the top, or a glacé cherry, which I fished out when she wasn't looking. Regardless, it was still the best gin and tonic in the world, simply because it was home.

"You all right, Tobes?" asked Lee, without taking his eyes away from Lizzie's ample décolletage. I might not have been the only gay man in the village—not by a long shot these days, but I was frequently the only gay man in the pub. I stole a furtive glance at Rob Langford. The only *out* gay man anyhow.

"Not bad, mate. You?"

"Fair to middling. Can't complain. I took her out for a drink last week."

"Who?"

"Lizzie."

I chuckled. He'd been asking the village's favourite barmaid out since I'd been tall enough to reach the dartboard.

"Finally. Congratulations! Where did you take her?"

He gave me a puzzled look. "What do you mean, where? Here, of course, on her night off. It was bingo night. I won a tenner."

And there it was; Rossingley in a nutshell. Half of the locals thought they needed their passports stamped just to drive to Bristol.

"Um...have you considered, like, taking her out for dinner somewhere? I don't know, like to that nice pub in Chadwick, maybe?"

Lee scoffed as if I'd suggested supper at the Ritz followed by front row seats in Covent Garden. "No. Christ, I want to get inside her kecks, not bloody marry the woman."

"I bet she's just gagging to marry you though."

Sarcasm was lost on Lee. "Too bloody right. She's got a pulse, hasn't she?"

Oh my God, give me strength. Lee's partner in crime, Joe, sauntered over, saving me from further detailed analysis of Lee's love life.

"Tobes, have you had a word yet with his lordship's husband about getting training started for the cricket season?"

"It's only January, Joe. There's no rush."

"You won't be saying that when we're all bowled out after

five overs, and that ugly lot propping up the bar over there are crowing and lifting the trophy. *Again.*"

'That ugly lot' were the young farmers, including Rob, who wasn't ugly at all, but that was beside the point. He and his well-built chums, currently manspreading across about a third of the surface area of the pub, made up the bulk of the village team in the hotly contested annual 'Estate versus Village' cricket match. Not only was Rob handsome, cocky, and boasted the biggest herd of cows on the estate, he was also the village team's number one batsman.

For the last five years, the village team had trounced the estate; even Jay's impressive skills with a bat and ball weren't enough to singlehandedly carry our ragtag team of gardeners and me to victory. Last year, pissed as a newt at the victory party afterwards, one of the young farmers let slip that they'd clubbed together to hire indoor practice nets in Allenmouth throughout the winter. And paid for a fucking batting coach. Cheating bastards. If they were going to play dirty, then this year, we'd play dirtier.

"Tell him it's time to get the practice nets up on the south lawn. I don't care how fucking cold it is. I'm sick of those smug bastards having their names all over that bloody trophy. Steve would be rolling in his grave."

"Steve's not dead. He's over there, drinking his fourth pint of Badgers."

I indicated to the estate's retired head gardener, who had joined my dad and Will.

"I know, I know. But imagine if he was. The disgrace. The shame of it."

Not that any of us were competitive or anything, but unless we did something different, we'd be humiliated yet again this year. We couldn't erect practice nets on the estate cricket pitch, even though technically, Lucien owned it, because it transformed into the village football pitch in the cricket off-season. The last match of the football season didn't take place until Easter, which only gave us a few weeks until the big head-to-head in June.

It took a bloody Frenchman of all people, someone who didn't know his googlies from his silly mid-off, to come up with a cunning plan. Reuben, Rossingley's current head gardener and husband of the earl's devastatingly, stupidly handsome cousin, Freddie, had used his influence to whisper in Jay's ear that we could practice in secret, on the south lawn, hidden from prying eyes. Which would totally trash his immaculate south lawn, but hey, even a Frenchman recognised it was all for a good cause. Fortunately, Lucien gave the plan his seal of approval, as I knew he would. Anyone who doubted *his* competitive spirit must have missed his sharp-elbowed appearance in the kindergarten parents' egg-and-spoon race last summer. That plastic trophy still held pride of place in the back scullery toilet.

"Yeah, I'll remind him," I conceded. "We'll see if we can get practice up and running for the beginning of Feb."

Now all we needed was to find some decent players.

CHAPTER FOUR

NOAH

SO, NOT ONLY was my sperm donor a cold-blooded killer, but he was gay too. Or possibly bi, seeing as he'd so thoughtfully and lovingly impregnated my mother. Seemed like a preponderance for settling arguments with brute force wasn't our only common ground after all.

God knew how he'd finagled his way into this geeky guy's home and bank balance though. Maybe he'd lied; perhaps this naive little man ushering a thug like me into his sitting room had no fucking idea about his husband's past life. Perhaps he'd sold him some cock and bullshit sob story, lonely pyjama man had fallen for it, and he was next in line if he forgot to butter the killer's croissant one morning. I would enjoy ruining sperm donor's cosy little setup when I spilled the beans.

"Guillaume... ah...my husband will be home any minute. He's dropping a friend off after football training. He...ah... manages our little town team."

Football. Good, I was definitely in the right place. The geek—my father's *husband*– hovered over me, repeatedly pushing up his glasses and tightening the belt of his robe as I sat on a prim little upright chair. Every couple of minutes he glanced anxiously at the clock. Having recovered from my little burst of emotion, I moodily studied the floor, gripping my backpack tightly on my lap.

"Can I get you something to drink. Or to eat?" Out of the corner of my eye, I saw him pull something blue out of his pocket and suck on it. An inhaler of some sort.

I shook my head.

At a rattle at the front door, the man jumped as if he'd been electrocuted.

"Thank goodness. He's here."

A deep voice sounded from the hallway, muffled by a clatter of keys being dropped into a bowl. I wiped my sweaty palms down my thighs.

"*Marcel, mon cœur. C'est moi.*"

I'd never met anyone who had deliberately killed another person. Not knowingly anyhow. So I wasn't sure what I expected. A sign that singled him out, maybe Jeffrey Dahmer-style thick-lensed glasses at the very least, a shifty stance, a greasy comb-over, his prisoner number tattooed up his neck. I didn't fucking know.

But not this. Not this cheerful, handsome man with skin the same hue as mine, dressed in a navy Adidas tracksuit. His close-cropped black hair, also the same as mine, was damp from a recent shower.

"*Marcel, j'ai...*"

Marcel—I now knew his name—had been mostly silent as we'd waited, his composure contained despite his nervousness, aside from more and more frequent puffs on his inhaler. With sperm donor's arrival, however, the floodgates burst open. He practically flew to his husband's side, clutched his arm, and began jabbering to him in incomprehensible French, growing increasingly short of breath. I watched the drama play out.

Colour drained from the killer's face. With barely a glance in my direction, he curved an arm around Marcel's skinny waist, protectively tugging him closer. Only with his husband safely tucked into his side did the killer deign to give me his attention; two dark eyes bored steadily into mine, radiating cold, calm fury. For the first time since I knocked on the door, I felt a flash of fear and got up from the chair, gripping my bag in front of me like a shield. He didn't need thick-lensed glasses or any other kind of prop to show me what he was capable of; his expression said it all. This man might not have had the demeanour of a murderer when he strolled into his own living room, but Christ, he stared at me now as if he wanted to rip my soul to shreds and, if I gave him a hint of provocation, was perfectly capable of doing so.

A pulse throbbed loudly in my ear as my body subconsciously kicked into fight-or-flight mode. Cold fingers of sweat dripped down my spine, my travel-bloated guts curdling like I might puke, or worse. As Marcel's stream of incomprehensible words petered out in a fit of wheezy coughing, the killer's attention switched from me back to his husband, instantly relegating my shocking presence to second place.

"Do not move."

I froze, rooted to the spot. His French accent was much

thicker than Marcel's, and he gave the order with a menacing harshness brooking no resistance from me. Then, in a softer tone, as if a different person spoke, he murmured soothing words in French to Marcel as he guided him to the sofa. As Marcel took some more puffs of his inhaler, gradually regaining control of his breathing, the killer rubbed slow circles on his back and kept up a stream of gently spoken French, almost as if he'd forgotten a young man claiming to be his son stood not four feet away from them. After a few minutes, when he deemed Marcel recovered enough, he addressed me once more.

"You. Come with me."

I trailed after him, excruciatingly aware that of all the scenarios I'd spun in my head, most of them circled around me having a starring role. My father pleading my forgiveness for having taken a man's life. Begging me to hear his confession. Not a single one had me meekly obeying his simply barked orders and quaking in fear. Somewhere in the soup of my confused, angry, fucked-up mind, I'd conveniently overlooked the fact that this man had not only killed another person in cold blood, but then spent fifteen years in an environment crammed with other brutes like him. And I expected *him* to be scared of *me*? In comparison, I was about as intimidating as a newborn kitten.

We reached the kitchen, where he rounded on me with such speed I stumbled back into the closed door, gasping in shock. Up close, his narrowed eyes shone darkly. He stood fractionally taller, with an older man's broader heft as he thrust his face into mine.

"You." A firm hand gripped my sweatshirt, tightly twisting the fabric, yanking me closer so our noses were almost touching. The bitter coffee smell on his breath triggered another wave of nausea. "You see that man in there?"

I gave a desperate nod.

"Good. His name is Marcel."

His eyes travelled slowly down my face and up again as if memorising my features. "I'm going to tell you something very important about him, and you are never going to forget it."

He'd got that right. Tonight would forever be imprinted on my brain, every last tiny detail of it. He twisted my sweatshirt a little tighter, just to make certain.

"That man—Marcel—is more precious to me than anybody else who has ever roamed this earth. Do you understand?"

His hot breath burned my cheek. I nodded vigorously.

"Say it."

I nodded again. "Yes."

"Yes? Good. Keep away from him, you piece of shit."

He let me go with a shove and stepped back, crossing his arms across his chest. "If you are who you say you are, then we will talk, and I will welcome you into our home. But if you ever, ever, *ever* pull a stunt like that again, and upset Marcel, then I will hunt you down. And trust me, you will wish you had never been born at all."

*

I SAT AT the kitchen table while, like a switch had been flicked, the killer tenderly fussed around Marcel. As far as I could tell, he was gently encouraging him to go upstairs to bed. Was that so no one would witness what he planned on doing to me? Before he left the kitchen, he handed me a beer from the fridge, so perhaps not. I thirstily sucked it down, hardly tasting it, but appreciating the faint zing of the alcohol as it hit my bloodstream. I couldn't work the man out. He cared for his husband like he was made of bone china, totally debunking my assumption he'd somehow conned his way into Marcel's life. No one could fake tenderness like that, and it swam in both directions between them; Marcel had sunk his head onto the killer's shoulder and let his exhausted frame droop as if he did it every night.

"Tell me your name. Tell me your mother's name."

The killer had silently re-entered the kitchen, or I may have briefly dozed. Adrenaline hadn't so much as leeched from me, more like flooded out across the floor. He calmly took the chair opposite, toying with a beer of his own, waiting for me to speak.

"Noah. Noah Bennett. My mother is Sally Bennett. You had sex with her, twenty-two years ago. On a beach in Ibiza. She was seventeen."

"If you say so." He took a long drag of his drink in noisy gulps before belching softly behind his hand. "I had sex with a lot of women back then."

I bit back a retort. Now wasn't the time to debate whether seventeen was a woman or a girl. If the guy felt any contrition at all, he hid it well.

"So, *Noah Bennett.*" He drew out my name in a low growl as if teaching his tongue the foreign vowels. "What now?"

Aggressive one minute, tender with Marcel the next. Suave. And in complete control. I couldn't work him out; he confounded my every expectation. Off balance and so fucking weary, I suddenly felt very young and foolish and a long fucking way from home.

I shrugged. "Dunno, really."

I studied the top of the pine table while the sperm donor studied me, feeling as if I'd been dragged in front of the headmaster. Or, I thought with a flash of irritation, as if I was the criminal and he'd caught me red-handed.

"Do you have somewhere to stay, *Noah?* Money?"

Miserably, I shrugged again. "Not really."

"Not really? Or no?"

"No," I answered defiantly.

"Did you have a plan at least, for once you'd tracked me down? Not really, or no?"

He'd already guessed the answer. "No."

Just like that, in three or four sentences, he'd sliced me apart. I shifted uncomfortably as he sighed, shaking his head. He took another leisurely swig of his beer.

"That bruise." He indicated towards the fading yellow smudge on my jaw. "Been in a fight?"

I nodded. "Yeah. My mum's husband."

A touch of anger flared in his dark eyes, then vanished.

"I punched him first."

He brought the beer bottle to his lips once more. The skin covering his hand was a light brown colour, like mine. A strong, capable hand, but clean and soft, with neat short nails. A hand that might belong to a teacher, a dentist, or an office worker. Not a strangler.

"Where are you staying tonight?"

"Dunno."

He laughed softly, shaking his head. "A well-planned trip, *non*? There's a five-star hotel across the port. Four hundred euros a night. They'll have rooms at this time of year. You could stay there."

The bastard was mocking me. Perhaps the loving shit in front of his husband was just an act, after all. Anyone else giving me that crap, I'd have socked them one with my left fist and told them exactly where to get off.

Having finished his drink, he clasped his hands together across the table. "Do you do drugs?"

A bit late to start caring now. "What fucking business is it of yours?"

He sighed, exhaling loudly through his nostrils. "Just answer the fucking question."

"No. I don't."

"Do you smoke?"

"Sometimes, yeah."

"Not while you're within one hundred kilometres of

Marcel, you don't."

He leaned back, folding his arms, and coolly appraising me. "Okay. Listen, Noah. By the look of things, you've had a long day. You're not the only one. And you and I have a few things to discuss, but not at this time of night. There's a bed for you in the spare room if you want it."

His voice hardened. "I can trust you won't take advantage of our hospitality, *non*?"

*

FOR A GUY in turmoil, I managed to sleep an impressive ten hours straight. At my mum's house, thin curtains and the swelling hum of early morning traffic woke me as reliably as any alarm clock. On my mate Gary's lumpy sofa, sleep had been a luxury snatched between his late-night coke deals and his missus's early factory shift. Whereas here, in this tall grey house, the bedroom window was shuttered, rendering the room pitch black despite the brightness of the day. Outside, seagulls enthusiastically gossiped with one another; muted foreign voices wafted upstairs from the living room below. Compared to anything I'd ever slept in before, the double bed was hella comfortable.

I found a clean, prettily tiled bathroom and did the

necessary, swapping yesterday's grubby clothes for my other, less grubby set. My stomach growled as my sulky reflection stared back at me in the handsome mirror above the sink. *What the fuck was I doing here?* The killer had asked me as much last night. Unfortunately, a refreshing night's rest hadn't provided the answer. In the front of my wallet lodged a return train ticket, taking me as far as Paris. If I could scrounge any food lying about downstairs, I'd have enough euros left to see me back on English soil. I would hitch home after that. I doubt I could hitch off the island; I'd ask someone if there was a bus.

I encountered Marcel seated at the huge desk in the living room, still dressed in the same pair of rumpled pyjamas despite the lateness of the morning. He appeared to be working; two computer screens were open, and a stack of papers vied for space next to a vase of freshly cut flowers I hadn't recalled being there the previous night.

"Good morning." He paused from his work, pen in hand.

His warm smile seemed genuine, and hovering uncertainly at the bottom of the stairs, I gave him a quick nod. Guillaume's fierce warning to stay away from him echoed in my head. Marcel's eyes darted to my cheap sports bag, repacked and ready to go.

"You must be hungry. There's bread and butter in the kitchen. And cereal in the cupboard next to the fridge, if you prefer. Help yourself—you'll find tea and coffee too."

"Where is he?" I asked.

"Guillaume? Oh, he's just popped to the bar to open up and to make sure everything is okay. Then he's waiting on a delivery. He should be back soon. He's looking forward to talking to you properly."

That sounded ominous, although Marcel spoke kindly. I felt caught between hunger and wanting to make a bolt for the door before my sperm donor returned. My head couldn't decide whether missing him this morning was a blessing or a disappointment.

"I can't wait that long." *I didn't want to wait that long.*

"Please stay until he comes back," urged Marcel. He gestured towards the kitchen. "Stay and eat something. You can't make sensible decisions on an empty stomach. Guillaume doesn't bite."

Swerving to the flowers, his gaze settled once more on me. "He...he really doesn't. He's not what he seems. You... aah...caught him unawares last night. Both of us, actually. So, if nothing else, have some breakfast. You must be starving."

I didn't have long to wait, but long enough to hungrily wolf down some bread and drink my coffee. This man—the killer—seemed less threatening in the cold light of day. As he pecked Marcel on the cheek, I could almost believe him the kind of guy who bought flowers for his lover. Or maybe I'd simply pulled myself into a better frame of mind after a good night's rest. He took his time making himself a coffee and then carried a hot chocolate to Marcel before rejoining me in the kitchen.

"Start at the beginning, Noah," he said simply. "Tell me what you think you know about me."

"I know you strangled a man."

Again, my eyes were drawn to his hands, innocuously cradling a steaming mug of coffee. Hands that had once wrapped around another person's neck.

"I did. Your information is correct." He took a placid sip.

"You fucked my mum, a random tourist. You didn't even know her name, let alone her age."

Another sip. "Guilty of that too."

I waited to see what he would add to either or both bald statements. Nothing apparently. In his homey kitchen, with the birds singing outside and his kind husband happily working in the room next door, the killer savoured his expensive ground coffee like a man untroubled by self-doubt or a shameful past.

"Do you regret it?"

He frowned slightly. "What? Fucking a pretty foreigner when I was pissed?" He paused as if actually considering the question. "Can't remember doing it. But regret?" He shook his head and shrugged in the careless manner favoured by European men, whether contemplating having another cigarette or unprotected sex with a naïve tourist. "*Non, absolument pas.* No regrets. Not now."

I'd never wanted to hit anyone in my life as much as I wanted to hit him then. If I hadn't known his past, what he was capable of, and had a glimpse of it last night when he shoved me up against the door, I wouldn't have hesitated. Every waking minute since I'd known of his existence had fed a bitter rage, a greedy cancer swollen inside me, poisoning my mind so I could focus on nothing but my furious desire to confront this man. Demand answers, remorse, explanations. Demand an understanding of who I was and who I was fearful I'd become.

Seemed none of those answers lay within him. Instead, he gave me polite, simply worded responses as if I were clarifying the details of background checks before approving him for car insurance or something equally mundane.

We might have sat in silence across from each other for minutes or hours. Trapped in my head, I had no idea. All I knew was that when his low-accented voice spoke again, rich and warm, my cheeks were wet with tears.

"Tell me what you want from me, Noah," he said softly. "Anything at all. And I'll do my best to give it."

I wanted him to roll the clocks back twenty-two years. I wanted my mum to have had a whirlwind holiday romance with a handsome young Frenchman. A real romance, not a quick drunken shag. For him to have tracked her down in England, like he would have done if we were characters from a film or a novel. To have had a baby with him—married him maybe. Grown older with him, worked out together how to be responsible, loving parents. Be cherished by him, to cherish him in return.

I wanted to not be fucking crying in front of him now.

Angrily, I wiped my eyes. We didn't always get what we wanted. I'd learned that lesson many times over the years. Especially around Christmastime and birthdays. And the pictures I'd painted in my head of how it was supposed to be? The white villa, the blazing sunshine? The fucking proud father with his arms opened wide? A fucking pipe dream. One

I needed to wake up from, and fast.

"I want you to get me back to England."

CHAPTER FIVE

TOBY

"OOH, THAT'S A...um...a pretty picture, Eliza."

I squinted at the headache-inducing abstract of purple and blue blobs pinned to the fridge. *What the fuck was it?* As far as five-year-olds went, she was a reliably decent artist, inasmuch as she mostly coloured inside the edges, and I could generally decipher what she'd set out to accomplish. If he hadn't gone for a trip to the play park with his daddy, I would have assumed it was one of baby Orlando's finger-painting creations or even something Arthur had hashed together on a bad day. I pointed to a phallic blue splodge.

"Erm...this part. What...what..?"

"Oh my gosh, Toby!" Eliza harrumphed, demonstrating an impressive degree of indignation for such a small child. "I can't believe you thought *I* had produced that rubbish!"

Swivelling in her chair, she eyed the monstrosity with distaste. "It's supposed to be the view of the lake from the house." She rolled her eyes dramatically. "Papa painted it. He was very pleased when he'd finished. So I thought I had better let him stick it on the fridge to show daddy. I'll take it off tomorrow when he's not looking."

I bit down hard on my lip. "And where is our resident Picasso?"

She threw me a withering look. "Don't be silly! The Picasso at the London house is much better than that, Toby."

Because that was the kind of conversation that passed for normal around here.

"Papa's on the phone. *Again.* Talking to Uncle Marcel. Toby, what's a paternity test?"

Aah. They were still having *that* discussion. Having arrived at Marcel's house in the dead of night, declaring himself Guillaume's long-lost offspring, this man—Noah—was still staying with them three days later. Apparently skint, he had nowhere else to go, having fallen out with his mother, with whom he had been living on and off in England. Trust Marcel to welcome someone in with that ridiculous sob story. Although I'd bet a pound to a penny Lucien would have done exactly the same.

"A paternity test is a test to see whether someone really belongs to the person they say they belong to. For instance, if you took a paternity test, it would show that you belonged to Papa."

"How do they do the test?" She screwed her face up into a little frown. "Do they ask you lots of questions, like a sort of spelling test?"

"Mmm, no. I don't think so. More that they test a little bit of your hair or your blood in a laboratory to see if it is the same as your papa's."

"My blood is the same as Papa's," she declared with a degree of satisfaction. "I saw it when he cut his finger once. It's exactly the same. And my eyes are the same, and my hair is definitely the same." She pulled a face. "Not his willy though."

"No," I agreed, stifling a laugh. "Not his willy."

"Orlando has black hair and brown eyes, like Daddy," she added thoughtfully. "Not like me and Arthur and Papa. But Orlando and Daddy still belong to us, don't they?"

I gave her a fond smile. Out of the mouths of babes. If only the rest of the world viewed families like theirs with such simple clarity.

"They certainly do, poppet. You all belong to one another, which makes you a very lucky girl. Let's get your school shoes on—it's nearly time to go. Surely Arthur has finished brushing his teeth by now."

"Gosh, that man can talk," announced Lucien as he breezed into the kitchen. A smudge of blue paint adorned his cheek; I decided it could stay there for a while. Last week he'd spent an entire day at work with a plastic Peppa Pig earring dangling from his right ear, which I can't imagine fit his scary Dr Avery persona at all.

"Honestly, Toby. Marcel has been bending my ear for nearly an hour. My jaw aches from rabbiting on for so long."

He massaged below his temple, rolling his jaw from side to side to ease the strain, then smiled mischievously. "I'll have to ask Jay to rub some of his special cream into it tonight to make it better."

I shook my head, chuckling silently. Eliza's papa was a

very naughty boy. I busied myself with the twin's breakfast leftovers while Lucien helped his daughter collect up her school things. Arthur was all ready to go and waiting in the hallway.

"Anyhow, darling," Lucien added, addressing me. "Long story short, they're coming to stay and maybe leaving the boy here for a while. He's still looking at poor Guillaume as if Guillaume's about to pull a knife and stab him. He'll hardly speak to him. And Marcel has work piling up. There aren't any jobs on the island at this time of year for this Noah chap, but it sounds like he's burned his bridges with his mother, and he doesn't speak a word of French. Marcel's worried he's going to vanish into the night, without any money, and end up on the streets. It sounds as if the poor man is very muddled and feeling very low."

He picked up the car keys and gave me a quick grin. "So Marcel is going to bring him to Rossingley, where he'll have to scroll past the likes of us before he reaches total rock bottom, won't he?"

People who didn't know him could say what they chose about Lucien Avery. And plenty did. That he was eccentric, reclusive, pernickety, sometimes downright awkward. They seldom mentioned beautiful, although he was that as well, especially now, gathering his beloved children up for the school run, pale eyes glittering with happiness and a piratical slash of blue across his chiselled cheekbone. But what really made him beautiful, what naysayers didn't see because he kept it a closely wrapped secret, was his heart of pure gold, more precious and beautiful than any of the bloody enormous pearls around his neck.

*

JAY, ON THE other hand, like his cute baby son, was an extremely straightforward sort of chap. With the twins at school and Lucien at work, a still calm settled over the house. After tidying the children's rooms and clutching his favourite toy tractor, Orlando and I tracked Jay down to the library, where he was busy replacing a piece of skirting board, whistling quietly to himself as he toiled. God knew they had the money and the maintenance staff to do these things, but some jobs Jay kept for himself. For pleasure and relaxation, apparently.

"We need to talk about the cricket," I began. "Lee and Joe collared me in the pub a few nights ago. Last year's team are revolting."

He grinned. "They've always been revolting."

"Allegedly, the young farmers have already had a few

training sessions in Allenmouth. We're going to be anni-hilated this summer if we don't get our act together soon."

"Don't worry, I'm already on it," Jay reassured. "I've told Reuben we're happy for the gardeners to erect the practice nets on the south lawn this weekend. Why don't you start a WhatsApp group today, and we'll have our first training session next Monday night? Then every Monday after that, weather permitting. Reuben's got the gardeners rigging up flood lights too."

Winter outdoor cricket. Yay! Not a prospect I relished, and I doubted anyone else would either. But needs must—anything to wipe the smile off those smug young farmers' faces. Off one face in particular.

On my seventeenth birthday, I came out to my family. With very little fanfare. I was the eldest of six kids which made for a chaotic household; very little shocked or surprised my parents these days. My mother's response to my momentous revelation was to hug me to her chest while simultaneously stirring a giant vat of chili. After planting a sloppy kiss on my cheek, she advised me to always carry a condom in my wallet. Not embarrassing at all when I'd never even experienced my first man-on-man kiss. My dad's response was a muttered, "There must be something in the water around these parts."

The gentle cuff around the ear that followed signalled "I love you" as clearly as if he'd written the words on a banner and hung it outside the front of our house. My next oldest brother, Ollie, just said, "Yeah, I know, dude, I've listened to your Spotify playlists."

And that was that. Apparently, straight guys don't download Lady Gaga.

"Who are our top eleven players for the team, then?" I whipped out my phone and tapped a few buttons. "I've marked you down as the captain, by the way."

Jay put his tools aside so Orlando could climb all over him. "Freddie, of course, but he needs to have the match date early in his diary. And put him in charge of kit, as usual. Add Reuben to the list, too, if only to get Freddie there on time."

I inputted their names underneath mine and Jay's. We might never be a trophy-winning amateur cricket team, but we guaranteed we'd always be the best dressed. And possibly the gayest. The first time Reuben donned a cricket sweater (cashmere Ralph Lauren, courtesy of Freddie), he'd spent most of the game repairing indentations in the pitch with his bat and tutting loudly every time anyone created a new divot. He'd had some intensive one-on-one tuition from Freddie since; suffice to say he'd been comprehensively bowled from the pavilion end on numerous occasions.

Seeing as we were on the subject of the dubious cricketing skills of the Duchamps-Averys, I might as well get it over and done with. I took a deep breath. "And...erm...what about Lucien?"

Jay and I exchanged knowing looks. Thank God, no words required. It spoke volumes that a guy with an obvious handicap like mine made it onto the team sheet ahead of Lucien. The sixteenth earl had many talents, none of them of the sporting variety.

"Yes, well...we'll need someone to keep an eye on the children, won't we?" Jay eventually offered diplomatically.

"Absolutely, couldn't agree more." I nodded with enthusiasm. "I mean, your perfectly able parents and sister really won't be able to manage all three on their own for an afternoon. No, not at all."

"We'll promise him he's first reserve. That should keep him happy. And then pray nobody gets injured."

I hurried on before he changed his mind. "I've added the gardeners, Joe and Lee, obviously. Although they're viewing it more as gang warfare than a village cricket match."

Jay chuckled and blew a raspberry on Orlando's scrumptious fat cheek, making him squeal with delight. "Your

Uncle Will has already volunteered. And your dad."

That made eight. "Gandalf and Lucien's Uncle Charlie will both be umpiring again, so we can't pinch them."

"How about we drag Steve out of retirement?" Jay suggested. "He'll bring us up to nine players. He's quite handy if we keep him away from the pub beforehand."

We hummed and hawed a while. Two more players needed, otherwise we'd be going cap in hand to the young farmers and asking them to donate someone. Last year, they'd smugly offered us a choice between a kid still in primary school and a guy who'd undergone hip replacement surgery a week earlier.

"We've forgotten Guillaume," Jay said with a flash of inspiration. "We'll ask him. They'll be over here from France, anyway, because Lucien usually strongarms Marcel to do the scoring. And I reckon Guillaume can turn his hand to any sport. He'll be fine with a cricket bat once we teach him the basics."

Which left us a player short. Once more, we gave one another a meaningful look.

"I suppose if we can't find anyone, then I could always ask you-know-who," Jay began carefully.

I pulled a sympathetic face. Once upon a time, although

it was hard to ever imagine now, Dr Jay Sorrentino had been engaged to a very nice person of the female variety, who herself was now happily married and expecting her second child. Following a mysterious homosexual epiphany, the details of which were a closely guarded secret, Jay had broken off the engagement a week before he was due to walk down the aisle. Unsurprisingly, this went down extremely badly with quite a number of people, and especially with his best friend at the time, a.k.a Evan, his putative best man. From thereon, Lucien had forever referred to Evan, with not a small degree of malice, as Second-Best Man. Being a genial soul, Second-Best Man had mended the bridge with Jay; Lucien, however, had never quite forgiven him.

"Evan's *such a* good player," Jay added. "So good. He was a county junior. He could make all the difference."

Was it worth starting World War Three over though?

"I suppose if there is the tiniest hint we may have to resort to asking him, it might spur Lucien on to find a more suitable eleventh man."

Jay chuckled. "Knowing Lucien, if I threaten him with the prospect of Second-Best Man, he'll hire Kevin Pietersen for the afternoon."

After agreeing to task Lucien with drumming up an

eleventh man, Orlando and I left Jay in peace and headed out for our regular afternoon walk in the crisp, wintry sunshine. Of all the routes through the estate, Orlando's favourites were the ones past the stables and the cows. Petting the twins' ponies and then mooing at cows tired him out, and it wasn't long before he was back in the pushchair, wrapped up like the Michelin man, and fast asleep. Once the twins returned from school, there wouldn't be any quiet until bedtime, so I took my time dawdling home, letting him snooze.

As I cut through the private lane heading back towards the dower house, home to Freddie and Reuben, a Land Rover pulled up beside me. I didn't need to turn to guess the driver. Bloody Rob Langford. He rolled the window down.

"Hey, Toby. This is a happy coincidence. I was just thinking about you, and here you are."

There was nothing coincidental about it; we both knew that. I took Orlando for a stroll every afternoon before the school run, and Rob knew the layout of the estate like the back of his hand. We all did. I wasn't so hard to track down.

"I'm busy." I increased my stride purposefully. "Don't you have cows to milk or something?"

"Not for another couple of hours, no."

He let me walk ahead then pulled the Land Rover in

behind and killed the engine. The door slammed, and he jogged to catch me up.

"Too busy to stop and talk to me?" He peered into the pushchair where Orlando snoozed blissfully, the tip of his button nose red and shiny from the chilled air. "Orlando won't mind."

With a scowl, I prepared to tell him to bugger off, then made the schoolboy error of looking up at Rob Langford's fucking lovely face.

Rob Langford was not gay. *Allegedly.* Not even bisexual. Absolutely not, who would ever think such a thing? After all, a different dollybird hung off his arm practically every time he set foot inside the Rossingley Arms. None of them lasted very long, but as Lee pointed out, why would they when he could have his pick of the bunch?

I wasn't aware that anyone except me knew Rob's little secret. No witnesses saw him kissing me behind the marquee at the earl's wedding all those years ago. Still wet behind the ears, I'd thought this rugged young farmer, with his mop of blond curls and brawny shoulders, was all my Christmases come at once. A week later, no one saw him push my head down behind one of the potting sheds, his strong hands holding me in place until I gagged on his hot spunk shooting down my throat. That wasn't to say I hadn't been willing; I'd wanted it as much as he had— on that day and on all the furtive occasions afterwards.

I could have stopped it. I *should* have stopped it. Because when he wasn't slamming me up against dark walls in the dead of night or snatching hand jobs across the front seat of the Land Rover parked in the estate's fallow east fields, far from curious eyes, Rob Langford blanked me. He'd lean on the bar with his cocky gang of heterosexual friends, hoovering down his manly pints, laughing uproariously at shitty misogynistic, heterosexual banter, and fucking blank me.

It was natural that we knew each other, of course. Everyone knew everyone else in Rossingley. We occasionally found ourselves at the same gatherings—the earl's Christmas drinks party, for example; the annual cricket match; the village fete; the Christmas carol service. Or side by side at the fucking urinals in the pub. In front of an audience, he'd throw me a friendly hello, clap me on the back, ask how life up at the big house suited me, then send his regards to my parents. But he didn't ever *talk* to me. Not really. He didn't show a real interest, he didn't want to get to know me.

Because he most definitely, 100 per cent, was not gay. Except for when he was. Like now, as Orlando slept, and we were alone. And when his blue-grey eyes, shining all the colours of a stormy sea, caught mine and held until I was forced to tear my gaze away.

"Quiet around here at this time of day, isn't it?" he began pleasantly. It always began pleasantly. "Not bumped into anyone except you and Orlando."

His arm brushed against mine as he walked alongside. "I've missed you, you know."

Whatever. The damned annoying thing was I'd missed him too. I'd deliberately avoided him, convinced myself I'd never let him do this to me again, what he was doing now. That his words and promises were hollow. That he could take his secret predilection for men with him to the grave for all I cared. That I was a convenient gay man for him and nothing else.

But all that was much easier to believe when he wasn't loping along next to me, radiating warmth and health and fucking pheromones. I attempted to play it cool.

"You know where I live. I guess you know how to use a phone too. And you could do something really radical like say hello and stand next to me in the pub. Or are you scared everyone will think, I don't know, that you have a thing for fellas?"

"If I did that, I wouldn't be able to keep my hands off you. I'd be ravishing you up against the dartboard."

His words were light, teasing. And even though we both recognised them for the fucking old baloney they were, they still managed to push my hidden masochistic buttons. The odds were higher on finding life on Mars than Rob Langford outing himself in the Rossingley Arms.

"As I said," he continued, that arm nudging against mine again. "There's no one about. I didn't see a single soul as I drove down the lane."

He stopped, and like an idiot, I stopped too. He lifted up my chin, holding it firmly. Possessively. Those fucking eyes, today matching the blue of the clear afternoon sky, gazed mockingly into mine, and I swore to myself this time would be the last.

"Just a kiss, sweetheart." He trailed his other hand across my hip.

"I'm working, Rob."

"Orlando's asleep," he countered.

We kissed, silently and hurriedly, up against a cold damp tree trunk, me with my good hand tightly gripping Orlando's pushchair and my precious sleeping charge facing away from us so he wouldn't see if he woke. Our lips were cold, too,

Rob's chapped from all the time he spent outdoors. The scruff on his chin—dairy farmers shaved early in the day—scratched a path across my jaw, following a route down to the join of my shoulder and neck. Our breath puffed out between us, and as his coarse hand slipped between my thighs, he let out a deep moan. I pushed his hand away.

"No. Not with Orlando here."

Obeying for once, he pulled back. "You won't mind if I do, then, will you?"

I heard the zip of his trousers opening, his hiss of relief as he took out his dick and began bringing himself off. His tongue fucked my mouth in time to his hand pumping his dick. God, I knew exactly how good that big, callused hand felt wrapped around a hot shaft. I hated that I was here, so weakly giving in to him again. Guilt that this was happening with Orlando in my care flooded through me, and I screwed my eyes up tight, willing him to get it done as quickly as possible so I could take us both far away from him.

He came with a low grunt of satisfaction, the result spattering the dirt at our feet, and it was over as quickly as it had begun. As he stepped back, tucking himself in, I began marching away from him.

"Soon, Toby," he called, sounding out of breath. "Soon.

I promise."

Yeah, yeah. When hell froze over.

CHAPTER SIX

NOAH

"YOU SHOULDN'T TRUST me like this. Give me a few euros, and I'll go now. I'll pay you back when I've got some money."

Day three. The killer had left for work, and Marcel sat tapping keys at his computer, the plasticky irregular clicking setting my teeth on edge. I didn't think I could stand another minute in this silent, claustrophobic house. I didn't belong here; Marcel knew it, my sperm donor knew it, and I knew it the first morning I'd woken in that strange bedroom. Trouble was, I didn't belong anywhere. So why was Marcel so hell bent on trying to make me stay?

Marcel laughed. "It's funny. Your father said exactly the same to me when I suggested he come and live in the annexe as my lodger. That I shouldn't trust him. We hardly knew each other; he'd just been released from prison and didn't know which way was up."

I threw him a disbelieving look. The sperm donor behaved as if he'd been born with an answer for everything. He'd never experienced a second of self-doubt in his life.

Marcel waved me away. "It's true. You and he have more in common than you think; you just haven't realised it yet."

I tightened my fists at my sides. "Don't lump me in with him. I haven't murdered anyone."

"No, my dear." Marcel let out a long sigh. "You're right. You haven't done that."

"But you shouldn't have trusted him then, and you shouldn't trust me now. How do you know I'm not going to steal your wallet? How do you know I'm not going to pull out a knife? For that matter, how did you know he wasn't going to kill you?"

"I didn't," Marcel answered simply. "I trusted my

instincts and took a chance on him. It was the best decision I've ever made in my life. Just like I'm going to trust you. And if you were planning to steal my wallet, you would have done it by now. It's been lying on the kitchen table for three days."

"I might still do." Pointless posturing, and we both knew it. Even I wasn't that stupid. I'd done some idiotic things in my time but stealing a wallet belonging to the spouse of a convicted killer wasn't going to be one of them. "You don't know the first thing about me and what I'm capable of doing."

Marcel swivelled around in his chair, facing me full on. He'd dressed today in a hotchpotch of garments—ancient baggy beige cords, a striped shirt buttoned up incorrectly, and a cleanish oversized knitted cardigan. He could easily be mistaken for a tramp. Begrudgingly, I realised I quite liked him.

"Forgive me, my dear, but I beg to disagree." He crossed off his fingers as he spoke. "I know your name and your age. I know that you are who you say you are on your passport because I have ways of finding out these things. I actually have your mother's home address, too, but you can rest assured I won't contact her. I know you've mostly lived with her, but occasionally spent a few months at your grandmother's, particularly when you were a difficult younger teen and your mother remarried. I also know you spent a short period in social care before your grandmother took you on. I know you have a juvenile criminal record. Petty stuff, fighting mostly. Drunk and disorderly. Vandalism, particularly cars. You performed three months community service in lieu of a custodial sentence for repeatedly driving without insurance. And, I'm assuming, without your mother's permission to borrow her car. Although she didn't press charges."

I swung about to face him. "How the fuck do you know all of that?"

At least he had the grace to look slightly sheepish. "I...I studied at university with my opposite number in the British government. I may not look it, but as I once informed your father, I...am quite important."

His blue-grey eyes twinkled behind his glasses. It was shaming that Marcel knew all my flaws and showered me with kindness anyhow. His soft warm hand briefly squeezed mine, and I swallowed down a hard lump in my throat.

"And, Noah, my dear. More importantly, I know you are very brave because you came all the way here with very little money and no backup plan."

"That was just stupid, not brave." Blinking back tears, I looked away from him, to the vase of pretty flowers.

"Stupidity and bravery are not so very different," he

countered. "It is only the outcome which determines whether you are labelled one or the other. You're still here and not down and out on the streets of Paris, ergo, you are brave."

"You're the stupid one if you believe that."

He ignored my rudeness. "Let me think what else I know about you. I know you want to go back to England but have nothing to go back to. And I know you are terribly stubborn. Like your father," he added with a smile.

I counted the red flowers, that grapefruit-sized lump obstinately resisting my efforts to swallow it. And then I counted the yellow ones. Tulips possibly?

We looked alike, me and the killer, even I wasn't so dumb I couldn't see that. But I didn't want to hear I was like him. Not on the inside, anyhow, not where it mattered. Even if I suspected it to be true. A bitter heat billowed up inside me. Marcel's gentle calm voice continued on.

"And I know inside your strong, young man's body, and behind your angry, hostile words, there is a lost and lonely person who needs help. So, thank you for coming here and staying. Guillaume and I want to find a way to help you."

"He doesn't want to help me. He doesn't give a shit about me. He'd have said so if he did."

I'd never held another man's hand before. Not a lover's,

not a father's, not even a grandfather's. Marcel's hand was small, his skin smooth, his fingers slim. I wondered if he thought mine felt like the sperm donor's.

"My dear, if only you knew."

*

IT SOUNDED A crazy suggestion, but so far, it was the only one on the table. The alternatives were unthinkable. That first morning, I'd braced for a lie when I bluntly asked sperm donor if he'd committed the murder that had put him away for fifteen years. All criminals automatically denied guilt, right? Wrong. He'd confirmed it immediately. No hesitation, no remorse.

After telling him I wanted to go back to England, I'd stormed out of the house, half running, half walking, until I stumbled upon an empty beach. With rain lashing down and an icy sea breeze knocking me sideways, I played his words over and over. It had been an ugly scene; I hadn't thought it possible to hate him even more. I'd lashed out, attacked him verbally, screaming everything I loathed about being his son into his handsome, inscrutable face. And then, after I'd run out of words, my fist had come up, and I'd tried to hit him hard on the corner of his jaw. I might as well have not bothered; he'd seen my punch coming from five miles out, grabbed my hand, and twisted it behind my back until I'd cried out in pain. And then he'd let me go and apologised for hurting me as if I hadn't attacked him first.

He and his husband had this good cop, bad cop thing going. Twice, I'd stuffed my clothes back into my bag and Marcel had followed me up to my room, begging me not to walk out. Why wasn't it sperm donor blocking the doorway, insisting I stayed? Marcel pleaded with me to give the killer a chance to prove he wasn't the man I'd labelled him. He begged me to listen and try to understand. Guillaume was in shock, he said. He needed time to get his head around my existence, that the discovery he had a son who carried his genes, genes that were capable of murder, was as shameful for him as it was for me. It shamed him that I knew about his past, and he wished more than anything he could change it. That he'd been a better person. A better father.

I only stayed because Marcel was so goddamn nice. He didn't need to be; he could have shown me the door, given me enough cash to get back to the UK, and sent me on my merry way. He was a man of routine—his yoga, his work, his quiet evenings with his unlikely husband. He was ill, too, yet still, he wanted to help, which was how he persuaded me that his alternative to sleeping rough was worth a try.

Marcel had been a little woolly on detail, which in hindsight was just as well as I wouldn't have gone along with it otherwise. A friend with a big house, he'd said. Back in England, where everyone spoke a language I understood. With a decent spare room, he'd said. So I wouldn't have to sleep on someone else's floor or sofa, or in a dark doorway. Somewhere private to hang out, away from malign influences and temptation, a place where I could be alone, with time to consider my next step. To figure out what to do with my life. And I could stay for as long as that took. Maybe have another bash at college, maybe find a job, get a routine going. Put space between me and Guillaume and me and my mother. Maybe seek professional help.

At the very least, I'd get a free plane ride back to England.

*

I HADN'T PAID much attention to the journey, lost in my own world yet still acutely aware of the silent, brooding man in the seat next to mine on the plane. Still as much a stranger to me as before we'd met. He held his hand loosely in Marcel's, their fingers interlaced, the lines between who supported whom blurring the more time I spent with them both.

I'd expected a taxi to collect us from Bristol airport, not a posh Jag. An F-Pace SVR in Firenze Red if we were really splitting hairs. Once upon a time, I'd dreamed of becoming a car mechanic. I'd even done a few months at college learning the trade before it all felt like too much of a fucking bother. Especially when I didn't have a permanent place to bunk down. People like me didn't manage to finish courses like that, not when loafing around and causing trouble were more tempting and less hassle.

A guy with frizzy hair leapt out of the passenger seat and sprinted across to Guillaume as if his arse was on fire. Jabbering in French, he threw his scrawny arms around my sperm donor before doing that kissy thing French guys seemed to get off on. Meanwhile, a pair of long legs unfolded themselves from the driver's seat, attached to a tall blond man who instantly relegated every other hot guy I'd ever encountered into a minor league.

"Marcel, hi! And you must be Noah. Hi! Nice to meet you. I'm Freddie. Traffic was a bitch; we only just made it in time."

He turned to where my sperm donor and the other smaller guy were still squeezed together. "Any time you're ready to peel yourself away from Guillaume," Freddie drawled, his voice matching his car and his clothes. "Just let me know, Reuben. No rush."

"*Mon dieu*, Freddie. Calm down," responded the other guy in accented English, reluctantly releasing the killer but keeping an arm around his shoulders. "Always in such a hurry."

He spun around and, with a hand on his hip, looked me up and down, a happy grin splitting his lively features. "*Putain*, you and Guillaume are two beans in a pod."

"Peas, my sweet. Peas, not beans," Freddie murmured.

The smaller guy, Reuben, advanced on me, and I cringed as he repeated the kissy thing. "My husband corrects me because he is jealous of my good looks and charm, *non*? We have to pretend he is handsome, too, okay?"

Behind us, Marcel and the killer helped Freddie stow our bags into the boot of the car.

Reuben whispered in my ear, "I am Guillaume's oldest friend. I will be your friend too. You'll see; everything will work out fine. We are taking you to a magical place."

I doubted that very much. The guy had a screw loose, evidently. And I'd stopped believing in magic years ago, the first Christmas Santa forgot to pitch up.

They spent the journey talking about plants and gardens—

seemed they'd all visited the same stately home—the Reuben guy especially well informed. On the backseat, sandwiched uncomfortably between Marcel and my donor, I did my best not to touch either of them and switched off, preferring drab scenery and the near-silent hum of precision engineering to making small talk.

Before I knew what was happening, they'd elected to take a detour to the stately home they'd been blathering on about. Except it wasn't a detour at all because Freddie parked the car in a garage housing quite a few other cars as if he lived in the grounds of the stately home himself. Which, it turns out, he did.

A flurry of activity greeted our arrival. Two blond streaks dashed out to the car, squealing in that ear-piercing, high-pitched way only small children could. Joyfully, they wrapped themselves around Marcel's legs, Reuben chiding them and steadying Marcel to prevent them knocking him over. A chubby toddler waddled after them, gurgling and holding his fat arms out. For the first time since I'd clapped eyes on him, the killer smiled. Dropping his bag, he scooped the boy up, twirled him around, and kissed him, both of them laughing with delight.

A big guy followed the toddler at a more leisurely pace,

and he embraced the killer, not minding in the slightest that the small child evidently belonging to him was being cuddled in his arms. He disentangled the other kids from Marcel, and they scampered off back inside the house, shouting to someone that we'd arrived.

"I'm Jay," said the big guy pleasantly. "You must be Noah. Nice to meet you."

What the fuck was I doing here?

Grunting hello with the finesse of an acned fourteen-year-old, I shook his hand. In his sweatpants and hoodie, he appeared perfectly at ease, although he didn't look or sound like the sort of person who belonged in a place like this. Not like Freddie. But then what did I know about anything?

A second man appeared in the doorway, the two blond kids hanging off each arm. He didn't resemble the kind of person who'd live in a house like this either. Too young for a start—he was around my age—and with his gingery curls and freckles, much too ordinary. Too small and skinny as well—he only reached my shoulder.

One of the children released him so he could shake my hand. This ginger guy was fucking smiling too.

Why was everyone around this place so fucking happy?

"Hi! You must be Noah. I'm Toby." With the same hand

I'd shaken, he ruffled one of the blond kid's hair, which was when I noticed his other arm didn't have a hand on the end, it just petered out into a kind of stump. Realising I'd noticed, he pulled the sleeve of his baggy jumper over it, then fixed me with his bright smile again. "I work here. I have the misfortune to be in charge of this pair of toerags."

The girl let out a screech of protest, and Toby laughed easily as they dashed off again back to Marcel.

"They're Eliza and Arthur, and sorry, they appear to have forgotten their manners. Usually, they would have introduced themselves, but they're too excited at seeing Marcel and Guillaume. Everyone's favourite godfathers. The baby wrapped around your dad is Orlando, by the way—he took a shine to him from the moment they first met; he probably won't let go now until bedtime."

My dad. The first time anyone had said those words to me ever, my entire life. And this stranger—Toby—had dropped the phrase so casually into his greeting, seemingly without realising he'd uttered it. A tense pause stretched between us as he waited for me to make an appropriate response.

"I don't have a dad. He isn't that."

"God, sorry," said Toby with a slight frown. "I thought

you were..."

"Yes. I am. But that doesn't make him my fucking dad. Okay?"

Toby shrugged, backing off a little. "Sure. Whatever."

By now, we'd all trooped into the kitchen, a space the size of my old school assembly hall, except much more homey and cluttered with kitchen stuff and piles of laundry and kid's toys and stacks of washed dishes and...a...a person. Yet another man, and not a run-of-the-mill sort. I had to look twice, thinking it was Freddie at first, somehow zipped in ahead of us through another entrance. And then I realised it wasn't.

The new man wore a nightdress for a start, of the frumpy kind favoured by little old ladies.

Tall and slender, like Freddie, he had hair that looked as if it came from a bottle of bleach, except it didn't because the rest of him was very, very pale too; his skin tone matching the elegant pearl rope weighing heavily around his neck. Even his clever eyes, made up with a shimmery bronze halo, were pale, a cloudless light blue, and they crinkled around the edges as he smiled at me. Marcel stepped up to give him a hug.

"Gosh, darling," the man murmured in a whispery, fluttery sort of voice. With his slim arms around Marcel's bony shoulders, his warm gaze settled on me. There was a hint of mischief in his smile, revealing pointy sharp canines as he flicked his eyes down to my feet and back up again. "I don't think you need to bother wasting any of your filthy lucre on paternity testing, do you?"

Marcel gave a muffled laugh and shook his head.

So, this must be Lucien. The owner of this vast country pile and Marcel's best friend. The person who apparently was going to 'sort me out'. Yeah, right. I wouldn't bet money on it. How could someone who had all this, and who looked like that, ever understand how it felt to be me? They hadn't got a fucking clue, any of them. I should have parted ways with the killer and Marcel at Bristol airport, pretended to go to the bog, and sneaked off. This experiment would be over by the end of the week; I'd be out on my ear, sleeping rough in Bristol. A couple of nights kip here, and then I'd be gone.

Still tightly bound to his old friend, Lucien extended a bony hand towards me. I took it, his grip surprisingly firm, his palm cool and soft.

"I'm Lucien Avery. Welcome to Rossingley, darling."

*

AT LEAST WITH all these people crammed into the kitchen,

no one fired awkward questions or stared at me. Well, no one except the Orlando kid, who had draped himself over the sperm donor's shoulder and tracked my every move with his big sloe eyes as if making sure I didn't nick his daddies' silver teaspoons. In amongst the noise and chatter of folk catching up and sharing news, I was momentarily overlooked, which suited me fine and allowed me to study them all, one by one.

Lucien was a fucking weirdo in a way only very rich guys could afford to be. Enough said. Reuben, the friendly French guy, got to have regular sex with Freddie, so I deduced his life must be pretty fucking peachy too. That alone was enough to explain his apparent joy with the world. And Freddie himself, with his looks and obvious money, wouldn't recognise misery if it stared him in the face. Jay seemed a bit more straightforward, but even he had the air of a man totally chilled with himself and his surroundings. Which left the sperm donor and Marcel, and I'd already observed at close quarters what a happy existence they'd carved out together. The kids would be spoiled brats, obviously, which meant the only one remaining was the skinny one-handed ginger. The hired help—a fellow misfit, like me.

Maybe I wouldn't even stay two nights—I could slip out later after dark; God knew which way took me back to Bristol or to that other little town we'd passed on the way here, but if I carried on walking in a straight line, I'd find civilisation somewhere.

After twenty minutes or so, all the people began peeling off. Toby took the twins outside to groom the ponies. (Exactly how did Marcel imagine my problems could possibly be solved by white people rich enough to keep fucking *ponies*?). Reuben and Freddie disappeared to be witty and beautiful somewhere else, Marcel went for a lie-down, and the killer took Orlando out to feed the ducks. Which left me alone with Jay, the most normal out of the lot, and Lucien, the most peculiar.

"We're thrilled to have you staying here," began Lucien as soon as the door was firmly closed. Talk about over-egging the pudding; I was fairly certain I was an inconvenience the entire clan could have done without. But no doubt, helping charity cases like me ticked some box inside him that made him feel good about himself. Like those celebrities who visited Ethiopia with a film crew and rolled up the sleeves of their pristine camo shirts to sprinkle glamour and baskets of Mars bars over pot-bellied kids too weak to eat them, then getting back inside their chauffeur-driven jeeps and drenching themselves in hand sanitizer on the route back to private jets. Okay, maybe not quite as bad as that, but along the same lines.

"Although it will be terribly boring if we don't find you something to do. Idle hands are the devil's playthings, I find. Wouldn't you agree?"

Okay, so this guy was even worse than the celebs. African kids only had to look cute and allow a few fat flies to crawl over their eyelids. Whereas he was planning on making me *work* for my charitable handouts. Lucien's pale-blue eyes coolly regarded me, a hint of challenge dancing at his lips as if he could read my ugly thoughts and found them terribly amusing.

"I've had a word with Reuben, and he is very happy for you to tag along with the gardening team."

I bet. He'd be able to spend the day telling me how wonderful his murdering best friend Guillaume was if only I could see beyond the murdering part.

"If that isn't to your liking," the weird earl continued, "then Will, my estate manager, can find plenty of chores to keep you busy. An alternative suggestion is that you enrol in a course of some description at Allenmouth College?"

No fucking chance. I'd tried college and not been very good at it when I found out they expected me to turn up every day.

Lucien's smile was exchanged for a firmer expression. "What you can't do, I'm afraid, is *loaf*. Contrary to first impressions, I run a rather tight ship, which you will come to appreciate if you hang around long enough."

He threw me a sudden impish grin, so at odds with everything else about him. "And I hope you do. We like to have our home filled with...extended family. The more the merrier."

Whatever. If he expected me to fall to his feet and grovel with gratitude or smile for the cameras, he was shit out of luck.

Jay stood up from the table. "I'll show you where you can stay."

I picked up my bag to follow. It was heavier than when I'd first arrived in France. On realising I scarcely owned anything, Marcel had left some tracksuit bottoms, a pair of jeans, a couple of T-shirts and some sweaters out on the bed. Old stuff, about to be passed on to a charity shop apparently, although they seemed pretty new to me and suspiciously in keeping with the sperm donor's sartorial choices. As soon as I had some funds of my own, I'd ditch them in the nearest wheelie bin.

"Noah, darling."

Dear and *darling*, both in the same week. Fucking ridiculous, not to mention so fucking gay.

Lucien's pale gaze openly appraised my physique, which, especially dressed in these clothes, was horrifically similar to the sperm donor's. To give him credit, he'd been the only one with the balls to say out loud what everyone had been thinking; formal paternity testing would be a waste of bloody time and money.

"I must ask you an exceedingly important question. It may seem a little odd, but I do require an answer, and the sooner, the better."

Jay threw him a quizzical look, and I tensed. *Here we go already.* Why had I pitched up? Would I leave without a fuss as soon as my presence became an inconvenience? How much money would I accept to clear off? Was I after Guillaume's money? Did I promise not to nick the silver?

Thieving wasn't on my list of juvenile crimes. But perhaps I would give it a go—thieve something and leave tonight after everyone had fucked off to bed. Steal enough to get me to Bristol. Forget the silver, hotwiring that posh Jag would do it. Those hypnotic pale eyes glinted at me with amusement.

"Tell me, Noah darling. How do you feel about playing

some cricket?"

*

"DO YOU HAVE everything you need?" Jay asked politely as I traipsed after him up one staircase, along a spooky dark hallway, then down another.

Yes, aside from a map to find my way back down to the kitchen in the morning.

"Phone charger? Toothbrush?" he continued, casting a glance back at me.

I nodded.

"We've given you a room in the east wing. Next to Toby. He'll show you where everything is. Lucien, me, and the children have quarters in the west wing. Marcel and Guillaume are on the floor below."

"Why are you doing this?" The question came out more aggressively than I intended, although Jay seemed unfazed. "Why are you both taking me in?"

"Trust me, mate, it wasn't my idea."

We turned a corner onto yet another long dim corridor. I bet this house was haunted.

"You'd better not cause Luce any trouble," Jay continued. "You'll be answering to me if you do."

Seemed I'd finally met someone in this place who spoke my own language.

He opened a door, revealing a plainly decorated blue bedroom. A double bed with a flowery eiderdown faced the sash window. A heavy oak wardrobe and matching drawers took up two walls. The view looked out onto a courtyard and the stables. With his arms folded across his impressive chest, Jay sized me up, the only person I'd met in this mad house who didn't mind showing me his trust had to be earned, not gifted. In another life, maybe, we'd have been friends.

"The public relations answer is that Lucien is fully aware of his aristocratic inherited privilege and likes to give something back to those less fortunate than himself whenever he can."

I huffed, indicating exactly how underwhelmed I was by that statement. Playing Lady Bountiful and sprinkling crumbs to the poor was easy when you already had so much you wouldn't notice if some of it was given away.

Jay leaned down to fiddle with the radiator. "I'd keep this turned on if I were you. It's bloody freezing at night along this corridor, according to Toby."

Straightening again, he fixed me with a softer expression. "That's part of it. The other part is he knows what it feels like to be cast adrift and alone. And to hit rock bottom. It's hard to believe looking at him now. But trust me, he's the best chance you've got. Don't fuck it up."

Chapter Seven

Toby

GUESS WHO GOT himself saddled with the new guy? I should have seen that coming a mile off. For a childless man, Marcel was extraordinarily adept at entertaining small children, more so now his alleged dental situation commanded 100 per cent of Arthur and Eliza's attention. Orlando, as usual, clung to Guillaume like a limpet on a rock from the second he opened his wide, brown eyes until his doting godfather tucked him up and read him his bedtime story. Which left me slightly twiddling my thumbs. Fifth rule of Rossingley: look busy, otherwise Lucien would find you something to do.

Guillaume's long-lost son would be drop-dead gorgeous if he cracked a smile occasionally, but there was no sign of one of those on the horizon. If brooding, introspective sullenness were an Olympic sport, Noah would trounce everybody on his path to claiming gold. Aside from the addition of a couple of eyebrow piercings and a burgeoning flesh tunnel in his left ear, he was the spit of his dad. Sensibly, I thought it best not to draw attention to that elephant in the room and focused on Rossingley instead, a topic on which I boasted an entire medal cabinet myself. Lucien had suggested/commanded I fill my time by offering Noah a tour of the estate.

"Why are those cows all fucking staring at us?"

We'd begun the tour by broadly surveying the grounds from the elevated position of the house. I'd pointed out riveting landmarks such as the chapel, the lake, and the distant cricket club, then taken him towards the village. Instead of winding our way down the drive, I chose the more scenic shortcut across the fields. Not recommended in the dead of night after several drinks at the Rossingley Arms—I still had the scars to prove it.

"Which cows?"

"Those huge fucking brown ones, over there!"

We were skirting the edge of Rob's dairy farm, crossing a wooden stile that cut through one of his pastures. There was zero chance of bumping into him at this time of day, which mostly felt like a good thing, and yes, we had attracted the attention of several of his charges, who had inquisitively edged towards us.

"Because that's what cows do. They're Ayrshires, by the way. That farmer has around two hundred and fifty of them. The other dairy farm beyond has sixty Friesians. The milk yield is—"

"When?" he interrupted.

I frowned. "When what?"

"When did I ask?"

Sometimes, bad behaviour was better ignored. Childcare college had taught me that. Thus, cursing my employer under my breath, I ploughed on.

"I suppose if the only thing you did was eat grass all day, you'd find us desperately fascinating too. That's why they stare."

One cow took a couple of definitive paces towards us, and cows being cows, five or six others all stopped grazing and copied.

"Is that electric fence switched on?" Noah quickened his step. Oh my God, spot the townie.

"Maybe? If the farmer remembered?" I shrugged casually. "Why don't you touch it and find out?"

He gave me a look. "I'm not that fucking stupid."

"Anyhow," I carried on, as if I didn't have a care in the world. "I wouldn't worry about cows, not unless they've just calved, which this lot haven't. I'd be more concerned about the fucking huge bull behind us. Especially with you dressed in that bright red sweater."

To give him credit, Noah avoided the majority of the cowpats as he legged it to the next stile. I very much doubted I'd gained myself a new mate though. In the distance, Rob's placid longhorn lounged under his favourite oak, not giving a shit that two blokes wandered through his pasture.

"Have you really lived here all your life?" Noah asked, not hiding his incredulous tone. I'd filled ten minutes of our time together outlining a potted history of the village and my own unremarkable footnote within it.

"Yes, my parent's house is about half a mile in that direction." I pointed to my left. "I went away to college in Bristol for three years, but then I came back."

"Why the fuck?"

We'd left the fields of grazing livestock behind us, much to Noah's relief, and hit the lane taking us into the village. I was on the cusp of pointing out another tranche of enthralling local landmarks, such as an ancient gravestone marked with a skull and crossbones (disappointingly, not a pirate burial but a plague victim) and the row of terraced cottages purportedly the longest stretch of uninterrupted thatched roofing south of the M25. If we had time, I had plans to show him the tiny cottage belonging to Mrs Hannon, aged 109, the ninety-eighth oldest person alive in the UK, although that ranking tended to be rather fluid, especially after a cold snap. So, all things considered, his question came across as a tad rude, but seeing as it was the first time he'd spoken since I'd pulled the bull trick, I let it pass.

"Uh, because I like it here?"

Reaching a fork in the road, I nudged him in the direction of the village green. His eyes strayed down to my deformed left arm and just as quickly back up again. So, yes, that might have something to do with it too. With so many oddities inhabiting this village, a man with a withered arm barely registered. Especially when he'd been here all his life. Whereas in town, at college, or on the bus, every stranger and his dog considered it their divine right to stare or ask about it. Like this guy. I might as well get it over with.

"No, it doesn't hurt, and no, it's not an injury or cancer. I was born this way. The medical term is phocomelia. No, I know you haven't heard of it; no one has. Yes, the rest of me is normal. And no, I can't paint watercolours with my feet. Nor do I ever find 'can I give you a hand' jokes amusing, no matter how well I know that person."

I recited the drill in a dull monotone, hating every second but knowing from bitter experience it was the best way of shutting someone up. No doubt it endeared me to Noah even less.

"All right, keep yer hair on. You brought it up, not me."

One of the young farmers chugged past in a shiny new John Deere, the flash bastard, and he threw me a cheery wave. Noah narrowed his eyes suspiciously.

"Who's that?"

"Oh, that's Rich, a guy who farms Fernlea, over on the east of the estate. Wheat, barley, and oil seed rape mostly."

Crawling along in a clapped-out Mini behind the tractor was Mrs Laycock, the school secretary. We waved to each other as well.

"Do you know everyone?"

"Yeah, of course I do. I've been here my whole life."

"Are there any shops?"

"There's a bread van." I felt a desperate urge to defend my home, to justify to this urbanite my own decision to stay in such a backwater. "Sharon delivers every day, pretty much any sort of bread. As long as it is bread and not a cake. You won't catch her out with banana bread, for instance. Because in her book, that's a cake. She scratches you off her Christmas card list if you ask her about cakes."

I frowned, trying to make Rossingley sound vaguely appealing to this miserable out of towner but fully aware it made me come across as a local yokel. Fuck it, I *was* a local yokel. A proud one.

"Eddie, the milkman, also brings cheese and cream if you order it a week in advance. And if you slip him an extra fiver, he'll drop off some fags too. Honestly, we've got everything. Mick, the mechanic who owns the garage, mends hedge trimmers. Hairdryers and vacuum cleaners, too, as long as they aren't Dysons. He doesn't do Dysons."

He harrumphed so I gamely carried on.

"The tractor rally at Easter isn't to be missed. The highlight of the Rossingley calendar. And there's the pub, of course."

"I should fucking think so. Living in this bleeding backwater, you'd need somewhere to drown yourself in alcohol."

As if on cue, the mobile library trundled past and came to a halt in the defibrillator layby.

"See? There's a whole vanful of entertainment, right there," I pointed out. "As long as Barbara Cartland and James Patterson are your jam. And if racy historical romance or thrillers prove too much and your heart packs up, then in that converted red phone box—you see where there are green stickers? We've successfully campaigned for a..."

"This whole village is dull as fuck," Noah declared and thrust his hands in his pockets. Conversation over.

*

"I'M NOT ENTIRELY sure he's going to stay," I confided in Lucien on Friday. "He's...um...not best pleased to be here." That was putting it mildly.

"We must remember, darling, Rome wasn't built in a day." He shot me a knowing look. "Partly because they didn't have us mixing the cement, did they? You're doing a marvellous job with him. He totally hides from Jay and myself. At least he talks to you. And don't pretend to me he's not a pretty addition to the scenery."

A blush heated my cheeks—being a ginger frequently annoyed me on many levels. Yeah, so maybe I had noticed that

Noah's eyes, a diabolical shade of brown, were fringed by equally diabolical thick eyelashes. And that he had inherited his dad's almost arrogant way of taunting you with them, practically spoiling for a fight or a fuck. The latter, I could *so* get on board with.

"Lucien Duchamps-Avery," admonished Freddie from his sprawl on the kitchen sofa. (A catwalk model loitering around the house was an occasional perk of the job.) "You're a married man and father. You have tubs of lip gloss older than Toby and Noah."

"I may have you thrown in the tower for that comment, darling." Lucien pouted at him. "Just making an innocent observation; that's all. And somebody around here has to keep their eyes peeled for a suitable young man for Toby."

Another flush surged up my neck, so my face now annoyingly matched the colour of my hair. I already had a man, sort of, although his suitability was questionable.

"I don't think Noah's gay," I mumbled. "And I certainly haven't got the guts to ask him."

"I'm not sure he is either," Lucien concurred. "But we can live in hope." He frowned slightly. "Under that stubborn, angry exterior, I think there is a very big heart straining to get out. Just like his father. He's craving love and affection;

everyone can see that. I have a feeling he hasn't ever experienced much of either."

"I agree," Freddie interjected. "He wouldn't have gone to France otherwise, to track down Guillaume, whatever he's told himself his reasons were."

Lucien gave me one of his quick naughty grins. "I promise you, Toby, do that little shimmying walk of yours in front of him, and he'll be rolling over, asking you to tickle his underbelly in no time."

I conceded Lucien might have a point regarding the love and affection part, but I didn't think he'd be craving it from me anytime soon. Or from any of us, to be honest. When Noah erected his sky-high barrier topped with barbed wire around himself, it had been with the express intention of keeping all of us out.

Sensing my discomfort, Freddie pitched in. "Toby, have you asked Noah about the cricket? Perhaps he'll feel more at ease if he gets involved in something physical, instead of skulking in his room or wandering the estate on his own. You never know, joining everyone in a team sport might thaw him a little."

I applauded Freddie's optimism. "Yes, I have. And he wanted to know why everyone keeps asking him about the cricket."

"More importantly, does he play?" Lucien demanded. "Because Jay has tickets to watch a rugby match at Twickenham with you-know-who in a couple of weeks. If we don't have an answer by then, I'm going to find myself having to be vaguely pleasant to his Second-Best Man every Monday evening. I'll have to offer him a heterosexual pint of real ale, with a stupid made-up name like Badger's Arse, then feign an interest in televised snooker while he spreads his testosterone all over my cream sofas and monopolises my husband."

"It's good for you, Luce," laughed Freddie. "Anyhow, if you want him to clear off, you could always come downstairs in that lacy baby doll number. It kept him away for six months last time. Poor guy was petrified.

"Probably best not to parade it in front of our newest house guest, though," he added thoughtfully. "Sounds like you need to break him in gently. Where is he anyhow?"

The two days Noah had been with us, as Freddie had observed, he'd spent hiding out in his room or trudging around the estate, hands thrust deep in his pockets and his eyes glued to the ground. Kind of avoiding everyone, including the herd of cows. The cool, tortured look suited him, but God, it must be wearying keeping it up all day every day. Even baby Orlando's charms had failed to coax a smile out of him.

With work commitments and busy lives to return to, the time came for Marcel and Guillaume to say *au revoir* and regretfully fly back to France. Putting a brave face on it, Guillaume suggested that without him hanging around, his son might feel more at ease and come out of his shell. No one was holding their breath.

Noah didn't exactly give them a jolly send off. As they loaded their bags into the boot of Reuben's car, he could barely bring himself to look at his father. To make it worse, he ignored Guillaume's outstretched handshake, shoving his own hands into the pockets of his jeans instead and kicking at the gravel drive. Simple good manners cost nothing; if he'd been my mother's son, she'd have pulled him up on it, not caring who was listening. But everyone, including Lucien, let it go. Despite wanting to grab him by the shoulders and give him a jolly good shake, I kept my mouth shut too.

Attempting to make it up to his oldest friend, Reuben hung off Guillaume's neck and reminded him he was wonderful, which was cute, and hopefully gave sulky Noah something to chew on. Marcel, taking the initiative into his own hands, issued Noah with a firm hug and a promise to call the house every day to see how he was faring, which Noah accepted with the charm and grace of a lamppost.

*

EVEN THOUGH HE wasn't exactly a great conversationalist at breakfast—and by that, I mean he drank his tea and munched toast in stony silence—Noah's presence or absence was noticeable, nonetheless. And at breakfast next morning, the Noah-sized hole was difficult to miss. After packing the kids off to school and putting Orlando down for a midmorning nap, ten o'clock came and went with still with no sign of him, so I went upstairs to investigate. No surprises, the fucker had repaid everyone's kindness by doing a runner.

"Okay, let's not panic." Lucien wrung his hands together, doing an excellent impression of a man on the verge of panicking. Most likely, he was imagining breaking Noah's disappearance to Marcel and Guillaume. "He can't have gone far."

His optimism was misplaced. If the guy had set off late last night when we'd all been tucked up in bed, he could be halfway across the world by now.

Lucien immediately began thumbing into his phone. "I'll ask Will to put a message out onto the farming WhatsApp group. It's not yet lunchtime. If he left early this morning, then someone is sure to have spotted him."

I endured half an hour of Lucien alternately drumming on the table and pacing the kitchen before he received a reply. He used the time to inform Guillaume that his newly minted son had gone AWOL, and from the tense expression on his face, the news didn't go down too well.

"I know, Gui, I know," he repeated. "I'll do everything I can. I promise. We're on it already."

More nodding. "I'll track him down," he promised again with feeling. A pause. "Gosh, don't be ridiculous. He wouldn't have stolen from us. Any rate, I don't care if he has pinched something. In some ways, I sincerely hope he has. It means he won't starve or freeze to death."

He put the phone back on the table. "This is merely a stumble in the road, Toby. Let's remember that." He sighed. "That poor boy. Gosh, I hope we find him. For Guillaume's sake too. He's beside himself."

Personally, I thought *that poor boy* needed a kick up his backside. Ungrateful toerag.

Turning up out of the blue and having all these kind men bending over backwards to help him out? He had a charming way of thanking them for their efforts.

Lucien's phone chirped. Uncle Will reported that one of the farmhands had spotted a guy fitting Noah's description trudging along the Allenmouth road at around seven this morning. He'd swerved to avoid hitting him in the fog. Lucien thanked him, hung up, and sprang into action. Or rather, sprang me into action.

"Right, Toby. Why don't I stay here and look after the children? I need you to drive to Allenmouth and start searching for Noah."

"Me?" I couldn't recall a clause in my manny contract mentioning I had to go running after miserable grumpy northerners, no matter how good their arses looked in stonewashed denim.

"Yes, you, darling. I'm...um... It's incredibly hard to believe, I know, but I'm possibly not quite his cup of tea. He's much less likely to run if he sees you."

I wasn't so sure. "I can't say we exactly hit it off either."

Lucien handed me the car keys. "Toby, you are the only person in this household who managed to cajole Arthur to try broccoli." His voice had taken on a familiar fluttery persuasive tone, his command-wrapped-up-as-a-suggestion voice. "If anyone can coax Noah back, it's you."

"Tricking a five-year-old into eating his veggies is hardly in the same skill set as luring a sullen young man back to a house full of people he clearly detests!"

Not to be deterred, he wrapped his arms about himself. "Goodness me, it's so cold out today. Don't you think it's cold, Toby? Did Noah have a decent coat?"

I shrugged as if I'd scarcely glanced at the moody vision of hotness that had glowered at all of us for the past week, as if I couldn't possibly recollect any of his attire. Truth was, I'd studied him so hard I could probably recite his entire meagre wardrobe. "Um...I think he maybe had one of those thin quilted jacket things?"

"Gosh, so not waterproof either. Poor, poor man. It's hat, scarf, and gloves weather today."

I glanced out across the frosty lawns. Yes, a little chilly.

"I'm praying he's stayed in Allenmouth," Lucien continued, "and not taken it upon himself to hitch to Bristol. I'll send Lee and Joe on the hunt too. They haven't met Noah, but they know what Guillaume looks like. There can't be that many young men as gorgeous and unhappy as Noah wandering aimlessly around Allenmouth."

He lingered on the gorgeous and unhappy bit, the bugger.

"The poor man is in desperate need of a friend, Toby, don't you think?"

Quite possibly, but Noah wouldn't choose the plain-and-ginger variety.

With his mind made up, Lucien went for the kill, dangling his car keys between us like a bag of gold sovereigns. "Naturally, you had better take my car. That way, you'll leave me with the Land Rover so I can pick up the twins later."

With a pained sigh, I agreed. Sixth rule of Rossingley: save time, see things Lucien's way. Taking the proffered keys, I reminded myself my agreement had everything to do with tracking down that grumpy, ungrateful git and absolutely nothing to do with the opportunity to drive Lucien's fabulous Aston Martin. Nothing at all.

*

OH MY GOD. By the end of day one, I didn't care how gorgeous Noah was, because I seriously wished I'd stayed back home with the kids. Don't get me wrong, being behind the wheel of the Aston, purring underneath me like a cat that had worked out how to use a tin opener, was still exceptionally cool. And sinking into the soft, buttery leather seat and cranking up the heat felt pretty awesome too. Nevertheless, chilled to the bone and footsore, I became increasingly convinced we wouldn't find him and starting not to care very much if we didn't. Despite the treat of the luxury car. The guy was twenty-two and behaving like a spoiled fifteen-year-old. Between them, Lucien and Jay and Marcel and Guillaume were handing him a chance at a new beginning on a plate, and he'd tossed it aside and flounced off.

"Not a sausage," I declared to Lucien, draping myself across the Aga. "I hung around the park, the main bus shelter, and the market. All day. Nada."

Lucien gave Marcel a FaceTime update, attempting and failing to reassure one of the sweetest men on the planet. Seeing Guillaume, a haggard, worried mess next to him, I found myself resolving to try all over again tomorrow. But with an extra layer of thermals.

I'd choose running after three small children all day long over tramping the two main streets of Allenmouth on a wintry wet Tuesday in February. It wasn't a big town, but the sort of touristy, smallish place that old people retired to and young people escaped. A Saturday night punch-up outside Wetherspoons was about as exciting as it got. If Noah was camped out and homeless, then it was hard to believe we wouldn't spot him, or that a suspicious Neighbourhood Watch type hadn't reported him to the police. Nonetheless, I diligently endured another day of loitering around the park, the college, and the cemetery, not to mention several laps of the shopping areas.

Lee and Joe hadn't had any luck either, although I had a
sneaking suspicion their searches had concentrated on checking he wasn't hiding out in one of the pubs.

By the end of the day, as dusk fell and the air turned icy,
I'd convinced myself Noah had somehow transported himself
to Bristol, where we didn't stand a cat in hell's chance of tracking him down. That evening, hugging the Aga like a long-lost
friend, my irritation became gradually superseded by a growing concern. With temperatures dropping below freezing, Jay
had reported the road gritters were out and a heavy snowfall
forecast. Which gave Lucien the opportunity to lighten the
mood with his favourite joke—that he was expecting at least a
good six inches at the back door—and was, frankly, way more
about their sex life than an innocent youngster like me ever
needed to hear. To be honest, none of us were feeling the
humour because we all knew the only place to be on a night
like this was in bed, with a hot chocolate and a warm body to
snuggle up against. I had to settle for two of those, Noah had
none. Once I'd thawed out, they took a late evening drive
around town, only to come back as despondent as I felt.

When I took a final circuit of the play park on day three,
we'd almost given up. The snow lay only about two inches
thick, but it was the horrible kind, a mix of muddy slush and

icy chips. Some lads optimistically kicking a ball about at lunchtime reckoned they'd seen a guy they hadn't recognised hanging around the day before. Unenthusiastically, I swept the snow off one of the metal benches lining the nearby skate park and perched for a while, trying to convince myself that the numbness spreading across my backside wouldn't be permanent. My brain might have become anaesthetised with cold, too, because when I turned away from watching a gang of foolhardy girls zipping up and down the icy skate ramps like their skateboards were glued to it, Noah, the bloody sod, was sat at the other end of the bench.

"Oh my God, it's you. Thank fuck for that. I can go home now."

His face was ashen, skin matching the wintry blanket of low cloud above our heads. Gripping the cheap sports bag on his lap, his gloveless hands looked frozen in place. He stared resolutely at the ground. I had a horrible certainty that while I'd been moaning about incipient chilblains from a couple of days spent tramping the streets of Allenmouth, he'd suffered the freezing nights out on them too. I pulled my woollen beanie off my head and held it out to him.

"Hey. Put this on. Your need is greater than mine. Take my gloves too."

He didn't move, so I scooted across and pushed the beanie into one of his hands. "Go on, take it. You look bloody freezing."

As if his fingers were knotted with arthritis, he painfully let go of the bag. Raising my beanie up to his head, he pulled it down low over his ears. With my teeth, I tugged the woollen mitten off my right hand, then passed it to him, along with the matching sock my mum had knitted, which I used to cover my left stump. I flushed with embarrassment.

"Better than nothing. At least it's been prewarmed."

"Thanks," he answered softly, through chattering teeth. "Were you looking for me?"

"Good lord, no." I gave an involuntary shiver. "I actively chose to spend the last three days sitting on a cold metal bench freezing my balls off. Of course I was looking for you! Everyone's been worried sick."

He nodded, almost in a daze, and briefly closed his eyes.

I stood and tried to rub some circulation back into my dead legs. "Come on. There's a Maccie D's the other side of the park. I bet you haven't had anything to eat today either, have you?"

He shook his head. "Ran out of money. Can you lend me some? I'll pay you back when I get to Bristol and find some work."

Evidently, no one had clued this guy into how stuff worked or, more to the point, how Lucien worked. "Um...no can do, I'm afraid. I'm not here to give you money and send you on your way. I'm taking you back."

"I don't want to go back."

Fleetingly, I imagined returning to Rossingley empty-handed and Lucien sadly explaining to Marcel and Guillaume that I'd let him get away. Or giving the guy fifty quid, then seeing him onto a bus bound for Bristol, a city where he knew nobody and had nowhere to go except maybe a homeless shelter. Lucien would have my guts for garters.

"Tough, mate. Because two of Lucien's gardeners are sitting in a toasty pub about three hundred yards from here. Much bigger blokes than me, and they won't take any shit from anyone. So, you can come for a warm and some grub before I take you back to Rossingley, or I'll give Lee and Joe a call. If you still want to hoof it, now's your moment to start running. But I reckon Orlando could trot across this park quicker than you right now."

CHAPTER EIGHT

NOAH

A BEANIE HAT, a mitten, and a homemade knitted sock. Someone loved Toby enough to knit him a bloody sock to fit over his deformed arm. And he'd lent it to me. Didn't sound like much, but after two nights fighting off hypothermia, it tipped me over the edge. The only thing stopping me from collapsing against him, sobbing my heart out and never letting go, was that I hadn't changed my clothes for three days and stank to high heaven.

I knew where to find McDonalds because I'd lingered inside on day one for so long the manager chucked me out and threatened to call the police if I reappeared. I couldn't spot her when Toby pushed open the door, but anyhow, Toby was a paying customer.

He sat me at a table, fiercely ordered me to stay put, then never took his eyes off me as he waited at the counter as if I was about to leg it. He needn't have worried; I was all-out broken. I'd have landed flat on my face before I'd got halfway across the street. Not breaking down completely in front of him took up every last ounce of energy I had left.

My fingers tingled, then throbbed unpleasantly as the warmth of the fast-food restaurant began to take effect. In a bleary daze, I watched Toby as he paid, gathered our order, and walked back to me. After setting the food down, he pulled out his phone.

"I'm texting Lucien to call off the search. And I need to phone Marcel and Guillaume—they've been calling every hour—they were about to get on a plane to come and join in."

I felt a pang of guilt at stressing Marcel. I hoped his asthma hadn't flared up because of it. The other man...I wasn't sure how I felt about his apparent concern.

"Guillaume told me he wasn't sorry for fucking a

seventeen-year-old on the beach, taking advantage of her. No regrets, he said. That's why I ran. I had to—"

I stopped abruptly, ambushed by a film of tears. With blurry vision, I ripped the plastic lid off the polystyrene coffee cup, hoping to redirect Toby's attention away from my face. *Non, absolument pas*, the sperm donor had said. None. Absolutely no regrets. Not a glimmer of regard for the consequences. A butterfly flaps its wings on a moonlit beach in one country, and a shitty existence is created nine months later in another. And then, as he prepared to fly back to his cosy nest with Marcel, he'd stuck out his hand in front of all those fucking people and expected me to shake it.

"I'm...I'm...I mean, obviously I don't know the whole story," Toby began. "Are you sure that's what..."

"No. You're right. You don't."

I grabbed a handful of fries and forced them down. Hunger. If I could just get some food inside me, warm me up from the inside out, and then sleep, I'd feel more myself again, less out of control. My hatred of that man would be more contained.

Toby eyed me warily. "Let me just text Marcel, then, okay?"

As Toby's thumb flew across the screen, I tried not to

scarf my burger like a fucking animal. His rusty hair stuck up in all directions after being under the knitted hat; his nose and freckled cheeks shone red from the cold. I should be saying thank-you to him for not giving up on me, Lucien, too, but I didn't know how to start. Thank-you. Two incredibly difficult words to vocalise, probably because I hadn't had an opportunity to say them very often.

As a teen, I'd run away plenty of times, but nobody had seemed to notice very much, let alone care enough to send out a search party. In those days, I'd had places to go, mates who let me crash. Here, I'd made do with hunkering down in a park hedge. Last night had been so cold I'd got up every hour and wandered around, scared that if I nodded off, I might never wake up again. The public toilets had been locked, and even if the pubs hadn't all been closed by midnight, I hadn't enough cash to buy a drink and pass the hours in one anyhow. A surge of shame flooded through me as I remembered something.

"I nicked a blanket off the bed at the house," I confessed as Toby tucked his phone away. "I'm not a thief, honestly. I didn't pinch anything else. I'd have sent Lucien the money for it. I'll still give him the money because he won't want the blanket back. I've got it here, in my bag, but it's covered in dirt."

Toby wrapped his palm around his coffee and took a sip. "Lucien won't give a fuck about the blanket. He'll be glad you had the warmth of it. Although there can't be that many people sleeping rough wrapped in Mongolian cashmere."

He smiled, two cute dimples appearing. Under any other circumstances, I might have...yeah. Whatever. I was ruining this guy's week; he was paid to look after three pampered kids, not wander around town in the freezing cold all day. With filthy fingers, I picked at the remainder of my fries then stopped, revolted by the grime packed under my nails. Revolted by what I'd been reduced to, a charity case, accepting free food from someone I hardly knew, and nicking blankets. Toby likely found me fairly revolting too. A fresh wave of tears threatened to spill over, and I quickly stood.

"I'm going to the bogs."

Toby stood too. "Do I need to come? You're not going to scarper again, are you? I promised not to let you out of my sight."

"I think I can manage a slash on my own." I escaped before my wet eyes gave me away.

The men's toilets in McDonalds were only marginally cleaner than me. I scrubbed at my hands and face, then studied my reflection in the mirror, wondering what a nice, wholesome guy like Toby saw when he looked at me. The bastard son of a killer probably. A filthy loser he'd been ordered to track down when he could have been sitting in that snug kitchen playing games and singing songs to kids who'd never have a clue what being on the outside felt like.

"Just give me some money to tide me over. I'm not going back with you," I announced when I sat down opposite him again. "Please. I don't belong with all those rich white people and their fancy cars and their happy lives."

"What, and I do?" He waggled his stump at me.

"You do more than me."

He dimpled again. "It's not a bloody competition."

I nearly smiled back at him.

"I knew you'd say that," he continued, waving a chip around before popping it in his mouth. "But tell me what your alternatives are? Will there be a nice warm girlfriend waiting in bed for you if I drop you at the train station with a ticket pointing north?"

Instead of answering, I stared out of the window. My mum had texted me a few days ago after my mate Gary told her no one had seen me for a while. In an answering text, I'd confirmed I was alive, and that's how we'd left it. That's how we always left it. She wouldn't get in touch again, not unless I did first. The day I'd left for France, Gary's missus had told me their sofa wouldn't be available when I got back. Nights up there with the full force of the winds blasting over the Pennines made a night in Allenmouth tropical in comparison.

"I didn't think so." Toby pushed the rest of his chips over to me. "You could always contact Centrepoint. I suppose they would direct you to a homeless shelter in Bristol run by some really nice, helpful volunteers, but it would be a shame to take one of those beds and deprive someone who needed it more. Because you've got a bed at Rossingley. A comfier bed probably. And hotter showers and better food."

His phone buzzed, and pulling it out of his pocket, he glanced down, then handed it to me. "It's for you. One of those awful rich people, worrying about you."

Marcel. *Thank goodness he's safe. Send him my love, and tell him to rest and recover xx.*

"'Send him my love'? I barely know the guy," I mumbled.

Toby drained the last of his coffee and wiped his mouth with the back of his stump. I guessed he forgot he had it most of the time. "Listen," he said. "They're good people. I know Lucien is one of a kind and takes some knowing, but Jay's an ordinary bloke, honestly. Reuben's got a story, too, if you can be bothered to hear it. Trust me; you're not the only person up at that house with less than pristine white bed sheets."

He shouldered on his coat and cocked his head towards the door. "At any rate, if I don't bring you back, Lucien will kill me, and my death will be on your conscience for the rest of your days."

*

I'VE HAD THE pleasure of a few lifts in the back of police cars in my time. One of them was a souped-up Volvo, the sort they used to chase people down the motorway. I'd been around fourteen at the time, caught spraying graffiti in an underpass near my house and stupid enough to sign my own initials at the bottom. The bollocking had been worth it just to spend twenty minutes on the back seat of that flash car, sniffing the upholstery and asking the copper what all the dials were for. So my first reaction as Toby approached a swish Aston Martin and fished out a set of keys was to check over my shoulder for witnesses because if he was going to scrape them down the side of the immaculate paintwork, I wasn't in the mood for the police today.

As he pressed the fob and the car *blipped* in response, he caught me staring.

"It's not actually as much fun to drive as I thought it would be."

Those dimples again. Almost a good enough reason all on their own to return to Rossingley. "It feels like an even bigger responsibility than looking after three small children. Especially on icy country lanes."

He opened the door.

"Fuck, I'm too grubby to sit in there." The scent of luxurious leather assailed my nostrils, about fifteen cows' worth of the stuff, swathing every available surface from the compact sporty steering wheel to the couchlike bucket seats. On second thoughts, maybe I did belong with posh people and their fancy cars after all.

Toby laughed. "Don't be silly; get in. If it smells a bit whiffy, it's because Orlando puked in here a few weeks ago. Take it from me; half-digested milk is a devil to get out of leather creases. And Jay and Lucien probably have sex across the front seats regularly—I would if it were my car."

"Christ, I'm not sure I actually want to get in now."

Toby drove carefully and smoothly, although that could have been the car, not the driver. Before setting off, he attached a contraption to his stump, which slotted into another contraption on the steering wheel and a similar one on the gearstick. He saw me watching.

"Lucien and Jay sourced this from America and had it fitted for me. So I can drive automatic cars."

That was thoughtful. I nodded approvingly as my eyes roamed the interior. "It's a Vanquish S, isn't it?"

Toby side-eyed me. We were on a clear stretch of road, and he'd opened her up a little. The powerful engine growled underneath us, straining at the leash.

"Uh, maybe? If that's what the green ones are? With a wheel at each corner? You'd have to ask Jay. He's the one who really knows his cars."

Toby accelerated past a sign indicating the Rossingley village turn off a couple of miles up ahead. We overtook a tractor as we approached a straight.

"I bet you know what make and model that red tractor is though, don't you?" I asked him.

"I can go one better than that." Glancing in his rearview mirror, he pulled a face. "The driver's named Rob, and the tractor is an MF 3700. That herd of brown cows you're so fond of belongs to him."

Something or someone to do with that tractor had yanked his chain, and we sat next to each other in silence as he carefully threaded the Aston through the narrow village, giving an obligatory wave to a woman walking her dog and again to three kids pissing about on their bikes outside the church.

The heated seat had had my arse on a slow simmer for the last twenty minutes, and as I thawed out and our destination approached, my anxiety at facing them all rose. Seemed like Toby could sense it.

"Listen, Noah. I don't know much about you apart from what Lucien's told me about your da...about Guillaume. That must have been a horrible shock, finding out about his prison sentence and everything."

I nodded dumbly. Since walking away from Rossingley, I'd told myself the man who had impregnated my mother was dead to me. I'd disappear. Not back up north—there was nothing there for me either. Bristol perhaps, or London. I could find one of these Centrepoint places Toby had mentioned and try to get some help. See if I could find somewhere to hunker down indoors. But now I'd had a taste of winter homelessness, I wasn't so sure what I should do. Perhaps I should stay at Rossingley for a few days, do some work on the estate as Lucien suggested, and scrape a bit of money together.

"Maybe you should talk to Guillaume, about that stuff." He flicked me a wary look. "About your mother, on the beach. You might...um...have misunderstood what he meant? I haven't met him many times, but Guillaume seemed a..."

"I know what he said."

We coasted around the edge of the village, heading towards the long drive up to the house. A shower. A couple of nights sleep. More food.

Toby's steady voice with his soft country accent cut through my thoughts. "Are you worried you're like him? That's Lucien's theory. I mean, I can understand that. You look so much like him as well. My mum says I've been turning into my dad since I was about twelve."

I stared at him in shock. How had Lucien cottoned on to that? Or any of them, for that matter?

Toby caught me looking. "As I tried to explain, I don't know Guillaume very well, but if Marcel and Lucien accept him and love him, then that's good enough for me."

"Easy for you to say," I responded harshly. "Has your dad done a prison sentence for murder?"

"No, of course he hasn't," Toby answered. "He's a farm labourer. He's lived here all his life, just like me."

I stared out the window at the endless fucking fields and trees. Toby glanced over at me.

"It sounds like the world is a better place without the man

Guillaume killed anyhow."

"So do you think we should all go around killing people we don't like the look of?" Because I'd die an old man in prison if that was the case. Right now, I fucking hated everybody.

Toby frowned, his eyes back on the road. "No, of course, I don't. I just think...even if it was wrong, I can understand why he did it, you know? The man was molesting his disabled sister."

"Allegedly."

"Yes, allegedly, but from what Lucien says, she wasn't his only victim. And I don't think any of us can say how we'd react in the heat of that type of situation."

Was Toby's viewpoint a reasonable one? Probably. Did I care? Abso-fucking-lutely not.

"Murder, mate. Look it up in the dictionary. Usually has the words 'malice aforethought' written next to it. Not fucking 'heat of the situation'."

We'd arrived; I'd scarcely noticed. Toby switched off the engine but made no move to get out.

"Okay. But are you going to let what Guillaume's done in the past prevent you from sorting your life out? Whatever his crimes, he's served his time and he's now making the most of things. He's a good citizen and doing his best to help you now. That's got to count for something."

"I think we've just established he's a bloody murderer."

"Yes, and he's bloody served a very long prison sentence for it! Are you going to punish him all over again?"

He glared at me, then carried on before I could think of a suitable response. "When were you appointed judge, jury, and executioner, Noah? And why the hell did you go and track him down anyway, just so you could tell him to fuck off? It would have been much easier to do that by text message, you know. And cheaper."

No sign of the dimples now. Just a cold and tired feisty redhead, telling me how it was. Well, I wasn't in the mood to listen.

"Who are you, my fucking mother? You've just told me you know fuck all about anything beyond this pissy village. Thanks for the lift; I'd have walked if I'd known it was going to come with a frigging lecture."

I got out and slammed the door behind me, more of an unsatisfyingly cushioned *thunk*, to be honest, but he got the message. And then I wrenched it open again because, like a dick, I'd left my bag on the back seat.

Toby smirked at me from across the roof of the car. "You

think this is a frigging lecture? You wait until Lucien gets his hands on you. And consider taking a shower first, by the way. You stink."

*

IT WAS LESS of a lecture and more of a hypnotic persuasion that I kind of let myself go along with, probably because I needed to close my eyes for a week. Although, how a rich guy dressed in a purple jumpsuit with matching eyeshadow managed to con me into agreeing to anything, I had no idea. When I shuffled into the kitchen, head down and feeling pretty sheepish, he acted as if I'd only popped out for a loaf of bread, not sparked a three-day man hunt.

"There you are, my darling. Exactly the person I'm looking for. Have you ever done any bar work?"

A complete non sequitur, but I nodded dumbly anyhow, too knackered to care. I'd had a whole host of mindless cash-in-hand jobs. One way or another, I'd never held any of them down.

"Marvellous. They're short-staffed up at the Rossingley Arms; the lovely Donna has broken her ankle in three places tripping over a pregnant ewe. Poor Lizzie-the-landlady can't possibly manage on her own, not with Alf's mother being so poorly. And the early beetroot needs planting, so Henry will have to be roped in to do that as well as pull pints."

He flashed me a pointy grin. "I'll tell her you're free four nights a week and Sunday lunches. The tractor rally is only a month away, so they'll need some help with the pop-up stall too; it sounds like Donna may not be fully fit until the cricket match in June."

Either my hypothermia was worse than I'd thought, or I'd accidentally strolled onto the set of *The Archers*. Who the fuck were these people? And what was the obsession with fucking cricket?

"You can start tomorrow, which gives you time for a nice hot bath and a good night's sleep. We all missed you dreadfully, you know."

CHAPTER NINE

TOBY

AS TO BE expected, the mysterious surly 'foreigner' behind the bar was the talk of the village.

"I hope by 'foreigner', you aren't referring to the colour of Noah's skin, Lee," I commented sharply after Noah had poured him a perfect pint. From his apparent ease, bar work appeared to be employment Noah had picked up and dropped at some point in his past. Although more likely, he'd been fired. His customer service skills required serious finessing before he stood any chance of taking Lizzie's mantle as the Rossingley Arms most popular member of staff.

"Nah, mate, chill. But he's not from round these parts, is he?"

In Lee's world, foreign was basically anywhere beyond Allenmouth. "No," I conceded, watching Noah sulkily serve a couple of my mum's friends. Twice his age, they were giggling and batting their eyelashes at him like a pair of teenagers, not married dinner ladies with seven kids between them. Sunday night was darts league night, and the place was busy. "He's from up north somewhere."

"Don't they teach them how to crack a smile up there?"

It would appear not. That's not to say the mean and moody vibe he had going didn't suit him because it most definitely did, as did his low-slung Levi's and one of his dad's old, faded Olympique Marseille T-shirts. Sheila, one of the dinner ladies, caught me checking him out, raised her drink, and then her eyebrows at me across the bar. Not embarrassing at all—that would be reported straight back to my mother before closing time.

Joe joined us. I wasn't sure how much to divulge regarding Noah, but I needn't have worried, the Rossingley grapevine had been well fertilized. "He's Reuben's French mate's boy, isn't he? That Guillaume fella. Spitting image of him too."

Lee furrowed his brow. "How's a bender like 'im produce a boy like that?"

Not the sharpest rake in the potting shed, our Lee. Nor indeed, the most politically correct. I sighed heavily.

"Do I need to get my pink and blue felt-tipped pens out for you, Lee, and draw a diagram?"

"Well, you might have to because two blue pens ain't gonna get the job done, are they?" He openly stared at Noah in the way only country folk did, as if he was the result of some kind of immaculate conception.

I leaned up and whispered in his ear. "Brace yourself, Lee. Some men like to have sex with women *and* other men." I brought my finger to my lips and made a hushing sound. "But keep it a secret, yeah? Otherwise, all you straight boys will be jumping on the bandwagon, and then who's going to be left for the likes of me?"

I wasn't entirely sure Lee was convinced, but the first darts match had begun, and his attention had started to wander. As had mine because Rob Langford had stepped up to the oche and effortlessly thrown three darts in a neat grouping, to low grunts of approval from his blokeish teammates. As he cockily sauntered to the board to retrieve them, my gaze dropped to his meaty backside, where blue denim stretched tight over an arse and thigh muscles honed from years of hard outdoor graft. As he spun around, darts in hand, his eyes met mine, and a brief look of annoyance crossed his ruddy features before he looked away.

Irritated myself, I turned back to the bar and my drink, only to find Noah casually leaning against the optics, his arms folded and observing the whole thing.

"What's your problem?" I asked him.

He shrugged. "You should be asking yourself that, mate. I thought this place was paradise?"

A fool's paradise, more like. Rob fucking Langford, ruining my evening with one sneer. Of course, after that I had to have three more warm gins, only splitting one small bottle of tonic between the lot. Rob's team hammered the visitors, which meant his gang strutted about the place like a bunch of fucking randy peacocks, while the man himself pawed yet another of his short-lived female acquaintances. By closing time, I wasn't fit company for anyone. I could have gone home for the night—my parents place was much closer—but not fancying my mum's twenty questions at breakfast in the morning, I pulled my hoodie up over my ears and began trudging up the hill towards the big house.

"Hey, wait. Toby!"

In the gloom, Noah jogged to catch me up.

"It's not like you to want company." I carried on walking, making no effort to slow for him.

"Don't flatter yourself, mate. I just don't want to get lost and my body be pulled from the lake in a week's time. Or mauled by that bloody enormous bull. Why aren't there any fucking streetlights in this place?"

"Don't need them," I answered gruffly. "We all know where we're headed."

Wasn't that the truth.

We stomped on in silence, our boots making a satisfying crunch on the gravel drive. I had an early start with the kids in the morning and was already regretting the booze. Eliza's incessant chatter and a hangover were never a good combination.

"What's with you and Farmer Giles, then?" Noah asked as we rounded the first bend. The big house loomed ahead of us, a few lights twinkling from the west wing windows but otherwise shrouded in darkness.

"Nothing."

"Didn't look like nothing. He's the guy we overtook in

the tractor yesterday, isn't he?"

Christ, he didn't miss much. I kicked at some loose gravel. "Believe me, it's nothing."

"Is everyone in this village gay?"

I gave a hollow laugh. "No. And what makes you think I am?"

He made a show of scratching his head. "Let me think. You work as a nanny for two gay blokes, and you were checking out Farmer Giles's arse. "

Variations on shit I'd heard loads of times added to my crap night sent me rocketing straight into orbit. "I prefer the term manny, not nanny. And I'm sorry if in your world being a *manny* isn't a proper masculine job. But I'll have you know, there are plenty of straight men who enjoy childcare too. Are you about to tell me all male nurses and hairdressers and models must be gay too? Because that's going to be terribly regressive of you."

"No," he countered. "I had a mate back home who was a hairdresser. He wasn't gay. I'm just asking if you are; that's all. And there's nothing wrong with a bloke looking after kids. I'd have loved to have someone to kick a ball around with when I was growing up."

Okay, so I'd misjudged him, but I wasn't about to

apologise. My legs still ached as a reminder that I'd tramped round Allenmouth for three days. I kicked at a pebble again.

"Not that it's any of your business, but, yes, I am gay. Even if I wasn't, I'd still be a manny and happy to work for Lucien. And for your information, it's not a secret. I came out years ago."

I think I preferred silent, grumpy-chops Noah to this talkative, needling version of him.

"He's not out, though, is he?"

"Who?"

"Farmer Giles."

"That's none of your business either. And his name is Rob."

"So you know who I meant, then."

I swore under my breath. Four gins had loosened my tongue.

We reached the house and let ourselves in through the side door. I wanted to be alone to lick my wounds in peace, but unfortunately, in his wisdom, Lucien had allocated Noah the room next to mine in the east wing, so I had to endure his company a few minutes longer.

I bolted the door and reset the alarm. Knowing my way by heart, I didn't bother switching on the lights, so Noah stayed close to me as we padded through the silent house. Very close. Invading my personal space kind of close.

"Are you scared of the dark or something?"

"No."

As we left the familiarity of the kitchen and library, his arm had brushed against me several times. By the time we reached the main staircase, I'd realised he was practically clutching my coat.

"Are you sure?"

"'Course I'm bloody not! But the age and the size of this place would give anyone the heebie-jeebies. There must be all sorts of weird sounds and things going bump in the night."

"*Whooo.*" I chuckled as he flinched.

"You fucker. Don't do that!"

After a year of living there, I was totally used to the house and all its idiosyncratic creaks and draughts. Nevertheless, I knew how he felt; winding up and down these corridors at night on my own had been a bit spooky the first few times. Not that I would ever let on. I was going to have some gin-soaked fun instead.

"They say the ghost of the first Lady Louisa haunts the landing up here at night," I lied in a hushed voice as we trod soundlessly up the main staircase. "The story goes she was beheaded. By *her own husband*!"

Noah gasped in awe behind me. "Really? No way!"

"Yes, way. Jay is convinced he saw her once, just after he first moved in here. Wandering around the galleried landing with her mangled head tucked under her arm. A trail of blood covered the carpet behind her. He nearly shat himself."

"Oh my God. You're fucking kidding me, right?"

"Nope. You know Jay; he wouldn't make that sort of crap up. She had long blonde hair hanging from her head and dripping with blood from where her neck had been severed."

As I'd dropped my voice even lower, his warm hand fumbled next to me, then suddenly gripped my stump. I smothered a laugh; the oddness of that must have spooked him even more. Very few people aside from my family and Lucien's kids had ever touched it. As we tripped down three steps and along another dark corridor towards the east wing, he still held on, even tighter if anything.

Without warning, I rapped sharply on a dimly lit portrait of a stern-looking, long forgotten Duchamps-Avery. Noah jumped as the sound echoed menacingly around us, then let out an expletive as he tripped over his own feet.

"Shit! Don't fucking do stuff like that!"

"That's a painting of her. Before she lost her head,

obviously. We've probably woken her up, like in those Harry Potter films, remember? Where the people in the paintings walk around and hop from frame to frame? She'll be creeping after us down the corridor."

Behind me, he sucked in another sharp gulp of air, and I choked back a snort.

"Freddie says that when he used to stay in the east wing as a kid, he woke once in the night to see her standing at the end of his bed. Damn near screamed his own head off when he spotted her. He's never slept in the east wing since."

"No. Shit." Noah gripped me even tighter, his hand clammy.

"Yeah, I know, right? Stuff of fucking nightmares. Makes me glad my bedroom door has a bloody enormous bolt across it."

"Mine fucking hasn't!"

Oops.

I carried on, trying to keep my voice even and absolutely not dissolve into a fit of giggles. "Sometimes, when there's a full moon, like tonight, you can hear Lady Louisa's favourite pet cow mooing. Like it's crying—mourning her or something."

"No way. Oh my God."

"Yeah, I'm surprised we haven't heard her already. Buttercup, she was called. A beautiful big brown one. Used to follow Lady Louisa around like a puppy. Apparently, at her mistress's funeral, Buttercup trampled Lady Louisa's husband to death, then ate most of him. Now she moos at the full moon, like a werewolf, pining for her dead mistress."

"Oh, fuck. Just switch the bloody lights on, Toby. Turn your phone torch on or something. Just fucking turn it on."

I lost it then. Unable to suppress it any longer, a sudden shriek of laughter burst out of me. Noah yelped with shock and leapt three feet in the air. Flicking on the light switch next to us, I discovered him trembling and white as a sheet, his brow covered in a sheen of sweat. I collapsed in a heap of giggles on the floor.

"You absolute fucker! Is any of that true?"

"What? Buttercup? Yeah! Damn right! If you shut up a second, you can hear her."

Bless him, the townie idiot actually went quiet. I made a low-pitched mooing noise, honed over twenty-five years of living next door to a field of cows.

"You absolute fucker." He wiped his brow and narrowed his eyes at me. "I nearly pissed myself, Toby! None of that bollocks is true, is it?"

I pulled myself together. "Nope, not a word. Come on, you bloody scaredy-cat. I promise I'll keep the lights on."

I sniggered all the way to our bedrooms while Noah kept up a steady stream of swear words until we reached our adjacent doors. We paused, giving each other a quick nod.

"You seemed to get on all right working behind the bar tonight," I said.

"Yeah, I did." His throat emitted a low noise, alarmingly similar to a laugh—a sound I hadn't believed him capable of producing. "First time I've ever poured a half of shandy for a bloke's ferret though."

I smiled. After the tales I'd just spun, he'd never believe me if I told him the ferret owner, Old Sam, had a twin brother who came in with two more ferrets on Wednesdays and arranged them on barstools so they could share a bag of pork scratchings.

"Old Sam's finally weaned Banjo off the Jack Daniels and coke, then?"

I raise my hand to the door handle. In the gloom, I spied a brief flash of white teeth, transforming his face from merely drop-dead gorgeous to heart-stoppingly sensational.

"You're taking the piss, aren't you?"

CHAPTER TEN

NOAH

SO, ONE WEEK passed by. And then another. I got paid in cash for the hours I'd worked at the pub and left most of it on the kitchen table. It probably covered the cost of two square inches of Mongolian cashmere, but the principle mattered more. I'd googled Lucien Avery. The guy didn't need my few quid; he was fucking loaded. But it stuck in my craw, being even more beholden to him than I was already. I'd pay Marcel and Guillaume back for the airfare, too, one day.

Every day brought a text from Marcel. Sometimes it was chatty, telling me about the weather, his work, or reporting on the killer's latest football match. Sometimes, brief. One included a photo of him and Guillaume, wrapped up warm and huddled together, a pair of old queens enjoying hot chocolates outside a restaurant, with a port full of fishing boats as a backdrop. They looked happy and in love. The killer was smiling. Marcel always did that older person thing of putting his name at the end of his texts—both of their names, actually—followed by a kiss, as though I wouldn't know who had sent it otherwise. Which was cute. I hadn't answered any of them, mostly because I didn't know how to respond, apart from the photo, which I deliberated over for way longer than I should before giving it a thumbs-up emoji.

I had planned to leave Rossingley at the end of one week; I even went so far as stuffing some clothes into my bag and checking the bus timetables. But then I overheard Reuben telling Jay how much Lizzie would have struggled by herself on darts night without my help. And Lucien mentioned, again in my hearing, that a sharp frost was forecast; temperatures were expected to plummet below freezing and hit a new record low. So I unpacked, deciding that watching TV with Toby in the library when Lucien and Jay went on date night wasn't the worst way to while away a midweek wintry evening. I promised myself I'd leave when the weather improved, and I'd gathered a bit more cash together.

Since his ridiculous spooky tales, Toby and I had rubbed along. I told him I'd enrolled in, then abandoned, a car maintenance course at college, and the next thing I knew, Jay was looming over me wondering out loud why I didn't use my existing credits and sign up for the second year of the course at Allenmouth college. Along with Toby, Jay was the most normal person in the whole crazy Rossingley village, so to keep him happy, I lied and agreed to look into it. Sometimes I wondered if they were all competing to see who could be the most philanthropic, whether they had a list somewhere. Because Lucien, Marcel, Jay—all of them—clearly got off on being fucking nice to me.

It got me thinking about my future though. I loved cars, and I couldn't be their pet charitable project for much longer. Maybe I could find a course or an apprenticeship when I left here.

Although my bar job kept me busy, it didn't leave me with enough ready cash to swan off into Allenmouth whenever I felt like it. So I started finding myself in the kitchen most mornings, with Toby and the baby, having had enough of the four walls of my room or wandering around on my tod.

"How do you know what to do?" I asked him as he deftly extracted the baby—Orlando—out of a complicated contraption around his middle and onto the floor, all the time singing an out of tune version of Humpty Dumpty. A well-used satin-trimmed blanket hung from his shoulder. He handed the blanket to Orlando who promptly stuffed a corner of it into his gummy mouth.

"Erm...three years at childcare college? And I'm the eldest child in my family. I've been clearing up sick and changing nappies for as long as I can remember."

"Do Lucien and Jay know you tie him up in a straitjacket?"

Toby laughed. "It's a papoose, you moron." He began untangling himself from it. "And not just any papoose, I'll have you know. Tibetan monks have handwoven this one from organic hemp. Orlando owns this model in three more colours, and he also has a leopard print version, too, with diamanté studs around the seams."

He rolled his eyes. "Guess which is Lucien's favourite? Jay thinks it looks like some sort of kinky sex restraint. Trust me, he'd know."

Toby folded the papoose and put it to one side. "Me and

him tend to go a little more low-key with this one. I'll put the kettle on."

I watched him as he set about preparing toasted soldiers for Orlando and some tea for us. He moved about the vast kitchen with a quiet confidence, perfectly at home as he held a one-sided conversation with Orlando. So adept, a new-comer would easily miss that he only had one hand. On my first day at Rossingley, surrounded by men as extraordinarily attractive as Freddie and as classically handsome as Jay, and in this fabulous house, littered with beautiful things, I'd dis-missed Toby as ordinary-looking. A smallish, slender youth with reddish hair and a freckled nose. Like a plain green leaf, out of place amongst a priceless vase of roses. I watched him surreptitiously as he gracefully reached for a plate, humming tunelessly to Orlando, and realised I'd done him a disservice.

"By the way, there's a letter for you on the side," he said with his back to me. He pointed in the vague direction of an ornate dresser. "From France."

Foreign stamps and loopy writing covered the front of a white envelope. Addressed to Noah Bennett. It had to be from Marcel; he was exactly the sort of person who would send a letter when an email or text did the job more efficiently. All the same, receiving it gave me an unexpected shot of pleasure, and I folded it in half before stuffing it in my jeans pocket to read later.

With an unfeasibly large amount of blanket jammed into his mouth, Orlando waddled over to where I sat at the kitchen table. He pulled it out of his mouth again, with the satisfaction of a magician producing a rabbit out of a top hat, and triumphantly presented it to me in all its soggy glory.

"Uh, Toby, what does he want me to do?"

"Take it of course." He grinned, twin dimples coming into play. "You're honoured. He doesn't let just anyone touch his favourite blankie, you know."

"I don't feel very honoured." I plucked it out of Orlando's podgy hand, holding it gingerly by a dry corner.

"He's been desperate to make friends with the scary, grumpy man that's started keeping us company in his kitchen, haven't you, my poppet?"

I gave Toby a look. "He told you that, did he?"

"Of course he did." He ruffled Orlando's mop of black hair. "I speak fluent Orlandish, don't I, sweetie pie?"

Orlando burbled delightedly. As babies went, even I had to admit he was a cutey. I had a feeling it was probably uncool to speculate about parentage with same-sex couples, but this boy was obviously Jay's progeny, all the way from his soulful brown eyes and thick head of dark hair down to his chunky future rugby player thighs. I guessed people thought as much when they saw me and my sperm donor side by side. Especially on a day like today, when I was modelling yet another of his cast-off sweatshirts.

"He wants to climb into your lap," observed Toby, pouring tea into a mug. "Without his godfathers around, he thinks you're the next best thing."

I'd never held a baby before. It showed.

"Go on," Toby urged. "He doesn't bite."

"I'm scared I'll hurt him."

"You won't. Orlando is pretty indestructible."

I picked him up—he weighed a ton—and balanced the little boy carefully on one of my thighs. Snatching his disgusting blanket off me, he contentedly began chewing it.

"There you are," said Toby, reaching into the fridge for the milk. "Bezzies for life."

There was something quite peaceful about the warm weight of Orlando's sturdy body resting on my lap. Toby handed me my mug, and we both sat for a few minutes watching him do his thing.

"I'm surprised Jay and Lucien leave him alone with one of his godfathers," I said suddenly. I hadn't quite worked out how to refer to Guillaume out loud, but Toby knew which one I meant. The names I used for him in my mind weren't appropriate in polite company, and I couldn't bring myself to refer to him as my father. The observation hadn't randomly popped into my head; I'd been mulling it over for a while, ever since the day I arrived here, when my sperm donor had tucked Orlando into a pushchair, and they'd gone out alone to visit the ducks.

"Why?" answered Toby, half laughing. "He's really good with him. He's a great godfather."

"Aren't they worried he'll, I dunno, do something to him?"

He laughed again. "Like what?"

"I dunno. Something bad, I guess."

Toby put his mug down and gave me a hard look. "Listen, Noah. I know you've got a lot of stuff going on. And I know some of it will be to do with Guillaume. But I think I've already made it pretty clear the way I see it. He's done his time. If Lucien and Jay are happy to welcome him into their home and make him Orlando's godfather, then that's good enough for me. Maybe you should try to accept that. Maybe— and I'm going out on a limb here—their attitudes are the right one?"

I had a tendency to ignore unsolicited good advice. But Toby had no axe to grind; resolving my inner turmoil mattered not one jot to him. A couple of weeks ago, our similar heated discussion across the front seats of the Aston had me slamming the car door and flouncing off, gravely offended. Now, I had a baby on my lap, a cup of tea in my hand, and a cute guy diplomatically trying to chisel away at the rotten lump of hatred squatting in my core. I had no intention of flouncing anywhere.

"Easy for you to say," I answered mildly. "You haven't inherited his gene pool."

"More's the pity." He smirked. "He's not freckly and ginger for a start. And"—he gave me an eyebrow wiggle—"I've seen him in his blue swimming trunks. Very Daniel Craig. He's got some damn good genes going."

I laughed and groaned; at the same time, Toby's millions of freckles flushed a delightful pink as he realised he'd paid me a backhanded compliment. "That's gross, Toby. My d— He's about twenty years older than us!"

He shook his head and tutted. "So's Daniel Craig. Oh dear, don't tell me you're an age queen, Noah."

Bloody hell, Toby was flirting with me, albeit in a flustered way. Dimples and freckles were popping up all over the place, and it was kind of adorable.

Bored with his blanket and recognising he was no longer the centre of our attention, Orlando held out an arm for his lidded cup. Gripping it in both plump hands, he took a long draught from it, his two big eyes staring at me over the rim. I heard a click and looked across to see Toby had snapped a photo.

"What's that for?"

He thumbed a few keys on his phone. "I'm sending it to Lucien and Jay at work. I usually send them at least one a day. And he looks very sweet propped on your lap."

"They'll probably text back and say I'm a bad influence on him or something." Cuddling Orlando suddenly felt a little less comfortable.

"Don't be ridiculous. I haven't seen you do or say anything I would be unhappy for Orlando to witness. Listen, when he's finished his toast, I'm taking him out for a walk to say hello to all his animal friends, starting with Harkin and Penelope. And finishing by feeding the ducks. You can come with us if you like."

I liked the sound of that a hell of a lot more than I should. Not that Toby needed to know.

"Might as well. There's bugger all else to do."

Toby made a show of clapping his right hand and his left lower arm firmly over Orlando's ears. "What you meant to say was, 'I'm at a loose end, Toby. I'd love to join you and Orlando.'"

A thought struck me. "Hang on, are Harkin and Penelope cows?"

"Yeah. We've named all of them. Harkin and Penelope are Orlando's favourites, and then we have Snowdrop and Flora—those two are my favourites, and..." He was trying not to smile as his eyes searched around the kitchen. "And then there are Milky and Teabag and...um...Lurpack and..."

The fucker was taking the piss. "They're the kid's horses, aren't they?"

Toby gave me a mock gasp and tutted. "Ponies, darling," he answered in an excellent impression of his ultra-posh boss. "I think you'll find, here at Rossingley, we prefer the term *ponies.*"

"There's a difference?"

He cleared his throat with dramatic flair and carried on in his false posh voice. "Gosh, as even Eliza would be able to tell you, a horse is an animal larger than fourteen point two hands. On the *other hand*"—I winced at his really bad pun— "a pony is an equine under that height."

Dimples and freckles and shy flirting. A winning combination.

"So we're not visiting the cows, then," I confirmed with my sternest look.

"Only if you promise to be very, very good."

We took a slow stroll around the perimeter. Some school kids were having a sports lesson, and several of them waved at Toby, a couple even coming over to pet Orlando. It was kind of...nice. Toby was easy company, cute, too, although he had no idea I saw him that way. I'd known I was bi for years, and while a heap of girlfriends had come and gone, I'd never had any experience with boys. More through lack of opportunity rather than a grand master plan. But I now knew I had a type: skinny, freckly, and ginger.

I forgot about the letter until much later, long after Orlando had giggled with delight as one of the ponies snaffled a sugar cube from his outstretched hand. And long after I'd tried my hardest to pretend I didn't care either way if I accompanied them to the duck pond or not. Nor whether I kept them company as they wandered down to the football pitch. Not a cow in sight, thank God.

Dear Noah,

This is from me, not Marcel, although Marcel has helped with my written English. And anyhow, I have no secrets from him. If you stop reading now and throw this letter away, then I'll understand. If you never want to see or hear from me again, tell Lucien, and I'll understand.

I penned hundreds of letters during my years in prison. Reuben has piles of them. But none as important as this one, a letter I never anticipated writing, to a son I never dreamed of having. Coming home that evening and finding you in my living room was a profound shock, yet also one of the happiest moments of my life. I'm deeply sorry I couldn't show you that at the time.

Travelling alone to find me in France took a lot of courage. We're both very proud of you.

Can we give each other a chance? I don't deserve one, but I'm asking anyway.

I think of you as my son, but I don't expect you to think of me as your father—that title is earned. One day, perhaps.

Lucien says you seem okay, and Reuben says you are quite a hit with the village ladies at the pub.

Yours, Guillaume.

PS. Have they roped you into the cricket yet?

CHAPTER ELEVEN

TOBY

THIS SUMMER WE were going to show those cocky young farmers a lesson they would never forget. Or so Jay insisted we keep telling ourselves.

"Who votes we move this practice inside, into the ballroom?" Freddie asked, hidden somewhere within the most luxuriously padded skiing jacket I'd ever clapped eyes on. Eight hands shot up. Jay, a leading proponent of the 'you'll only feel the cold if you stand still' school of winter training, and only wearing a lightweight sweatshirt, shook his head. Seeing as the sport we were training for was cricket, standing still was difficult to avoid, which probably accounted for it being a pastime conducive to the summer months and not the second week of March.

"'Fraid not, lads," Jay said. "Something to do with a rare, early example of forest glass and a priceless sixteenth-century frieze on a section of the wooden panelling."

To warm up, he sent us on a run around the perimeter of the lawn. Noah and I jogged out ahead. Not because we were super fit, but because Steve needed to finish smoking his fag first; Freddie launched into some complicated stretches, monopolising Reuben's attention; my dad and Uncle Will were middle-aged men; and Lee and Joe hadn't run anywhere in living memory. In his usual cheery fashion, Noah cursed with every step.

"I thought you northerners were immune to the cold?" I puffed.

"So did I! Brass monkey weather, this is. I'm gonna have to stop thinking of you lot as southern softies if the forecast carries on like this."

With our breath misting in front of our faces, we passed alongside the walled garden. Bloody freezing, considering spring had officially sprung. I was beginning to wish I'd stayed indoors and helped put the kiddies to bed with Lucien. A heavier tread sounded behind and Jay overtook, cheekily ruffling my hair. "Come on, Tobes. Put your back into it."

"Bastard."

"He's all right, isn't he?" panted Noah.

"When he's not forcing us to do this, then yeah," I agreed.

I looked over my shoulder. My dad and Uncle Will were making progress at a slow trot, and Freddie and Reuben had finally set off. Reuben's chatter floated towards us. Steve, Joe, and Lee ambled along behind them.

"He wants to know if you'll still be here for the grudge match in the summer," I said as we rounded a bend. "Otherwise, we'll have to rope in Second-Best Man to take your place. Which means Lucien will have to buy a crate of IPA and cultivate a hipster beard."

"You lost me at Second-Best Man. I swear this village has its own fucking dialect."

"So are you?"

"Am I what?"

"Going to be here?"

He thudded next to me for a few metres, adjusting his

longer stride so it matched mine. This morning, I'd discovered that young men unconfidently dangling chubby babies on their knee was an extreme fucking turn-on. I'd snapped that photo as much for me as for Orlando's parents. Noah had hung around afterwards too; we hadn't talked about anything in particular, but he'd asked questions about Lucien and Jay, and I'd filled him in on a few details. Such as Lucien's family tragedy and his ongoing commitment to the village and its inhabitants. He'd been...surprised.

I'd half expected him not to turn up for cricket training, but here he was, dressed in something suspiciously similar to a tracksuit I'd seen his dad wearing, not that I had the stupidity to point that out.

"I don't know," he huffed out. "They might have moved on to their next charity case by then." He nudged my shoulder with his own. "I'll race you back."

The bloody idiot. One step forward and two steps back. How would we ever get him to believe that he wasn't a bloody charity case? That his dad and Marcel would walk over hot coals to see him happy because that's what good fathers did? Especially ones with chequered pasts, who hadn't even known they had a child and were determined to make up for it. I watched him sprint on ahead, annoyed despite the chance to enjoy his easy athletic grace.

"He is his father's son, *non*?" Reuben jogged up alongside me. Seems he'd spotted the easy athletic grace too.

"Yeah, but whatever you do, don't say that out loud. He's a touch sensitive, to put it mildly."

Freddie swept past, and Reuben swore in French, then smiled. "These sporty types, they sulk if we don't let them win. Does Noah ever mention *mon ami* Guillaume?"

I shook my head. "No, not much, but at least he's stopped pulling a face whenever anyone else brings him up in conversation. Marcel texts him regularly, and as far as I can tell, he usually replies. I might be wrong, but I think he likes receiving Marcel's news."

Reuben seemed pleased with this, and I knew he'd report back to Guillaume later. "So, you think he will stay?"

I watched Noah round a corner ahead of us alongside Freddie. It made for a good view; one I'd be happy to see a lot more.

"I don't know," I answered honestly. "He's a stubborn bugger. He finds accepting help really difficult, as if he can't trust that Guillaume and Lucien don't have some sort of ulterior motive."

"They do, though," Reuben contradicted. "It's that they

want him to be part of our lives, Guillaume's especially."

He made it sound so simple. It was a pity we couldn't persuade Noah to see it that way. "He loves his cars apparently, so Jay had the idea of subtly trying to persuade him to sign up for a trainee mechanic course at college, without him noticing that we're in cahoots. To get him to put down some sort of roots here."

"That's good. I'll tell Guillaume; he will be pleased."

For a few steps, Reuben jogged alongside me in silence. Noah and Freddie had reached the end, turned around, and were running back towards us, seemingly hardly out of puff at all. Reuben and I gave them both an appreciative look as they passed; it was difficult not to. Reuben spoke.

"We say in France that a tree's beauty lies in its branches, but its strength lies in its roots." He tapped my shoulder. "I will work on the college course too. We concentrate together on developing Noah's roots, *non*? The beauty, he has already mastered."

*

"WHAT DID MARCEL have to say in his letter?" I asked Noah, pretty bravely, all things considered. Having completed the warmup loop, Jay had chucked me a cricket ball and now had us doing catching practice in pairs. I steeled myself, half expecting Noah to tell me to mind my own fucking business. He didn't—significant progress in itself.

"It wasn't from Marcel. It was from him."

We concentrated on tossing the ball between us for a few minutes. I was beginning to think he wouldn't say anything else, but then he lobbed it at me with a little more force than strictly necessary.

"He wants me to give him a chance," he said.

"Are you going to?"

"Dunno. I haven't decided yet."

"It's not an unreasonable request." I possibly had a death wish. "After all, you reached out to him first."

He cocked his head to the left slightly, sooty eyes narrowed and locked onto mine, hopefully contemplating my words and not which part of my anatomy to punch. He pursed his lips in an extremely kissable pout, which, funnily enough, I elected not to point out. "Huh," he responded eventually.

Jay had four sets of cricket nets lined up, which was three more than most village cricket teams owned, but then most village cricket teams weren't bankrolled by a benevolent earl. In pairs, we began batting and bowling at one another. Behind Freddie's relaxed, self-deprecating demeanour and goose-down Moncler jacket hid a rather decent batsman. The rest of us, however, had quite a lot of ground to cover prior to the summer. My bowling would become passable after a few more net practice sessions; no one expected much of me with a bat, for obvious reasons.

"The farmers are going to bloody thrash us again," I commented despondently after watching Joe lunge with his bat and miss a simple underarm toss from Jay. Eliza and Arthur could have done better with their plastic toy versions.

"Why do you care?" asked Noah. "It's only a game. Or is it one farmer in particular you want to beat?"

"I told you, Noah. He's a guy I know; that's all. I'm just fed up with them thrashing us every year."

Divulging Rob Langford's sexuality wasn't my call, even though I hated the effect he had on me. I'd been lucky, my parents had taken my coming out in stride; not everyone had that solid family support. Even so, it bloody hurt—the blowing hot and cold, the nagging knowledge I was being used for his convenience and still pathetically held out hope it would turn into something more.

"Let's swap; it's my turn to bat," I suggested, trying to divert his attention. No such luck.

"I suppose he's okay to look at." Noah casually paced out

his short run up. "I've seen better. You could do better."

My belly performed a sort of swoop, preventing my brain from functioning at the precise moment Noah bowled, tossing the ball out towards me as casually as his compliment. Swiping wildly, I missed, losing my balance, and performing a clumsy pirouette. I landed heavily in an untidy heap of pads, helmet, glove, and bat. The bales behind me clattered to the ground.

"Ouch."

I'd have an impressive bruise on my hipbone by tomorrow morning. My pride already boasted one.

As a one-handed batsman, my aims were modest: stay in, defend my wicket, let my batting partner score runs when he was on strike. I gathered myself together, acknowledging that even by my low standards, I'd made a pig's ear of things.

"You've got a bigger swing than Tarzan, mate," chortled Lee from the nets next door. Trust him to have noticed me being shite; him and Joe would be taking the piss from now until practice finished.

"Are you okay?" Noah stood over me, holding out a hand to help me up.

"Yeah, I'll live. Thanks."

I clambered to my feet and replaced the bales. Lee was still pissing himself laughing, and I gave him the finger. I sensed Noah throwing him a hard look as I retrieved the ball from the depths of the netting and chucked it back to him. Rubbing it dry on his sweatpants, he paced to the start of his run up again. I braced myself, then resumed the position. After I indicated I was ready, he bowled, and sure enough, another ball sailed past me. Followed by another.

Noah bowled spin, not even particularly quickly, but bloody hell, he was accurate. And his smooth action, his lean body arching up into the overarm release—I could happily admire that all night long. Which possibly accounted for why I never managed to get my bat on the ball, but at least I stayed on my feet. I wasn't brave enough to tell it to Noah, but being gifted at sport, as well as good looks, must run in his genes. Jay had only given him a couple of technique pointers, and already he was on his way to becoming the second-best bowler on the team, behind Jay himself.

I steadied my position for the last ball of the over, hopefully protecting my wicket as Noah jogged forwards, winding up for release. My last chance to appear vaguely competent. From the corner of my eye, I spotted Joe had joined Lee in the spectator's gallery, and predictably, the fuckers were keeping up a running commentary on my failings. Noah's ball was plumb; it spun inwards at an impossible angle, and as the bales tumbled with a rattle behind me, I cursed at being the one bearing the brunt of his improved technique.

"Maybe turn the bat over next time, Tobes," goaded Lee. "It might have the instructions written on it."

I was about to suggest that I turn it over, then use it to clatter him over the head, when Noah straightened from his run up and beat me to it. Only in a much less friendly fashion.

"Do you want a closer look at the bat yourself, mate? 'Cos that can be arranged if you don't shut the fuck up."

"Hey, Noah, relax. He's only trying to wind me up. Let it go."

Lee snorted. "Catch a load of this guy, Joe! Been here five minutes, thinks he's bloody running the place! Tobes can take a bit of stick, can't you, Tobes?"

"Takes a lot of stick, from what I've heard," Joe cackled.

To be honest, that was pretty sharp for him. I rolled my eyes; it was nothing I'd not had before. They'd been taking the piss out of me all my life. I was about to applaud his surprising burst of wit and then see if Jay could give me some bowling tips, when it registered that Noah had abandoned our cricket net and dived into theirs, clinching Joe against one of the netting posts. And not clinched in an impulsive, romantic way, although him defending my virtue was all kinds of hot.

His hooded eyes took on that smouldering, fight-or-fuck look again, most definitely leaning more towards the former than the latter.

"Say that again, mate, and I'll shove a stick up *your* arse."

"Gonna shove one up mine as well, are you?" One of Lee's fat fingers poked into Noah's chest, and for a second, I fancied Noah was preparing to take both of them on.

As if by magic, Jay appeared, Reuben at his side. "Settle down, lads."

Something about Jay's tone and possibly the fact that he was six foot four with the build of a Transformer made Noah loosen his hold on Joe. But from the look on Joe's face, it wasn't before he'd frightened the bejesus out of him. Jay pulled them apart, keeping a firm hand on each man's shoulder.

"We're all on the same team, guys. So cool it. Save the sledging and your tempers for when we face the young farmers, all right?"

Taking the heat out of the situation, Reuben hung around with Noah and me, while Jay dragged Lee and Joe off to the far nets to let them blow off steam by taking the piss out of a genial Freddie for half an hour. Arms folded across his chest, Noah took up a sulky, sexy-as-fuck stance against one of the netting uprights. Seemed he'd decided practice was over for the evening. For all I knew, he'd decided his time at Rossingley was over too.

"I have a red Volkswagen Polo," began Reuben.

I stifled a snort. As if that would entice Noah to announce he'd stay and sign up for the mechanic course first thing tomorrow. Unsurprisingly, he didn't bite.

"It's a nice car," Reuben continued gamely. "Nice colour. Three years old. *Économique.*"

Apparently, Reuben's car knowledge was on a par with my own. With a distinct lack of audience participation, he changed tack as I swapped my bat and pads with him. "My gardeners are little charmers, *non?*"

He took up a position in front of the wicket and glanced up at Noah, clearly unafraid to take him on. Such a sweet, happy guy; it was very easy to forget Reuben had spent a number of years behind bars himself. "You have a temper, Noah. You think you are a chip off the old potato, *non?*"

Noah eyed him balefully, his chin jutting. How was I expected to concentrate on my bowling with him smouldering like that?

"Maybe," he acknowledged sourly. "In some ways. And yeah, I have a temper. But I like to think if I was going to fuck a woman I'd only just met, I'd at least check her age and wear a johnnie."

A heavy silence fell, and the temperature of the night air rose by a few degrees.

Reuben's lips thinned as he contemplated Noah. "You are quick to criticise, yes? Is that because you've never made a mistake yourself, *mon ami*?"

Reuben took a step closer. "In France, we say speak your mind freely, but make sure you drive a fast car. So, you watch your words, Noah. Only one of us is holding a cricket bat."

I quickly glanced around. Jay was nowhere in sight.

"Sure, I'm happy to criticise." With a cool shrug, Noah ignored Reuben's implied threat. Still in the same relaxed pose, propped against the netting, he continued, "And I've made plenty of mistakes. But if that had been one of them, I'd at least have the grace to regret it afterwards."

Reuben's eyes widened with astonishment before he started to laugh with genuine warmth. "*Mon dieu*, you think Guillaume *should* regret it?" He shook his head, still smiling. "Yes, now I know you are chip off the stubborn old potato for sure. Of course he doesn't! Are you too cross with the world to work out why?"

One look at Noah, fists clenched and seconds from

lashing out, should have given him the answer to that. "What the fuck do you know? You don't fucking know anything."

Reuben sighed and raised a pointed finger at Noah. "I know your *papa*, my friend. I know him like a brother."

They eyed each other from a couple of metres apart. Reuben, not for backing down, and Noah, seething with fury. Tension radiated from his every pore. Where the fuck was Jay? This whole bloody confrontation had spiralled out of nothing; if I hadn't fallen arse over tit, we'd be packing up and going to the pub for last orders by now.

"Listen, Reuben. You said Guillaume has a temper too," I interrupted, coming to Noah's defence. I jerked my head in the direction of Joe and Lee. "What would he have done with those two yanking his chain?"

Shrugging carelessly, Reuben knocked the tip of his bat against the ground.

"*Rien*. Nothing at all. He only fights the important battles; he lets everything else go."

"Was he always like that?" I was genuinely curious. Reuben and Guillaume had first met as prisoners together, way back when Reuben was a teenager and Guillaume himself wasn't much older than Noah was now. Reuben screwed up his face as he cast his mind back.

"Yes, I think. He had a...how do you say? A short fuse. But *mon dieu*, doesn't everyone in prison?"

I anticipated never finding out, to be honest.

"He controlled it though," Reuben continued with a small smile, remembering. "He scared people without violence. He had a look, you know?"

Yes, I did know. Someone else, who'd inherited that same look, was now staring at his feet.

"So, Noah, you are not the old potato. Your hot fuse is your own and not my dear friend's. There is no place for it here, against my gardeners, nor against me. Save it, and use it wisely, *non*?"

*

"COULD I HAVE a saucer, please, Toby?" asked Arthur. "A really, really big one?"

"Of course, poppet. I heard Obélix meowing at the back door earlier. I'll help you pour him some milk."

Arthur's twin, and partner in crime, appeared at my elbow. "It's not for Obélix, Toby. It's for these. Look! Uncle Gandalf has given us some special seeds to plant."

Carefully, I put down the knife I'd been using to cut an apple into cubes. "Has he now. That's nice of him. Lucien, isn't that nice of him?"

Lucien's tapping on his laptop stopped, and he peered at the twins in the same circumspect 'let's not scare the horses' manner as me. Orlando, once more in his new favourite spot across Noah's lap, burbled on, oblivious.

"Uncle Gandalf says it's very, very important to give baby seeds lots and lots of water and sunlight, and to keep them somewhere very, very warm," added Eliza helpfully.

"Erm...did he say what...um...sort of baby seeds?"

"No." Eliza shook her head. "But he says if we look after them properly that they will grow big and strong and smell really, really nice."

"Is that so?" replied Lucien slowly, with one beautifully arched eyebrow raised. "How terribly thoughtful of him." He pursed his lips. "Toby, darling. In the gardening section of my diary, would you be an absolute honey and add a note reminding me to discuss the...um...*cannabaceae* supplies with Uncle Gandalf?"

With an amused smile, he turned his attention back to the children. "Use the ghastly Spode dinner service, darlings. I'm trying to accidentally smash it, plate by plate. It's proving horribly robust. And how about we grow these...um...seeds next to the warm Aga, so we can all enjoy watching them sprout?"

The children ran off in the direction of the dining room.

"I think I'll be needing a firm chat with my uncle's paramour," he declared before leaning across and giving Orlando a chuck under his chin. "Noah, darling. I haven't seen you for a few days. How are you? You appear to have stolen my youngest child."

My favourite mornings at work were the ones when Lucien was around, for the principal reason that I would forever be a little bit in love with him. Partly because he trusted his three small children to the care of a man with only one functioning hand and partly because I never knew what would come out of his mouth next. Noah, yet to feel so comfortable in his presence, flushed at being the centre of his attention.

"I'm okay," he mumbled. "Sorry. Orlando wanted me to pick him up. I won't if you prefer me not to."

"Of course, you should!" Lucien exclaimed. "He's clearly extremely happy in your lap. And why wouldn't he be?"

When the crafty bugger threw me a sly look, I may or may not have pointed the paring knife at him. He'd been all mischievous Lady Louisa this morning and dressed as her too.

"Jay tells me you were my Toby's knight in shining

armour on Monday evening. Cricket bats at dusk." He
fluttered his eyelashes at Noah, who all of a sudden developed
a fascination with the thick dark crown of Orlando's head.
"How terribly *virile*, if I may say so."

"I'd rather you didn't say so, thank you, Lucien," I responded briskly. "And I don't imagine for a second that's how
Jay reported it."

"God, no, but one has to make one's own entertainment
in the countryside, don't you find? Would you like to hear
how I embellished the story further?"

I wasn't sure whether Noah or I had turned the brighter
beetroot, and I waved the paring knife at Lucien menacingly.

Fortunately for both of us, his laptop buzzed, signalling
an incoming call, diverting Lucien's attention.

"Ooh, look. It's Marcel," he declared happily. "Goody.
Probably about to whinge that I finished *The Telegraph* cryp-
tic crossword before he did yesterday. Let's put him on
FaceTime and see what horrific clothing combination he's
come up with today. I'm predicting beige corduroy, from
head to toe."

Which was pretty rich coming from a man dressed in a
tangerine kimono paired with one of Jay's soft blue hoodies.
As Lucien tilted the laptop screen, Marcel's beaming face

came into focus.

"You googled thirteen down, Lucien," he began. "No way did you know the word for a lieutenant in the Egyptian navy."

"Gosh, I very much hope you aren't accusing me of cheating, darling."

"I am," replied Marcel stoutly. "And you did. And before you say it, no, I didn't get dressed in the dark. Unlike yourself. And don't tell me that you once had a romantic liaison with a dashing Egyptian sailor on board a luxury yacht in the Med because I shan't believe you. I've seen your maritime activities, and they mostly centre around clutching a vomit bowl. Now, I'm a busy man, so where are my adorable godchildren hiding?"

Lucien smiled at him. "If I told you Eliza and Arthur are in the playroom unwittingly trying to grow marijuana on a soggy paper towel, you may not believe me, so I'll show you my scrumptious Orlando instead."

He spun the computer slightly so it faced Noah. Embarrassed, he gave Marcel a quick wave of hello, then concentrated his gaze down at Orlando. Marcel cooed with delight.

"Well! Somebody looks like he's found himself a very comfortable seat. So cute! Look at this, Guillaume! You are yesterday's news, I'm afraid!"

Guillaume's handsome face popped into view over Marcel's shoulder, and I sensed Noah stiffen.

"Would you like me to take Orlando?" murmured Lucien, but Noah shook his head.

"No, it's okay, I can..."

"Hello, Noah. You look well."

"Hi."

A drawn-out pause was filled by Orlando, who had realised where his favourite person's voice was coming from and started chattering delightedly to the screen.

"How is the work going at the pub?" Marcel asked, ignoring the awkwardness. "Lucien says you're still considering the car maintenance course too. That's excellent news. Well done, my dear."

"Uh...yeah. It's...uh...yeah, the pub's fine," answered Noah, glancing up and then away.

Marcel, sensing he needed a second, began talking gibberish to Orlando.

"Reuben says you've joined the house cricket team." That was Guillaume again. He spoke softly, but only a fool would miss the anxiety etched into his voice. Reuben would have relayed their frank exchange of views by now. I willed

Noah to say something.

"He's going to be our secret weapon," pitched in Lucien smoothly. "And a much, much more pleasing one than...the alternative. Very pleasing. Toby totally agrees with me, don't you, darling?"

Have I mentioned I was a little bit in love with my boss? I was rapidly revising that status downwards. Noah shifted Orlando in his lap and then looked straight into the camera.

"I received your letter."

Lucien gave a sharp intake of breath. Noah nodded nervously, his eyes once more on Orlando.

"Do you want us to go?" Lucien whispered, and Noah shook his head.

"Did you read it?" Guillaume asked hesitantly.

I'd met Guillaume quite a few times now. Not a great talker, but not shy either. Just quiet, I guessed. On the screen, Marcel reached up to find Guillaume's hand and held it tightly.

"Yeah, I read it."

"And?"

God knows what was in the letter, but from the hope in Guillaume's voice, it evidently mattered a lot to him.

"Yeah, all right," said Noah.

CHAPTER TWELVE

NOAH

"ARE YOU OKAY?"

Toby knocked on my bedroom door before tentatively pushing it open to find me lying on the bed, fully dressed and busily occupied doing fuck all.

"You were blindsided down in the kitchen, yeah?" he said. "Sorry, they can all be a bit much sometimes. It takes some getting used to."

I sighed and nodded slowly. He was right; I'd been totally

caught off-guard, although it hadn't been Lucien's fault or Marcel's really. He hadn't known when he called that I'd be there. Toby edged into the room and sat in the small armchair next to the window.

"Guillaume looked anxious," he observed, carefully avoiding referring to him as my father or my dad.

"Yeah. He wants to get to know me. Fuck knows why."

"I'm not sure why either. You're a right miserable sod."

I flicked him the V sign, and we shared a comfortable silence for a moment. *Can we give each other a chance?* That's what he'd written, and I'd said yes. The word had spilled out of me before I'd had time to think.

I'd begun looking forward to my daily text from Marcel. I'd started composing short answers in return. If I was being honest, his banter game was a little staid, but I'd found some memes on Insta about the French president and sent him a few, which he said Guillaume and he had chuckled over.

It had taken my altercation with Reuben for the penny to finally drop. Guillaume had no regrets about his one-night stand because I was the result of it. An almost visceral confusion had swirled around my head ever since.

"I know you're taking the piss, but you're right, Toby. I don't exactly bring much to the party, do I?"

"Duh..." Toby slapped his forehead. "You don't get it, do you? Apart from his husband, you're the only family he's got. He must be chuffed to bits you found him. Once he got over the shock of you turning up on his doorstep, obviously."

"He'd have been more pleased if I wasn't some homeless loser." I was doing an excellent impression of a miserable sod. "And not everyone wants kids or a bigger family. He and Marcel look pretty happy, wrapped up in each other, to be honest."

"You're not a homeless loser." His mouth split into a grin, the twin dimples putting in an appearance. "Not homeless anyhow."

The bugger thought he was so funny. I hurled a pillow at him, which he caught and threw back. More dimples, so I threw it again, low-key flirting. We'd done a lot of that lately.

"Seriously, Noah. They'd love to have you in their lives. Did you not notice how thrilled Marcel was to see you? He's brought you here, to Rossingley, for Christ's sake. That says something about how much they want you to be a part of them, doesn't it?"

When Toby became animated, he wheeled his arms around like he was bringing a plane into land. I'm not sure why I'd thought he was ordinary when we first met; watching him now, as he pushed his hand frustratedly through his rust-coloured hair, in his own way, he was as striking as Freddie. To me at least.

"They've brought me to the arse end of nowhere." I smiled to show I was teasing him.

"You love it." He scoffed. "You're becoming a local already. You're pulling pints in the pub, you've fed the ducks with Orlando, you've got into your first fight, you nearly had another one with Reu..."

"I don't care what you say, those blokes at cricket shouldn't have been taking the piss out of you."

Toby just laughed. "Yes, I think they received that message loud and clear."

I thought back to cricket practice and how much I'd been enjoying myself until those twats began teasing Toby. How was I to know they were his mates? And if a killer like Guillaume was capable of reining in his temper, like Reuben said, then why couldn't I?

"Anyway, as I was saying," Toby continued. "You're such a local you'll be entering your home produce in the biggest turnip competition before the year's out. Although you won't win—you have to have been born here and have three generations stacked up in the graveyard to be in with a chance of winning. That goes for the guess-the-weight-of-the-turkey competition at Christmas too. So don't waste your money entering *that*. Or the tombola at the village fête. Oh my God, when Donna's cousin came over from Canada and had the winning tickets for both the bottle of Glenfiddich *and* the Sainsbury's prosecco, the church warden nearly combusted on the spot. And the tractor rally in a fortnight's time—once you've experienced the dizzy heights of that trip around the estate, you'll regret not having found Rossingley sooner."

I rolled my eyes at him, and he stuck out his tongue.

"You're funny," I heard myself say softly, and my neck heated even as the words tumbled out of my mouth. He'd started dropping by my room almost daily, and his presence felt as if someone had thrown the curtains wide and flooded the room with sunshine.

"I'm never going to live it down, you coming to my rescue like that. My dad and Uncle Will found it hilarious."

He looked around, studying the room as we both pretended that neither of us were reliving my awkward, over-the-top response to his mates' banter. A couple of years older than me, Toby was a grown man with a proper job, a home, and friends. He didn't need me looking out for him.

"I haven't got much stuff," I said defensively, following

the direction of his gaze. That was an understatement. I owned the grand total of a toothbrush, deodorant, shampoo, a pay-as-you-go phone and charger, a pair of trainers, and a few items of clothing. Most of which had been donated by Marcel.

"I'm driving into Allenmouth later, if there's anything you need," Toby offered. "I usually pop into town once a week."

"Yeah, okay. I'm craving another McDonald's. And another pair of trainers might be good. They'd have to be cheap though."

"Trainers, yes," he answered. "McDonalds, no. My mum has invited you over for dinner."

"Why the hell?" Okay, so not the politest of responses.

"I think what you meant is, thank you, Toby. That's a very kind invitation. I'd love to."

I stuttered. "Sorry. But why?"

"Because you're new to Rossingley, your presence behind the bar has been reported, and that's what she does. It will be very casual, but if you don't come, she'll be knocking on this bedroom door with food parcels and giving you the third degree. Believe me, it will be much easier to just say yes."

*

I DIDN'T DO religion, which I explained in no uncertain terms to Toby as I hung my coat up next to his on the front porch of the ramshackle old house, slap-bang next door to the church, with its painted sign boasting, The Vicarage. He hadn't bothered mentioning his mum was the bloody *vicar*. A deliberate oversight, I was fairly sure, because if he had, I'd have declined the invitation with the same amount of grace as I'd accepted. I'd climbed on my high horse, all revved up with my charity-case spiel, and then had to dismount again because even I knew that welcoming people to new communities and then trying to persuade them to join the church was kind of the vicar's job.

"Just relax! FYI, I don't do religion either. My mum doesn't care—her theological philosophy is a broad church. That's a religious joke, by the way."

Fucking hilarious. Unfortunately, it was too late to make a run for it because a fearful-looking woman in a dog collar, with the same mad red hair as her son but also equipped with a pair of shot-putter shoulders he hadn't inherited, marched down the hallway towards me. Three spaniels and two small children in scruffy school uniforms followed hot on her heels, swerving around a kid's bike, a row of welly boots, various school satchels, and a side table heaped with old parish newsletters.

"Hi, Toby's friend, and welcome! I'm Victoria—but everyone calls me Vic-the-Vicar."

Vic-the-Vicar. You couldn't fucking make this place up.

"I'm Noah. The northerner." I shook her hand—from her grip she may have actually been a shot-putter in her youth—then watched as Toby was swept up and squeezed as if he'd been gone six months and not roughly twenty-four hours. The two kids gave him the same treatment but with screeching sound effects, while the dogs attempted to lick him to death. The noise of more kids emanated from the back of the house. Toby waited while I unlaced my new trainers.

"Noah-the-northerner? Did you just make a *joke*?"

"It has been known." I smiled up at him, wondering how he'd react if I grabbed his face in my hands and kissed it. "Don't tell anyone."

I followed him down the hallway. "Who are all the kids? Does she run some sort of after school club?"

"Hah! If only. They're my younger siblings. And no, we're not Catholic. But I did grow up in a house without a telly, so I guess my parents made their own amusement on long winter evenings."

Eew. Having negotiated the obstacle course of the

hallway, we entered the sitting room, which was in a similar state of chaos but with the added blare of a children's colourful television programme. The youngest child glued to it looked to be around five, so maybe Toby's parents had finally discovered TV as effective birth control. An older teen, surrounded by homework, coolly nodded his chin at me from his seat at the table. Toby's dad, a slight, unassuming chap whom I'd already met in the pub and at cricket training, peered around the kitchen doorway and gave me a wave, a tea towel over his shoulder.

An old-fashioned highbacked armchair occupied one corner of the room, itself occupied by an ancient man. Like a wonky portcullis, a top set of dentures lolled in his open mouth. Slumped down, he was apparently asleep, although how the hell anyone could possibly take a kip in this madhouse defeated me. Concluding he must be dead and that no one else seemed to have noticed, I nudged Toby, wondering how to gently break the news.

"Oh, he's fine," he said airily. "That's Derek. He lives on his own in one of the cottages next to the pub. He used to come over every day for a chat after his wife died because he was lonely. Eventually my mum gave him his own key. Trust me, he'll soon wake up when his dinner's put in front of him."

Gesturing that I should take a seat on a sofa littered with cushions, a longhaired tabby cat, and numerous books and magazines, Toby then disappeared into the kitchen to help his mum. Gingerly, I made space to sit down, surveying the scene of devastation.

So, this was what happy family life looked like. Different to Lucien's, but with obvious similarities. Lots of smiles for a start. Plenty of noise, too, like when Eliza and Arthur came home from school, bursting into the kitchen full of news and proudly brandishing their latest artwork. One of Toby's siblings was pestering the older boy at the table in the way Orlando pestered me. The boy stuck his tongue out at him, then gathered him up anyhow. Perching him on his knee, he carried on with his homework.

Somebody decided the new visitor was more interesting than the telly.

"Are you Toby's boyfriend?"

The source of the question was a miniature version of Toby, dressed in a grubby yellow bunny-eared onesie and sucking on a lollipop. It may have been a female sibling, but I was having a hard time deciphering them all. With the background noise, her question could have passed unnoticed, but typically, the TV show ended, and suddenly it commanded everyone's attention.

"Toby's homosexual," added another child helpfully.

"If he was Toby's boyfriend, you dickhead, he'd know that already, wouldn't he?" drawled the boy with the homework. A fair point, succinctly made.

"Mummy wants you to be Toby's boyfriend." The first child again, ignoring her older brother. "She says she wants him to have a boyfriend who will take him on big adventures because he's not brave enough to go on them by himself."

"Because of his arm," the second one interrupted.

"That's why he came back home," added the first.

I had a feeling Toby wouldn't have wanted me to know all that. Nevertheless, it was interesting. Despite clearly loving Rossingley and his job, perhaps he'd felt other options weren't open to him.

"So, are you?" said the first, stepping closer and critically examining me. "Are you his boyfriend?"

I felt a bit like a lad planning on taking his bird out to the cinema, only to be accosted by her scary dad demanding to know his intentions. Except worse, because I had four inquisitors, not one. In need of support, I looked across to the boy doing his homework, the only one old enough to really appreciate my discomfort. But the bugger had Toby's sharp blue eyes, and they were lasered on me as keenly as his guileless younger siblings.

"No, I'm not," I said eventually. "Sorry."

A beat of disappointment bounced around the room, the kid in front of me crestfallen. Unaware his sex life was being discussed a few feet away, Toby's cheerful tones travelled from the kitchen, and I remembered how he'd shyly flirted with me earlier in my bedroom today. Crushing his siblings hope entirely felt cruel, and if I was being honest with myself, misplaced. The kid openly scrutinised me, making no effort to conceal her disappointment.

Smiling down at her, I added, "But I'd like to be."

Naturally, after that, I spent the duration of dinner—fish pie and peas, followed by homemade chocolate trifle—expecting one of the kids to report the news back to Toby. Or, even worse, announce my designs on their older brother across the dinner table to their parents. But that was before not-dead Derek woke up with a start, then commanded every child's entire attention by dropping peas down his front and interspersing the adult conversation with loud harrumphs each time his dentures fell out. To be fair, I was pretty fascinated myself.

Toby, his dad, and Vic-the-Vicar had clearly seen it all

before. From the lack of fanfare, inviting randoms to dinner at the vicarage was a regular occurrence, which made the whole thing much more relaxing. We settled on talking about the upcoming cricket match, the tractor rally (by all accounts an event only a fool would miss), the scandalous broken engagement of a farmhand called Neil, and the state of Alf's mother's lumbago. Dinner, therefore, passed uneventfully, and the younger kids were dispatched to wash up. Toby and I were soon walking back up the drive towards Rossingley without me embarrassing him or myself. I was almost disappointed it was over.

"Your parents are nice," I observed as we kicked a lump of gravel between us. "Your brothers and sisters don't take any prisoners though."

Toby clapped a hand to his mouth. "Oh my god, I knew I shouldn't have left them alone with you. What did they say? Did Clara tell you that we sit around the table and make our guests read three chapters of the bible between dinner and pudding? She pulled that trick on a couple who used to rent the cottage next to the school, and the guy actually nipped home to get his reading glasses. Honestly, she makes Eliza look like an angel in comparison."

"No," I answered, laughing. "But she did ask me if I was

your boyfriend."

During the pause that followed, Toby concentrated intently on kicking the stone. "Okay, so that's not embarrassing at all. Sorry about that."

I shrugged. "I didn't mind. She also said that maybe when you had a boyfriend, you might like to travel. 'Go on an adventure' were her actual words."

Toby stopped walking. "Bloody hell. Would you excuse me, Noah, while I just run back home and beat up my little sister?"

"Do you?" I asked. "Do you want to leave here? Because I thought you loved it."

He resumed kicking the stone again, his brow furrowed. "I do love it. I love Rossingley. And the people living here. I also love my job, and Lucien and Jay, and I really love their children. All in all, I love my life here."

Even though I sensed a 'but' coming, that was an impressive list of loves. I felt a pang of jealousy. I'd never loved anybody or anything very much, apart from flash cars I'd never be rich enough to own. Then again, no one had ever been terribly fond of me either, whereas Toby was surrounded by people who loved him. He sighed heavily.

"But yes, maybe one day, I'd like to see a bit of the world.

If only to discover how much I'd miss this place."

"Is it your phocomelia that stops you?"

He halted, clearly astonished. "You remembered the word!"

"Yeah, I looked it up."

"It sounds funny hearing you say it. I never hear anyone say it."

He resumed walking. "I'm happy if you call it a stump though. I do."

Asking him why he felt only having one hand held him back from seeing the world was tempting. But as someone with two hands, who the hell was I to judge? He'd lived with his condition all his life; if anyone knew what he was and wasn't comfortable with, it was Toby, not a well-meaning do-gooder. So I refrained from commenting further, nor did I tell him how amazingly he managed everything despite only having one hand, from wrestling Orlando into a fresh nappy to unflinchingly facing sixty-mile-per-hour cricket balls. He viewed himself and wanted others to see him as neither tragic nor inspirational—just a regular man living a regular life.

As we kicked the lump of gravel back and forth, more than anything, I wanted him to know he was the reason I was still at Rossingley, then ask him if I could follow him into his room tonight instead of mine. I wanted to know if the rest of his body was covered in pretty freckles too. If he felt the same way about me as I did about him, even if I was a grumpy northern bugger. But, being a grumpy northern bugger, I'd probably fuck it up. So instead, we carried on our makeshift game of football until we reached the house.

CHAPTER THIRTEEN

TOBY

HAVING FINALLY DRAWN a line through winter, spring celebrated the changing of the guard by blanketing the Rossingley estate in a fanfare of snowdrops and bluebells. A glorious sight, heralding only one occasion: the annual Rossingley village tractor rally.

At the close of the Second World War, the thirteenth earl, Lucien's great-grandfather, marked the blessed occasion of so many of his menfolk returning safe and sound by gifting them all an extra day's holiday, to enjoy however they saw fit. Being a provincial lot, they reminded themselves what a green and pleasant land they'd been fighting for by touring the local countryside in tractors and getting totally wasted in the process. Such fun, they did it the year after, too, and the tradition stuck.

While fundamentally unchanged, aside from the horsepower of the farm vehicles and the price of beer, the event had grown, and now around twenty-five tractors lined up through the village, with a variety of trailers accommodating as many villagers as wanted to join in.

Picking the best trailer for the daytrip had become tactical. My Uncle Will's trailer, for instance, tended to be fought over by older folk seeking comfort, not speed; he reliably filled it with straw bales, blankets, and hot toddies. He slowed for ruts in the road. In stark contrast, the young farmers rigged their trailers with sound systems, piled them high with bottles of cider, and saw being at the head of the rally as a badge of honour. Understandably, they tended to be magnets for the Rossingley youth, every bump in the track throwing up a raucous cheer. I'd joined them in the past in the pathetic hope Rob and I would find some alone time or, even better, that he'd acknowledge me out in the open. This year, however, I gave him a wide berth, plumping instead for a medium-paced ride on a trailer pulled by none other than my dad, high and proud behind the wheel of his vintage David Brown.

Noah joined me, along with Freddie and Reuben, doing the benevolent uncles thing with Eliza and Arthur, wrapped up so snugly in coats and scarves they resembled two fat chrysalises. Lucien avoided the tractor rally like the plague, quickly volunteering to stay behind with Orlando. Trust me, if he hadn't already had a baby at home as a ready excuse, he'd have gone out and adopted one. Jay's excuse was an extra shift at the hospital. My mum and the dinner ladies squeezed on board too. We even wedged in Donna-the-barmaid, on crutches with her healing ankle wrapped in a Velcro boot, thrilling the twins. Somehow, we made space for her to prop it up on a hay bale.

"Did your skellington come through your skin when you broke it?" enquired Arthur. "Was there lots and lots of blood?" He'd ripped the Velcro strapping open and closed enough times in the five minutes we'd been on board to set even my teeth on edge.

Donna patiently shook her head. "No, love, it wasn't that bad."

"But I bet you cried," said Eliza, palpably disappointed

by her response. "I'd have definitely cried. And screamed."

"And been sick all over yourself," Arthur added emphatically. More Velcro ripping.

Maybe we should have chosen a different trailer, although Donna, a kindly lady with her own grandkids, seemed happy to indulge them both.

"Do the broken bits hurt?"

"A little," she conceded. "Not as much as when I first fell over though."

"When our Papa hurts himself, Daddy rubs some of his special cream on it," announced Eliza proudly. "He keeps it in their bedroom. Shall I ask him if he can give you some of his special cream too?"

Oh my God, yet another scenario childcare college hadn't prepared me for. All credit to Freddie, he held himself together much better than the rest of us. Noah's shoulders heaved like he was having a grand mal seizure.

"Arnica," he chimed in smoothly. "Great stuff. Works wonders."

Reuben's eyes danced wickedly. "Comes in a fat pink tube. We have some in our bedroom too. We rub it on thick. Very good after a day of gardening."

"Papa says that..."

"Who'd like some fruit gums?" I asked with a flash of inspiration. My manny training had been good for something after all—fruit gums and tissues, essential to have at hand at all times. I rooted around in my pocket. "Fruit gums. For the first child that can count five oak trees."

In total, ten of us shared a trailer better suited to six, making it a cosy fit. Not that I had any complaints, not with Noah's long warm thigh tightly wedged against mine. Naturally, Reuben, in fine mischievous form, noticed our cosy juxtaposition almost immediately.

"Need a blanket over your lap, Tobes? To hide the...um...chill?"

"I have a snifter of sloe gin if the wind gets up," offered Freddie, holding aloft a silver hip flask to the assembled trailer. "I expect Toby will be warm enough, but anyone else?"

Fortunately, Noah seemed oblivious, too busy taking photos with his phone of the long stream of tractors and trailers snaking through the fields behind us as we headed towards the bluebell woods. The scene could have been a snapshot from any year in the last fifty if you didn't examine the tractor models too closely. No matter how many times I'd witnessed it, the whole village on the move was an impressive sight. Today was the only day of the year Lucien opened up Orlando's and my regular stomping ground to the rest of the village, and they were in for a treat. As the lead farmer hopped out and unlocked the gates, and we slowly trundled through a dense carpet of bluebells, Noah's phone snapped even more.

I threw him a sly grin. "If I didn't know better, I'd say you're doing a very good impression of someone enjoying themselves."

He scowled. "Just killing time; that's all. Until I can get off this bumpy uncomfortable contraption and away from the annoying country bumpkin currently using me as his personal electric blanket."

"If it's that tiresome, you could easily swap seats with Reuben or my mum."

"Nah, I'm good." As his eyes strayed to my mouth, I felt my cheeks flushing. "Someone needs to put up with you drivelling on about flowers and trees and the virtues of wholesome rural life."

"Who are you taking all these photos for?" I asked as he craned his neck to capture the view ahead. I'd taken a couple of pics myself, even though I walked through the woodlands every day en route to visit the cows.

"Um...myself." His face pinked. "To be honest, Toby,

it's amazing. I've never seen anything like it."

"Aaah!" I chucked his cheek and laughed as he pushed me away. "You've become a country boy! I knew we'd do it! Congratulations!"

"Fuck off." Noah pretended hard, but trundling through the picture-postcard bluebell wood, even he couldn't maintain his moody thing for long. "Look over there, Toby! At the colours!" As he pointed into the woods alongside us, I didn't have the heart to tell him Orlando and I tramped along this particular route daily.

"Yeah, this section of the woods is pretty cool," I agreed, smiling at his enthusiasm.

"Pretty cool? Is that all? The bluebells through those trees are unbelievable; there are literally millions! And the way the light catches them, it's...I dunno...like the sky has flipped and become the ground instead."

Which was pretty damn fucking romantic, especially coming out of Noah's sulky mouth. I might have needed that blanket after all. Embarrassed at his atypical outburst of energy, Noah clicked off his phone.

"You should send a picture to Guillaume and Marcel," I suggested, casually, as if I didn't care whether he did or didn't. "I'll take one of you with the bluebells as a backdrop, if you like."

Not giving him an opportunity to decline, I leaned away from him and took a quick snap. I'd captured him perfectly—attempting to look cross and failing miserably. It was a look I saw a lot lately. With a few taps of my thumb, I forwarded it to him, then tried not to appear too delighted as he forwarded it to Guillaume.

"I don't know why I'm bothering," he chuntered as he added a quick message. "He's probably seen these woods hundreds of times. Photos never look as good as the real thing."

I let him continue grumbling and settled back, breathing in the delicious scent of wild garlic and basking in the warm glow accompanying a good day out with friends and family. We'd all had a hefty tot of sloe gin, and my mum passed around crisps and sandwiches. Boisterous trailers with the lads were all well and good, but for comfort, decent grub, and better-quality booze, I'd fathomed long ago that sticking with the vicar was best. From the way he attacked her ham and pickle sandwiches, I think Noah agreed.

"She's not like I expected a vicar to be," he remarked as Donna told a smutty joke that had my mum cackling like a fishwife. "She's all right, isn't she?"

Praise indeed. "Mmm," I agreed. "Sometimes I think Lucien's house is actually more peaceful."

He studied my mum and her friends for a minute and smiled at Eliza hanging off Freddie's arm before switching his attention to the lads pissing about on the tractor behind. Finally, he turned his gaze back to the scenery. "But you'd still like to see more of the world?"

As always, as if by an unseen force, my eyes flicked down to my arm resting uselessly in my lap, my stump out of sight up my sleeve. Calling it useless was a disservice—I was actually pretty adept. Of course, I'd never play the trumpet, use a mobile phone in landscape mode or lead a round of applause, but it's not like I'd ever experienced a two-handed existence with which to compare. Merely a world designed for, and by, two-handed people. Plenty of folk much less able-bodied than me fearlessly got up to all sorts of mischief; sometimes I wondered if I used my arm as an excuse to never step out my comfort zone. Why fix what wasn't broken?

"Yeah, perhaps."

On a stretch of track that allowed two vehicles side by side, we found ourselves overtaken by old Mick-the-mechanic, on his beloved classic Triumph motorbike. With a glass of something fizzy balanced in her hand, his enormous wife was squashed into a vintage sidecar next to him. She bestowed on us a regal wave.

Chuckling, I shook my head. "But sometimes, I think this village is a microcosm of the whole world, and I don't need to travel anywhere."

As we chugged out of the woods, the bluebells thinned, to be replaced by bare fields ready for spring planting. A roar went up from the lad's tractor behind, followed by a chorus of "We know what you're doing" as three of them hopped out and legged it to do their business behind the nearest tree. All that beer had to go somewhere. An energetic straw fight broke out amongst a group of restless teens on the tractor behind them, my brother in the thick of it. He received a stern holler from my mum, much to the joy of his tipsy mates. Yep, tractor rallying at its finest. Somewhere in the melee, I heard Rob's voice, a sound which, in previous years, would have me craning my neck, trying to catch his eye, and changing trailers at halftime. Today, cosied up next to Noah, it didn't have its usual effect.

After ninety minutes of jiggling over potholed dirt tracks, we were all ready for a breather, no matter how beautiful the scenery. Freddie most definitely looked like he needed a break; preventing an excitable Arthur from toppling over the side had been a full-time job, even more now I'd given him a sugar hit. Reuben had resorted to looping one end of his scarf around Eliza and tying the other around his own waist; seemed she had designs on hugging the oak trees, not just spotting them.

"We usually stop for an hour up here," I informed Noah. "Lizzie should be there already, getting the bar up and running."

I pointed to a clearing with a panoramic view down the valley. Sure enough, Lizzie and her husband could be seen setting up trestle tables and unloading crates of drinks. Colourful bunting looped through the trees, greeting our approach.

"I never thought I'd say this," began Noah slowly. "But it's quite cool, isn't it, your village?"

I smiled at him. He still held traces of the sullen young man that had first arrived in Rossingley, especially when anyone broached the subject of Guillaume. And he still threatened to leave, most likely after the cricket match. His fear of cows remained healthy too. But today, with his cheeks flushed from a crisp breeze and sloe gin, I could almost imagine he'd lived in Rossingley all his life. Didn't want to push it though.

"I couldn't possibly comment."

CHAPTER FOURTEEN

NOAH

THIS TIME LAST year, I'd been kipping on Gary's lumpy secondhand sofa and signing on at the dole office. A long way from standing in the middle of a field, serving salt-and-vinegar crisps, and beer in plastic cups to a bunch of pissed hillbillies, half of whom probably assumed Taylor Swift's *Red* was the newest product in the John Deere catalogue. And I'd discovered an alarming number of them shared the same surname—any more inbred, they'd be sandwich filling. Nonetheless, I was happier than I could remember in a long time.

Guillaume and Marcel had replied to my bluebell text and photo almost immediately and separately. Marcel had cooed over the picture, ignoring the flowers to tell me how handsome I looked, in the way Gary's nan used to praise him even when he was covered in acne and his hair hung in a lank, greasy teenage mess. It made me feel peculiar, but not in a bad way. Guillaume replied a minute later, wisely not commenting on me, but saying how much he'd love to join the rally next year and see the bluebells for himself. I'd deliberated over answering and eventually sent him the thumbs-up emoji.

"Three pints of Badger, cheers, mate," said a thick voice. "And a medium white wine."

A drunk and overbearing Farmer Giles, with one of his darts buddies next to him, waved a tenner in my face. Wordlessly, I plonked four plastic beakers and three cans of beer down, then reached for the bottle of white wine. I knew what attracted Toby to him; I could see it myself, even though big muscly blonds weren't my type. He was older than us, probably pushing thirty-five, much too old for Toby, in my opinion. Or perhaps that was jealousy talking; I'd seen the sly appreciative glances he threw Toby at the pub when he thought no one was looking, and they pissed me off.

"Nine pounds ninety-two, please."

He handed me the note with barely a glance. "Keep the change."

Eight pence, the fucker. Irritatingly, him and his mates stayed nearby talking; he handed the wine to a woman who seemed way too pleased to be standing with him, and I switched my attention to locating Toby. Flicking my eyes back towards Farmer Giles, I saw he was doing the same, even if he was pretending otherwise. I couldn't blame him because Toby was looking all kinds of cute as he chatted with Reuben and his dad. A can of beer loosely dangled from his hand. A grey sock covered his stump, and an oversized parka swamped the rest of him. Either he felt the cold in his stump, or he covered it up so as not to draw attention to it. I'd touched it once by accident—well, more like grabbed it to be honest—when the bugger had scared me to death creeping through the house. It'd felt mostly normal, like anyone else's forearm, although, to be fair, I'd been focused on trying not to scream at the time.

A whistle blew, and one of the farmers shouted a ten-minute warning, which was excellent timing because we were running out of beer. Another thing I'd discovered about these country folk—when it came to booze, they had hollow legs.

The whistle was a signal for the women to start queuing at the Portaloos and for half the men to make a dash for the woods. Beer, cold weather, and a tractor engine juddering underneath your bladder were a potent combination. I was about ready to go myself.

I wandered into a quiet patch of woodland, checked I was alone, then did my thing against an old oak tree. As I zipped myself up, I became aware of voices, one familiar and to which I could happily listen all day; the other had recently left me a paltry tip at the bar. Being a nosy sod, I crept closer.

"I said no," Toby stated firmly. "I'm done, Rob. Get back to the tractors; yours will set off without you otherwise."

Something jangled. "No, it won't. I've got the bloody keys."

"Shit. I hope you aren't driving back."

The same thought had crossed my mind. Rob sounded decidedly slurred.

"Nah, it's Kev's turn."

"Good. Well, I need to get back even if you don't because my dad's tractor will be setting off any second. I don't fancy a long walk home."

"Just stay here with me for a sec." Slurred and wheedling. Not the most attractive of combinations. Toby seemed to agree, thank God,

"No. It's been at least ten minutes since the whistle. Anyway, aren't you worried someone will see you?"

As if on cue, a diesel engine roared to life, followed by another. I crept closer still until I spied them both. Toby had backed up against a tree, and Rob towered over him.

"Tobes." He laughed mockingly, shaking his head from side to side. "Your dad won't go without you. And everyone else is still pissing over on the other side of the wood. Any more excuses?"

"Um...how about I just don't want to?" Toby again, louder, and more forceful this time. "We haven't got time, and you don't appear to be paying much attention, but I said I'm not doing this anymore."

Rob took a step closer and ran his big farmer's hand roughly up the side of Toby's face. My fists clenched. If Toby leaned in and kissed him, I didn't know how I'd respond. What if they did more than kissing? I should have walked away, but now I was here, I desperately needed to see how it would end.

Toby slapped him away, and I let out the breath I hadn't realised I was holding. "Get off."

His tone was kind of humorous and kind of not. I didn't

understand their dynamic well enough to work out which. Toby wasn't acting as if he felt threatened, but then, he didn't seem to be playing a teasing sort of game either. Rob evidently interpreted it as a challenge and tried again.

"I said, stop it!" responded Toby, batting him away more determinedly this time. "Fuck off, okay?" Ducking down, he escaped from under Rob's arm, only to be pulled back. I'd seen enough.

"Hey, Tobes!" I made a deliberate song and dance of climbing through the undergrowth as though I'd only just stumbled upon them. "You okay? Your dad's been calling for you. He's waiting to go."

Cool as a cucumber, Rob stepped back and straightened his clothes as if he'd just been for a piss. Weaving slightly, he sauntered towards me and the path beyond, leading to where the tractors revved up to go. He tilted his head back at Toby and gave me a conspiratorial wink. "Be careful having a slash around this one, mate; know what I mean?"

It wasn't the lewd wink or his insinuating words but the obscene gesture he made with his tongue that tipped me over the edge.

"Nah, mate. I don't think I do. You'll have to explain it to me."

Perhaps it was because he didn't know me nor appreciate the nuances of my thick northern accent. Or maybe he'd simply downed one too many beers. Whichever; he took me at my word and mistook sarcasm for an honest answer. Signalling back at Toby with a jerk of his thumb, he said, "Gay fuck."

I smiled to myself. The poor sod had walked straight into it. "I'm kind of busy, Rob? But thanks; it's nice of you to offer."

He'd strolled about five paces beyond before his muzzy brain computed the insinuation. He returned pretty sharpish, mind, bringing up his fist, but not quickly enough to catch me with much more than a glancing swipe at my head. Still bloody hurt, mind.

"Ow, you fucker!"

The guy was way too hammered to be a serious danger to anyone. His boot slipped on the uneven ground; and reflexively, I stuck my left hand out to stop his fall, taking the opportunity to curl my right into a fist and punch him back. My knuckles connected cleanly with his handsome smug jaw. Stone-cold sober, I had more street brawling under my belt than this guy, even if he was older and beefier. He landed heavily as I loosened my grip on him, ruining a rather pretty patch of delicate bluebells.

"Christ, Noah!" Rooted to the spot, Toby stared at Rob, now dazedly lumbering to his feet. He clapped a hand over his mouth in shock. "Christ," he repeated. "What the hell?"

A trail of blood dribbled down Rob's chin from a blood-ied lip. Unless injured pride counted, he seemed stunned but otherwise fine. Heaving himself upright, he seemed to be half-heartedly contemplating round two, but in a fashion that was more bravado than fancying a punch-up. Before he came to his senses, I thumbed over my shoulder.

"Go on, mate. Off you fuck. Unless you want another."

Fingering his jaw as if reminding himself he'd just been smacked, Rob muttered a string of abuse and jumbled threats, then lurched off. Relieved I wasn't heading for a fight I might regret with a bigger man, I joined Toby.

"Are you okay?"

He nodded dumbly. "Yeah, I'm all right. But I'm not the one you just felled to the ground. Shit, is he going to be okay?"

"Yeah, he'll be fine. He's so half-cut, I doubt he'll even remember by tomorrow." I paused, then added, "Do you care?"

Toby huffed out a laugh. "No. Not really. Don't tell any-one about him, will you? Because it's up to him if he wants to pretend he's straight. Christ, why the fuck did you hit him?"

"Er...because he tried to hit me first?"

"Yeah, I know, but..." He trailed off, looking at my hand, almost in awe. "God, Noah. I've never hit anyone in my life. Did it hurt?"

I flexed my fingers experimentally. *Fuck, yes.* Hopefully, I hadn't broken anything. "Nah, not really. I'm not good for much, but I do know how to punch someone so they won't get up again and hit me back in a hurry."

Toby nodded, dumbstruck. I couldn't pretend I wasn't preening a little. It must have shown.

"You're such a dick," he said in a low amused tone. "You've developed a habit of attacking all my friends."

"Only when they attack you."

He shook his head of ginger curls, laughing softly. "Rob wasn't attacking me. Just trying it on, as usual. He's harmless, really. And lonely, I think."

All danger gone, he blew out a breath and once again leaned back against the tree. Sunlight glinted on his head through the branches, picking out the hazel flecks dancing across his hair. Tipping his face up to meet the watery warmth, he ran the tip of his tongue over his plump upper lip, from one perfect corner to the other.

Making up my mind that I wanted to taste that lip, too, I took a step towards him. "He's not much of a friend."

"I've known him a long time."

"That doesn't make him a friend."

"I know that. But I'm a pacifist. Fighting doesn't solve anything."

I took another pace forwards. Right in front of him now, I sucked in a deep breath. "You remember Reuben saying that Guillaume only saved his fists for the important stuff?"

He slowly nodded, head still tipped back and eyes half closed against the sun's cool glare. There was a hell of a lot of competition, but at that moment, I reckoned he was Rossingley's most beautiful inhabitant.

"Well, hitting that fucker felt like the important stuff," I said.

A tractor parped—ours probably. Fucking shit timing. Half the village was waiting for us on the other side of the bank of trees, but for all I cared, we could have been the only people in the whole of Rossingley woods. A lairy cheer went up, probably at the sight of a battered Rob clambering out of the shrubbery.

Toby raised an eyebrow. "Come on. We'd better go."

"Yeah," I agreed. Neither of us moved. His irises were a

very similar shade to the bluebells; I didn't know why I hadn't noticed properly before. As I stared into them, adrenaline still coursing through my veins from the scuffle, I wondered how it would feel not to be a fucked-up mess. To be an ordinary boy from an ordinary home, standing in front of another ordinary boy and wanting nothing more than to kiss him. Again, I inhaled deeply, deciding the time had come to stop wondering and find out.

"You must spend ages practising that look," Toby murmured.

I frowned. "What look?"

His lips quirked in an amused smile. "That one, that you're giving me now."

Grabbing his arm, I tugged him closer and kissed him on his mouth, very hard and with the finesse of an eager fifteen-year-old. For a second, his plush lips opened for me; his hot tongue darted against mine. Then, just as suddenly, I pulled away. He softly moaned his annoyance. Slack with shock at my own boldness, I stared at him.

If a tractor hadn't parped again, more insistently, I could have gone on staring for another hour. A ragged sliver of bark had caught in his hair; his eyes widened as I reached up and carefully plucked it out. With one of his fingertips, he delicately wiped across his wet mouth.

"So, Noah. Um..." The bloom spreading across his cheeks was too pretty for words. "That was a thing."

"Yeah." Seemed we'd both regressed to the vocabulary of eager fifteen-year-olds too.

"Are we going to do it again?" A dimple accompanied his lopsided, shy smile. I shrugged as casually as I could and dropped my eyes to the few inches of lush, mossy ground separating his feet from mine.

"If you'd like to, yeah, we could."

Toby jerked his head in the direction of the noise. "Yeah, I would. But we should go. Can't keep the vicar waiting."

Walking out of the woods together, on a scale of one to ten, with one being not embarrassing at all and ten being a discussion about applying spunk to painful broken ankles in front of the vicar? A solid eleven.

Somebody wolf-whistled—my money was on Toby's dad, revving the engine like he was going to be first off the grid at Silverstone. He drove his point home a little excessively, given the other tractor drivers had become bored of waiting, and we would be playing catch up.

Like a pair of maiden aunts, Freddie and Reuben threw us pursed-lip looks that said they'd put two and two together and come up with an outlandish figure, which would be magnified by Lucien four times over when he heard about it. And Vic-the-Vicar—oh my God, I'd kissed a boy whose mum was a bloody vicar—grinned from ear to ear as if she'd personally hosted the Last Supper, then persuaded all the disciples to do the washing up afterwards. Fortunately, a fidgety Arthur chose that precise moment to drop his favourite toy rabbit over the side of the trailer, accompanied by squeals of dismay, which let us off the hook, allowing us to take our seats at the rear and most definitely not look at each other.

"Oh my God, your hand is swollen already," Toby remarked after the rabbit had been rescued unscathed and everyone's attention focused back on the bluebells. He added with a giggle, "I've heard there's a special cream for that."

Once more, my left thigh lay snug against his. My right lay snug against the sturdy flesh of one of his mum's dinner lady friends, and it was not having remotely the same effect. I glanced down at my hand and flexed my fingers.

"It hurts, doesn't it?" Toby remarked with a grin. "Don't pretend it doesn't."

"A bit." *Yep, I might have cracked something.* "I probably shouldn't have hit him." *I loved hitting him.*

"He won't tell anyone," Toby responded. "He'll say he

tripped."

I risked a quick glance at him and received a bashful one in return. He didn't look any different from before our kiss, which is to say his nose still had more freckles than the sky had stars, and his lips were still wonderfully swollen. I needed to kiss him again.

"I...um..." he began, his eyes skittering across to the other occupants of the trailer. A hurried check around reassured me the thrum of the tractor engine prevented our conversation reaching interested ears.

"What?"

"I...I didn't think you were gay. You don't...well...even Lucien didn't think you were."

Good to know my sexuality had been a topic of debate up at the big house. "I'm not."

He huffed, unamused. "You and Rob both, then. Lucky me."

"No," I contradicted. "You're wrong. It's not like that. I'm not hiding anything, not like him. Not shouting about it either, but not hiding."

"Bi, then?"

Like father, like son. "Yes, I think so." My face grew hot. "But I've...um...never done anything with boys. I've had plenty of girlfriends though; it's easier, I think."

"Something you and Rob would agree on, then."

I could tell he remained sceptical. "I don't mean that. I just mean easier because I like girls, too, and they were, or are, more available. I've always known, but never had the opportunity, I guess. Until I came here, I didn't really know any gay or bisexual blokes. Whereas Rossingley is littered with them. I should have moved to the country sooner."

He laughed at that, which eased the tension a bit, although I'd basically confessed I had zero experience as far as men were concerned, which was kind of embarrassing. Judging from the situation with that tosser, Rob, Toby had plenty.

"Two firsts for you in one afternoon, then," he remarked a minute later.

The return journey was more direct than the route out, and we were passing through a landscape I'd begun to recognise.

"Huh?"

With his thigh nudging mine, he leaned in, his breath warm on my neck. Soft lips brushed the shell of my ear. "You referred to your father as Guillaume. After you hit Rob. And you didn't even notice."

CHAPTER FIFTEEN

TOBY

THE GREATEST THING about living in a rural community was that gossip had done two laps of the village while truth was still putting its running shoes on. Lucien was practically tapping his foot at the front door when Noah and I delivered a set of overtired twins safely into his bony embrace.

"Hello, my treasures. Haven't you had a wonderful day out? Uncle Freddie's already phoned and told me how much *all* of the grown-ups enjoyed themselves too." An amused eyebrow raise accompanied that comment, causing me to groan inwardly.

Thanks, Freddie.

I braced myself for a verbal strip search. Noah, demonstrating mastery of the subtle art of fucking off, cited a pressing need to change his clothes before his evening shift behind the bar, vanishing quicker than leftover communion wine after Sunday service. Which left me with my annoying boss.

"Toby's been naughty," Eliza began. "He didn't come back to the tractor when they blew the whistle. We had to wait *ages* for him."

Tell-tale.

"It was only a minute or so," I protested, downplaying it. "Come on, poppet, let's get you..."

"Toby got lost in the woods," added Arthur, ever the dramatist.

"Now, hang on. I wasn't exactly..."

"With Noah," finished Eliza. "We waited ages and *ages* for them."

"It wasn't that..."

"Our tractor was the last one home!"

The speed with which Lucien fed, stripped, bathed, and tucked his children into bed was truly remarkable. Still reeling from Noah's impulsive kiss, I was nowhere near ready for his interrogation. Not that he had any intention of letting that hamper him.

"May I say, Toby, how much a sojourn in the fresh air has brought a healthy colour to your cheeks. Gosh, you seem positively *flushed*, darling. Doesn't Toby look flushed, Jay?"

Jay, flicking through the newspaper from his favourite position on the kitchen sofa, threw me a sympathetic look.

"Noah seemed rather spirited, too, wouldn't you agree?" Lucien continued. "I'd go so far as to describe him as *windswept*. Did he look windswept to you, Jay?"

What the hell had Freddie and Reuben reported back? I busied myself stacking the children's tea things into the dishwasher, refusing to bite. I'd put a laundry wash on next, keeping busy until I could escape to my room and relive the kiss in peace. Fat chance.

"It's such a relief when everyone comes back safe and sound from that event," Lucien added smoothly. "Tipsy farmers, small children, and heavy farm machinery never feel like a sensible combination. I'm surprised there aren't more accidents."

"Mmm," I agreed. "If only a pair of experienced doctors would join the rally, just in case."

"Absolutely not. I'd rather cultivate a chest rug and gobble steak and kidney pies with Second-Best Man than subject my skinny *derrière* to a spiky hay bale. Gosh, Jay, what a shame there isn't a place for him on the cricket team this year."

Phew, seemed Lucien had stopped fishing and moved on. Perhaps he was having an off day, and I'd avoid the full interrogation after all.

"Freddie said that Rob, the dairy farmer, took an awful tumble. In the woods near to where you and Noah managed to find yourselves, ahem, lost, by the sound of things. Split his lip open dreadfully."

Okay, so maybe not. I sensed Lucien's eyes burning a hole into the back of my neck and grunted acknowledgement.

"I daresay he'll find plenty of ladies willing to kiss it better," Jay murmured, turning a page. "I don't think I've ever seen him at the pub with the same woman twice."

"That's because he's *never with* the same woman twice," Lucien responded waspishly. "No surprise there. He's more interested in, ahem, soft furnishings than the rest of us queers put together."

"How the hell do you know that?" I said, realising a second too late I'd been well and truly outmanoeuvred. To his credit, Lucien endeavoured not to appear too smug.

"Darling, nothing happens in this village without it reaching my ears." He tutted fondly. "You should know that by now. And you should stop mooning after him. He's not good enough for you."

Funnily enough, Noah had said exactly the same thing.

"I'm not mooning after anyone."

Lucien raised his eyebrows.

"Not anymore, anyhow," I added.

"I'm very relieved to hear it. Your mother will be too."

What the fuck?

"And I've always thought he was too old for you," he continued as if he hadn't just revealed the earth-shattering news that my mother was fully abreast of my sex life. Were the congregation praying for me every Sunday morning too?

"That Rob Langford is a very naughty boy. He's always been the same, even when he was young. Goodness, I remember Freddie used to make any excuse to visit Rossingley during his school hols and then dash off to, ahem, assist at milking time. Rob and he milked each other for years, by all accounts. And one Christmas, if I recall correctly, Rob had an enormous...."

"I think Toby's probably been traumatised enough, don't

you, Luce?" interrupted Jay, folding his newspaper.

Yes, I had. Most definitely. I mean, on the one hand, the idea of a youthful Freddie and Rob rolling around together in the hay was kind of hot—like, super, porn video hot. But on the other, my boss had spelled out what I knew already. That I was not, and never would be, anything more to the hot dairy farmer than a convenience. Why would he bother with a trip into Bristol to find an anonymous man to suck him off, when the guy up the road was ready, usually willing, and perennially available?

"Somebody like...um...Noah, for instance, is a perfect age for you, Toby," Lucien swept on. "And don't you think he has such *brooding* good looks? Like a hero from a dark gothic novel, darling. Does he kiss like one too? Did he pin you up against a giant oak and *ravish* you from head to foot so that your tortured soul sang with joy and your aching heart throbbed wildly in your chest? And other less prosaic parts began *throbbing* too? Ooh, tell me he did."

Blushing didn't come close to how scarlet my face must have looked. Bloody hell, were there no secrets in this place? "Have you set up CCTV in the woods?" I demanded, only for my fabulous boss to squeal with delight.

"I knew it!"

Jay shook his head sadly. "Can't believe you fell for that, Tobes. How long have you worked here for?"

"Oh my gosh!" Lucien practically punched the air. "Sit down, Toby, this instant, and tell me everything."

"Tell him nothing." Jay had abandoned his newspaper and was doing that magical thing where he cloaked Lucien's bony frame from behind, causing Lucien to immediately fall back limply into his arms as if he'd been tasered. Or had his batteries removed. It was an impressive trick we could all do with mastering.

"Bedtime, love," he murmured in his husband's ear. "I need to examine your tortured soul a little more closely."

*

"WHOOO..."

I chuckled in the dark at the same time as a throbbing excitement started to build in the parts Lucien had alluded to. It had gone well beyond midnight when the rattle at the bedroom door disturbed me, not that I was objecting.

"Is that the original Lady Louisa?" I whispered. The responding low, throaty laugh had me chortling into my pillow and thrumming with pleasure.

"Yeah. Pre-beheading. And without Buttercup. Can I

come in?"

I switched on the bedside light and watched Noah contemplate taking the chair by the window for an entire half second before making himself comfy on the edge of the bed. He brought with him the scent of warm pub and fresh air. I bunched my pillows under my head, then rested my arms, with my hand covering my stump, on the duvet, chastely pulled up to my chest.

"Hi."

"Hi."

Because we were both damned suave.

"How was work?"

"Busy. How was home?"

I grinned. I liked it when he called Rossingley home. "Annoying."

We stared at each other for a moment.

"How's your punching hand?"

He glanced down at it. I couldn't tell in the dim light if it was more bruised or not. "A bit sore. But Rob's lip looks worse."

"Was he in the pub, then?"

"Yeah, he came along later." Noah gave me an assessing look. "Do you care?"

"Not especially."

He examined his hand again then laid it on top of my own, threading our fingers together loosely and dragging them into his lap. "Good. He'd sobered up a bit. He ignored me, to be honest, apart from an occasional dirty look, and ordered his drinks from Lizzie's end of the bar."

There was an extended silence as he studied our interlinked fingers. I became acutely aware of my stump, now lying on top of the duvet between us, exposed. He'd seen it plenty of times—I couldn't exactly hide it, but it wasn't the most alluring bit of my anatomy to wave under the nose of a guy I hoped would lean across and kiss me again. As casually as I could, I drew my arm up, with the idea of tucking it under the covers.

"You don't have to hide it," he remarked. "It's part of you. And it doesn't bother me at all."

As incredibly sweet as that was, and genuine, too, he'd made matters worse. My ugly limb now hung halfway between the top of the duvet and safely out of sight, making it the focus of our attention. Like every other bloody time I'd got vaguely near first or second base with anyone.

"Rob didn't like looking at it."

"Rob can go fuck himself. And he's not here. If I'd

known that, I'd have socked him even harder."

I didn't need a knight in shining armour. A grumpy northern lad with a bruised fist and dressed in one of his dad's old sweaters would do just fine. I shifted my stump under the bedclothes anyhow, but only so I could prop myself up on my elbow and edge closer to him. Noah was of the same mind; as I rose up, he dipped down, and we met in the middle, his expression caught between amusement and determination.

Grumpy northern lads were wonderful kissers, I discovered. Much better than sexually confused dairy farmers. His tongue parted my lips with a soft-mouthed tenderness I didn't expect, and certainly wasn't used to. A warm palm gently cupped the back of my neck, holding me in place as he sweetly and thoroughly explored my mouth. As a sigh of pleasure escaped my throat, I felt his mouth break into a smile, and he tugged on my bottom lip as he gently pulled away.

A squeeze of my hand, still held firmly in his. "Mmm. Kissing. Is this something we're doing now?"

God, I sincerely hoped so. "It's looking that way," I answered, trying to play it cool.

Bringing my hand up to his mouth, he leisurely dropped a kiss on each knuckle, eyeing me intently from under those diabolical sooty eyelashes. All attempts at coolness evaporated. Swoony as hell.

"Can I check you won't be doing anything like this with Rob anymore?" He turned my palm over, planting an open-mouthed kiss on the sensitive fleshy part in the centre. The look in his dark eyes as they slid across to latch onto mine should have carried a government health warning. "I'm the jealous type, just so you know."

An image of a dazed Rob, blood running down his chin as he staggered to his feet flitted through my head. I'd never done anything remotely like this with him. "Rob who?" I managed hoarsely, glad my throbbing parts, as Lucien coyly referred to them, were hidden under the thick duvet. My stump was hidden, too, which might not have mattered to Noah, especially in the dim light of my bedside lamp, but improved my comfort levels immeasurably.

More kissing followed; he brought his legs up, and we shifted until we lay side by side on the bed, me under the covers and him on top of them. Noah kissed me as if we had all the time in the world, like the kissing itself was the destination and not an obligatory way marker en route to more valuable treasure. As if pressing his mouth against mine was the feted pot of gold at the end of the rainbow.

Eventually, he pulled away and stroked a finger up my cheek before following the track of his finger with velvet-cushioned lips. Bloody hell. Grumpy northern lads had serious kissing game. Would highly recommend.

"Are you okay?" he asked, his eyes roaming across my face as if conducting a visual inspection. Apparently satisfied, he rested his head back on the pillow.

I conducted my own quick mental inventory of all the ways I was so much more than okay. "Yeah," I summarised inelegantly. "You?"

"Yeah."

I could tell from his voice he was smiling.

"I've never kissed a boy before today," he said. "I've wanted to, just never done it."

The gay community of his northern town had missed out big time. Their loss, my gain. "And?"

"Yeah. I like it. I'm going to need to do it a lot more."

Yay! "Practice makes perfect?" I wasn't going to be the one to tell him he had already completely nailed it. He could practice on me all he wanted.

Chuckling in the dark, he sat up and swung his legs over the side of the bed. "Yeah, but not tonight. I'd better go; you've got an early start with the kids."

He hovered over me, suddenly less assured, then darted down and delivered a very prim peck on my cheek before playfully mussing up my hair. In contrast to his confident kissing, he seemed nervous. "I had a text tonight from Marcel. He's coming to stay in a couple of days. With...with Guillaume."

He shrugged as if it was of no importance. "Seems a bit random. Are you going to be around?"

Random? If only he knew. More like a military campaign. I suspected Marcel and Guillaume had been impatiently counting down the days between their last visit and an acceptable interval in which to engineer another. By my calculations, they'd timed the visit with the weekend of the college open day, which must only be a happy coincidence. For a guy with such a great kissing game, Noah could be a complete dork sometimes. "Yeah, sure. I'm always around."

He let out a long exhale as though hugely relieved. "Great."

*

TWO THINGS HAPPENED after he left. The obvious, tension-releasing one, involving a wad of tissues and my fervent imagination; the other a more measured reliving of the tractor rally and Noah kissing me against the tree trunk. Curled on my side, I hugged my knees to my chest. Tonight had been a first for me, too, not that Noah needed to know. Not the kissing—I'd done that plenty, in dark clubs at college, in pub toilets, and in dimly lit doorways and carparks. A melange of tongues and hands and shared hurried releases I could barely recall and certainly not put faces to. Rob and I had also kissed plenty, in various hidden locations around the estate. But never on a bed. I lay in the dark, increasingly sleepy, and eventually nodded off, remembering the tender touch of Noah's tongue.

CHAPTER SIXTEEN

NOAH

"MY CHILDREN'S MANNY had a rather upbeat wiggle in his walk this morning," Lucien observed from his post at the kitchen table.

For a guy with a vast country estate to run, a demanding job, and three kids, he was surprisingly difficult to avoid. Still unused to his gentle teasing, I hadn't fully decided whether I liked him or not. My difficult, inner teenager kicked in, and I responded with a grunt. Wisely, Lucien took another tack.

"Jay mentioned you might be interested in the trainee mechanic course at Allenmouth college? They have an open day tomorrow. I have the details here."

He pushed a piece of paper over the table towards me, identical to one that had mysteriously appeared after Reuben dropped by one evening. And very similar to one Toby had left lying on our shared bathroom windowsill a couple of days ago, next to the cress farm that had sprung up virtually overnight. Why the hell was Toby cultivating cress in our bathroom?

I picked up the flyer and pocketed it. I could take a hint. "Yeah, I might go."

After bolting awake at six o'clock that morning, vibrant energy coursing through my veins to replace the blood pooled in my cock, I'd decided I would attend. For the first time in as long as I could remember, small pockets of happiness had begun poking through the cloud of anger and confusion hanging over me since the discovery I had a less than fairy tale father. Mind you, my father had an equally undesirable son, so maybe we could call it quits on that front.

So, yes, something approaching happy, and extremely horny. In the space of a few months, things were looking up. I'd gone from sofa surfing, dodgy cash-in-hand jobs, and finding out my dad had done time for murder, to living in a stately home and confirming my bisexuality. To hopefully starting something good with Toby, cossetting Orlando whenever I needed a cuddle, and feeling much fitter after all the cricket training. As if all that wasn't surreal enough, I'd served shandy to a ferret and punched a guy for abusing the local vicar's son. At the thought of Toby, my morning wood chose to join us at the breakfast table. Lucien gave a delicate cough, bringing me back to the present.

"Good news. I hear it has an excellent reputation."

The estate's regular visitors had arrived from France and were staying in the dower house with Freddie and Reuben. Their presence didn't fill me with half the trepidation it should, mostly because I had a hot date with Toby to the college open day. Afterwards, I planned on treating him to a burger at Wetherspoons. Who said romance was dead?

Thus, by my low standards, I was positively congenial when they joined us up at the big house for morning coffee and a gossip. Until I realised I'd been totally played.

Marcel kicked things off by professing a whim to visit the unremarkable graveyard at Allenmouth church. The final resting place of an obscure eighteenth-century poet, allegedly a particular favourite of his. No other day would do, apparently. Guillaume then joined in by declaring a burning need to stock up on English cheddar cheese, unavailable in their local French supermarket but freely available in the cheese shop in Allenmouth. Toby conveniently offered to show him the shop's location—because, apparently, everyone had forgotten Google Maps was a thing—and then hotly rebutted any suggestion the whole expedition might possibly be a finely orchestrated setup.

"Can I just point out, Toby, that Marcel has waited until today, after being a regular Rossingley guest for approximately three decades, to visit his favourite poet's gravestone? Don't you think that is a little suspicious?"

We had a few minutes alone, retrieving our coats from the cloakroom while Marcel and Guillaume gathered their own belongings in readiness for our expedition. My open day was rapidly turning into less hot date and more a jolly family outing.

"Oh, he pays his respects nearly every time he comes to stay," answered Toby airily. "A pilgrimage of sorts."

A likely story, quickly glossed over by Toby pushing me back against the welly rack for a sneaky kiss.

"You can try to distract me all you want," I said with a groan around his delving tongue, "but their stories are riddled with plot holes. For instance, the French have, like, two hundred and forty-six varieties of cheese. So...cheddar? Really? Shall we invite Lucien along, too, seeing as we're making a party of it?"

"Shut up and concentrate. We've only got a couple of minutes, and your sulky grumpy face is hot as hell."

I forgot about cheese, about being difficult, and about the welly boot prongs digging into the backs of my thighs because cloakroom snogging had entirely eliminated coherent thought processes. As had the heat of Toby's lean, tight body stretched up against mine. I pressed the heel of my hand against the hard outline of his cock, happily digging into my thigh, and gave it a few experimental rubs. And then nearly ejaculated on the spot myself when Toby let out the most gorgeous growl of pleasure known to mankind.

"You've got to stop," he panted, pushing up into my hand. "I'm not wandering around Allenmouth College covered in jizz. I thought you hadn't ever done anything with a man?"

"I haven't." I squeezed his arse as he writhed against me. "Fuck knows why."

"You were waiting for me." He let out a breathy laugh around my mouth and, with a final grind of his hips, pulled away.

"Later," he promised. "You and me. After cricket training."

*

THE FOUR OF us found ourselves wandering around the open day together, seeing as the church graveyard conveniently sat only a hop, skip, and a jump away from the college. Surprise, surprise, the cheese shop was virtually opposite. With relief, I discovered I wasn't the oldest prospective student, nor the only guy accompanied by his dad (although I bet I was the only one whose dad had done time for murder). On account of Marcel's asthma, we perused the stands and classroom displays at a snail's pace, Marcel winning the award for looking the least likely person interested in signing up for a motor vehicle maintenance course.

"It's a bit pricey," I observed sourly because, yes, even though each time I so much as glanced at Toby, my cock grew hard, I'd also regressed into the adolescent space that mushroomed in my head whenever I had to take a leap into the unknown. What I really meant, although no one managed to translate, was that the college and the course seemed fantastic, but I was scared I'd probably fuck it up and drop out after three months, exactly like the last time I attempted to make something of my life.

"That nice administrative lady said you'd be eligible for an adult-learner grant," Toby offered, ignoring my moodiness. He was quite good at that. "That would go part of the way to covering it."

I'd done the sums already. If I looked for a bar job with more hours, rented a cheap room somewhere in Allenmouth, like in a student house or something, then in a year or two, with the grant supplementing me, I could maybe afford the course. Better still, find a job in a garage and save up while learning the basics. Assuming I stuck at a job, of course.

"My bar work won't be enough to cover the rest."

Putting up barriers seemed to be my default. Each time one of the current students or enthusiastic tutors bounded over, I morphed into Kevin the Teenager. Interestingly, Guillaume appeared equally sullen; anyone would think we were related or something. Fortunately, Marcel and Toby negotiated every conversation with consummate ease—I learned a hell of a lot more about the course from their polite questioning of the tutors than I would ever have done on my own.

"I've already thought of that." Marcel patted my shoulder. Guillaume sensibly stayed quiet. In fact, he'd been quiet the whole time. He'd thumbed through a few brochures and given the appearance of listening when one of the teachers ran through the Level Two modules, but other than that, nothing. I wondered what he was thinking. And then wondered why I cared. We hardly knew each other.

"You could take out a loan."

I harrumphed. Marcel was a nice guy, but he lived in cloud cuckoo land. "Who the hell would give me a loan?"

I certainly wouldn't. I wasn't a safe bet. The bar job at the Rossingley Arms was the longest position I'd ever held, and if I hadn't fallen in love with the vicar's son, I'm not sure I'd still be doing that.

Shit, am I in love with the vicar's son? I pictured Toby, red hair splayed out on the pillow behind his head, lips parted in anticipation of my mouth on his. And then I dared look across at him, patiently flicking through a brochure on how to diagnose chassis system faults. Sensing my eyes on him, he looked up and gave me a flash of dimples. *Oh my God, I think I am.* I gasped aloud as comprehension dawned.

"It's not that stupid a suggestion," Marcel added, seeing my alarm.

"No...um...it's not that. It's...um...I don't think the bank would give me one."

"I would though. And you can pay me back a bit at a time when you qualify and begin working properly. Like a bank, except I wouldn't charge as much interest."

"What if I dropped out and didn't pay you back? Because I probably would drop out, you know. I never stick at anything."

He shrugged. "All investments carry risk." He shot his husband a sly smile. "But sometimes, I assure you, the gains can be enormous."

The offer stunned me and, at the same time, felt like an enormous responsibility. Why on earth would he volunteer to do something like that? He'd done so much for me already, not least dipping into his pocket to bring me back to the UK and finding me a place to stay with Lucien. He'd be throwing good money after bad.

"I...um..."

"My dear, you don't have to give me an answer today. The offer will stand for as long as you need it."

Toby tore himself away from his thrilling reading material and jerked his head towards the exit. He gave me a tentative thumbs-up, and I nodded back, ready to leave too. My brain was full of all the things I wanted to share but didn't know how to start—my feelings for Toby; Marcel's generous offer; my sullen father and me, mirroring each other perfectly; committing to the bloody course...

Marcel took my arm with an apologetic look. "Do you mind if I use you as a crutch? Guillaume has his hands full."

I glanced at Guillaume, who inexplicably had managed to spread carrying a small bag of cheese, Marcel's coat, and a pile of brochures over both his hands. Toby had engaged him in a conversation about Stilton cheese. As we continued dawdling along, Marcel with his arm through mine and keeping up a running commentary, I realised I didn't mind at all.

*

"HOW DO YOU think it went today?" asked Toby, lacing up his trainers. I tried not to stare, but it was difficult because he had an impressive technique of tucking the straight lace under his other foot to tauten it, then performing a very clever sleight of hand with his thumb and forefinger. For that feat alone, I needed to kiss him again, and maybe more, but it would have to wait because we had an audience, namely our shambolic estate cricket team.

"Yeah, good." My word power required some work. Seemed I was yet to emerge from the teenage regression mode I'd adopted after spending the morning with Guillaume and Marcel. The thing was, I'd enjoyed myself—they were good company and so dorkishly sweet on each other it made me laugh. So why did I have this ball of stubbornness curled inside that prevented me from smiling and joining in, from behaving fucking normally around them like I did when I was alone with Toby? Why couldn't I show them I could be lovable? Why did I hide the nice parts of myself away behind this tiresome shield of sullenness whenever they proffered the hand of friendship?

Because I'm an idiot, that's why.

Watching the vicar's son, who you have fallen in love with, covertly appreciating your father's athletic physique was kind of annoying. Especially when your father looked so damn good for his age and barely seemed aware of the fact. Seeing as he was going to be on the team for the summer match, he'd joined us at cricket practice, and from the way he filled out a tracksuit, he still took his football and fitness seriously.

"What?" Toby smirked, when he spotted me pouting. "I'm only checking out how you're gonna shape up in twenty years' time." His eyelashes lowered in a slow blink. "Not bad at all. Maybe you should visit me again tonight so I can compare notes."

Blood rushed to my cheeks en route to my groin, then settled in downstairs for the foreseeable future. Which made for an uncomfortable jog around the south garden. How was I supposed to concentrate on improving my off-spin bowling after a comment like that?

My father demonstrated his high level of fitness by lapping us in the warmup. Followed by an exhibition of his apparent ease wielding a cricket bat before almost absently performing uninterrupted keepy-uppys with a cricket ball while awaiting his turn to bowl.

"Stop ogling him. He's ancient. And I'm the jealous type, remember?"

Toby side-eyed me as he removed his cricket helmet. In unspoken agreement, we'd deliberately not spent the training session paired up. I might not have been able to keep my hands off him if we had.

"How much longer are we training for tonight?"

"Ages," Toby groaned. "Your father joining the squad has given us a new lease of life. Jay is treating us to drinks down the pub afterwards to celebrate our newest team member. It's a three-line whip."

*

BEING ON THE customer side of the bar in the pub felt strange. Even more strange was being part a group of blokes. Not only was I part of them, but dressed in similar sports kit, I looked like I belonged too. And while I didn't know everybody in the village, not like Toby, who had encyclopaedic knowledge of each inhabitant right down to their inside leg measurements, a few of the regulars gave me a nod in greeting before turning back to their pints.

Farmer Giles was there, of course, with his cronies. Toby's spies had informed him the young farmers team had been practising hard too. Since I'd sent him packing, our paths had crossed a couple of times, and I half expected some sort of retaliation. But as Toby predicted, he merely blanked me because to acknowledge what I'd done would be tacit acknowledgement of a hell of a lot more. I almost, but not quite, felt sorry for him. I might not have much to my name—for example, I didn't have two hundred and fifty head of cattle, a decent paying job, or a Land Rover—but neither did I live a lie every day, and I reckoned that had to count for something.

Seeing Guillaume squashed around a table, chinwagging with Reuben, also felt peculiar. Reuben, one slim leg elegantly crossed over the other, was smartly kitted out in high-end leisurewear, no doubt selected by Freddie. Guillaume, equally effortlessly chic and contained, sipped at a small cup of coffee. Every time Reuben demonstrated his point by madly waving his arms around, he nodded coolly and occasionally shrugged. Not a pint of ale or cheese-and-onion crisp between them. They couldn't have stood out as French any more than if they'd worn berets and looped strings of onions around their necks.

I wondered what they talked about in their slurring, indecipherable language. A lot of shared history probably.

"It was okay, wasn't it, being at the open day with Guillaume?"

Toby brought his gin and tonic over and took the stool next to me, no longer able to pretend he'd much rather listen to Joe and Lee arguing about who had the driest winter log store last year. His knee brushed against mine and stayed there, sending me a shivery preview of what was to come later. I glanced up to find Reuben gifting me a knowing raised eyebrow. Sometimes it felt as if this village was populated by MI5 agents.

"Yeah." I nodded because, weirdly, it had been. Although Guillaume had spent the morning as quiet and grumpy-looking as I'd probably sounded.

"He didn't seem to enjoy it though. He just followed Marcel around. So I don't know why he bothered coming, really."

"Yes, he did!" Toby contradicted. "But if you think about it, he's missed out on a lot of normal stuff that people do by being in prison. You know, like going to college, job-seeking, etcetera. It was as new for him as it was for you."

To be fair, that had never occurred to me. He threw me a sly grin. "And also, he was probably concentrating on not saying the wrong thing, such as 'Noah, please sign up for the bloody course because I want you to have a career and be secure and happy'. All parents, even unpractised ones like Guillaume, know that if they offer an opinion, their kids will likely do the exact opposite."

I shook my head at him; he reminded me of Eliza at breakfast this morning, explaining her five different excuses as to why she hadn't done her reading practice. Always with an answer for everything.

"And how could you possibly know that? Are you a mind reader now?"

Toby's look informed me I'd asked a stupid question—Eliza was quite adept at that too. "Listen. The defensive, hostile, pouty thing Guillaume had going all morning—like he'd got a set of knuckle dusters in his pocket he was itching to find an excuse to put to good use—was his 'I protect my own or die trying' face."

"You're ridiculous." I took a swig of beer to disguise how funny I found him.

He shrugged carelessly and hummed. "I suppose it could have been his 'I'm going to fuck you incredibly slowly and precisely until you beg and scream' face—I bet the two are quite similar. But I suspect he'd already done fucking that morning, judging from how his expression changed utterly every time he smiled at Marcel. So, by process of elimination, it must have been the 'you mess with my son, and I'll mess with you' version."

Snorting with laughter, I lifted my beer glass and attempted to swallow another mouthful without it spurting out of my nose. Fucking hell. Discussing my ex-con father's sex life with the son of the vicar. In a pub full of blokes, droning on about organic fertiliser and the price of red diesel. And both our fathers sitting not three feet away.

"You are so going to pay for that slow fucking comment later, Toby. You have been warned!"

"Can't wait," he teased, and nor could I. I really, really wanted to finish my pint and drag him back home so I could show him, slowly and precisely myself, exactly how I'd make him pay. Needing to touch him, I chanced a hand on his thigh under the table and let my fingers drift to the inner edge of his tracksuit bottoms, travelling along the rough seam. Which made my own trouser situation even worse, so I stopped before Reuben noticed.

The really funny thing was, Toby had bloody nailed Guillaume to a tee. Hostile and defensive was an excellent way to describe his behaviour that morning. And he was bang on about everything else too; all of Guillaume's expressions were exceedingly fierce unless aimed at Marcel. I grinned at Toby and let my foot rest lightly over his, but only because kissing him was not currently an option.

"And you are convinced of the reasons behind Guillaume's fucking scary expression at the open day how exactly?"

He shrugged again, and his lips quirked as he leaned closer, so his breath brushed my temple as he spoke. Suddenly, I didn't care if Reuben, Farmer Giles, or my father saw us together and drew conclusions. "Because, Noah, it's the same as the face you made when you tried to suffocate Joe with his own sweater for taking the piss out of me at training. And when you smacked Rob around the jaw."

A flush of scarlet swept across his cheeks. "The pouty look you gave me afterwards was the same too." He blushed even more. "You're giving it me now."

"I don't pout!"

"Yes, you do. You're pouting now."

CHAPTER SEVENTEEN

TOBY

HOW WAS IT that I could read the same four-page baby book with Orlando over and over, and never experience a smidgen of impatience, yet found watching the cricket team finish off their last pints at a *glacial* pace as tedious as hearing my mum's Easter sermon for at least the thousandth time?

I knew why, of course. Noah's innocent expression whenever his foot pressed down on top of mine under the table. And the bob of his Adam's apple each time he swallowed a mouthful of Guinness, followed by the mesmerising slow sweep of a thumb across his wet lower lip afterwards. His sinful dark eyes, the same colour as the ale he drank, snapped up to mine every time he did it, knowing exactly the effect it damn well had. Even the presence of both our fathers, my uncle, and Reuben, waffling on about the impact of climate change on crop harvesting times in southwestern France couldn't dampen my anticipation of what was to come later.

That frustrating tedium was nothing compared to the lift home in Jay's Land Rover, squashed in the back between Reuben, Guillaume, and a kid's booster seat, while Noah sat in the front with Jay, discussing the pros and cons of electric cars. An established alcoholic lightweight, Reuben had reached his absolute hard limit of two pints of lager and drunkenly embarked on a monologue in his native tongue, which from his lewd hand gestures, appeared to be an outline of Freddie's welcome home from his modelling assignment tomorrow.

"I'd love to, sounds great," I heard Noah respond to Jay over the din of Reuben and Guillaume's spontaneous French sing-along. He twisted around in his seat and smirked at me.

"Would you be able to take my bag inside? Jay's going to

show me under the bonnet of the E-Type."

"Cool," I replied through gritted teeth and pulled a face behind his back as he fiddled with his phone. My own vibrated in my pocket a second later.

Warm the bed up for me.

*

BY THE TIME Noah crept into my room, my body dangled by a thread off the far end of a spectrum progressing from sexually frustrated to volcanic eruption. A vigorous sneeze would have been enough to trigger my balls to explode. Thank God Noah was on the same page.

"That Jag is bloody awesome, but fuck, not tonight," he said, kicking my bedroom door closed behind him. He strode over to where I lay propped up on pillows and carelessly toed off his trainers. "For all I was taking it in, Jay could have been showing me a Reliant Robin."

Staring with restless eyes, he licked his lips. "God, Toby. I've thought about this all day."

Whereas last night had been all tender exploration and politely keeping his hands to himself, tonight, Noah had worked out that men didn't require a carefully choreographed dance prior to sex; they just needed to have a pulse and be breathing in and out. Straddling my hips, he dove straight for my mouth.

I inhaled the scent of warm beer and clean skin until his no-holds-barred kiss systematically cleared my mind of everything except the sweet sensation of his mouth invading mine. Could I come from being kissed by him alone? Probably. As his hands clawed my hair and panting noises of utter relief escaped both of us, I barely held on and thrust up through the duvet to find relief.

"Noah," I managed to get out. "I'm gonna..."

"Me too."

Pausing in his quest to suck out my tonsils, he tugged the duvet aside, then sat back and, in one swift movement, ripped off his sweater and T-shirt, revealing an acre of flawless caramel skin. A vibrant tattoo swept across his right shoulder down to the point of his elbow. In the dim light, I made out an open tiger's jaw swallowing black Celtic writing inside a green sundial or something. Who the fuck cared? The whole package was fucking glorious. If the brief separation of our bodies was meant to calm us down, it was having the opposite effect.

"That's more like it. I need to see you properly."

Removing the duvet exposed my significantly less

impressive physique, thankfully covered in a white T-shirt. My bloody arm was on show, too, not that Noah appeared remotely bothered by it. His dick bulged heavily in his sweatpants, and he kneaded it as he swept his tongue across wet lips.

"Come on, you too. Take that off."

As Noah nestled between my legs, pale, freckled ordinariness contrasted with honeyed perfection. Once more, he captured my mouth in his, and stroking my hand down the smooth sweep of his back, I hooked my withered arm around his neck and out of sight. Hot skin melded into hot skin as our heartbeats galloped against each other. I licked at the heat of him, at his neck and the dip of his collar bones, tasting salt and fresh sweat. Underneath the fabric of his sweatpants, Noah's hardness stood ramrod straight, his frustrated moan when I arched up against him, lost in the tangle of our tongues.

"Not enough," he panted. "I need to touch you there too." His hand slipped under the waistband of my boxers and teased them down. My dick sprang free, sliding against him, dribbling wetness against his flat belly. With his mouth not leaving mine, he shoved his own underwear down onto his thighs, too, so our dicks rubbed. The velvet skin of his balls kissed mine, and he let out a hiss, grinding himself against me like he was trying to close every tiny gap between our bodies. For a guy who'd never been with another guy, his confidence was sexy as fuck. Contagious too. I squeezed my hand down between us and took hold of us both, our natural lubrication easing the way. Not expecting it, Noah pulled off my mouth, his firelit brown eyes shot with wonder as they stared incredulously into mine.

"I didn't know we could do this."

With a grin, I licked off the beads of sweat gathered on his upper lip and breathed hot air into the open cave of his mouth. "We can do all sorts of things." I panted as, in time to the shuttling of my hand, I fucked and stroked my tongue against his.

A deep moan of discovery and desire escaped his throat as we thrust together into my fist. "Christ, Toby, that feels so fucking good."

I wasn't going to last long; I'd been half-hard and aching for release all evening. A flood of heat unfurled from the base of my spine and spread to my tightening balls, warning me I was close. I quickened the pace and tightened my grip.

"Coming." Noah shuddered, his whole body taut above me.

I caught a glimpse of him stretched like a bowstring, lean sinews straining, honeyed flesh darkening before my vision whited out. His liquid heat spilled between our bellies sent me crashing over the edge to join him; I came, too, leaping from a great height, hard and fast.

"Oh my God," he panted, crashing all his weight down on top of me. With a loud groan, I sank, boneless, into the mattress, letting myself be crushed. Like a spent ragdoll, I flung my arms out to the sides, my head lolling back on the pillows. I had a vague awareness of Noah kicking off our remaining clothing, then pulling the duvet over us and slightly shifting his weight—thank God—to the side. If any seismic world events had chosen to occur at precisely that moment, I'd have missed them entirely.

*

"ARE YOU AWAKE?" Noah asked.

Five minutes or five hours could have passed. Long enough for a rather unpleasant crustiness to have glued our pubes together but not sufficiently unpleasant I wanted us to separate. I shook my head, a sudden rush of shyness keeping my eyes closed.

Pliant lips landed on my jaw, trailing a path down my

neck as I hid behind my eyelids. If I played dead, the delicious nibbling and sucking might never stop. Noah, with one heavy thigh slung across mine, rolled his hips against me. Light fingers confidently waltzed a path across my soft belly. He chuckled lightly at my happy noise of appreciation and brushed the backs of his knuckles against my fast-growing dick.

"No, not awake," he whispered and ground his hips against me once more. So fucking nice. "I'd better be quiet, then."

From his shuffling around, I sensed he'd propped himself up on one elbow the better to explore with his eyes and his hands. I kept my own eyes shut, embarrassed that his were tracking every average pasty inch of me—my non-existent abs, every imperfect freckle covering them, and my small-to middling-sized knob. My repulsive arm. With his hardness rammed against my hip, his fingertips traced slow circles over my belly, advancing towards my slender shaft. Without hesitation, his soft palm curled around it.

"Is that good?" His thumb circled my slit, dipping into the steady stream of wetness and spreading it around the head. I made an incomprehensible sound in response, and he laughed softly. "I'll interpret that as a yes."

He brought me off with steady assuredness, almost lazily,

taking his own pleasure by frotting against my thigh. My with-ered arm rested on the sheet alongside us, my hand trapped behind him. I made a half-hearted attempt to retrieve it and reciprocate before he stilled me with a determined press on my shoulder.

"No." His voice sounded gravelly and determined. "You stay just as you are. Like an earl."

I came with less force than the first time, but no less sat-isfactorily. Then almost came again, despite being wrung out twice, because I dared open my eyes to find Noah straddling me, lips parted, broad chest heaving, and energetically bring-ing himself to climax.

"Christ," he gasped as the first jet painted my neck. "Christ, Toby."

*

"CAN I ASK you a question?"

"Yeah," I answered, amused at the hesitation in his voice.

We'd cleaned up, taking turns alone in the bathroom, neither of us yet ready for that degree of intimacy. I'd assumed he'd head back to his bed next door, but he spread himself in the middle of mine as if he owned it, then stretched an arm out wide, inviting me in for a snuggle. Needless to say, I accepted his invite.

"Why do we have two saucers of cress growing in the bathroom?"

I vaguely wondered if Lucien and Jay's postcoital conversations were as prosaic and decided they were probably much filthier.

"To surreptitiously swap them with Gandalf's saucers of marijuana being cultivated next to the Aga. I don't know whether you've noticed, but every time a leaf grows on the plants downstairs, we're trimming them with nail scissors so that they're shaped more like cress."

He laughed with delight. "This place is fucking crazy."

I agreed. Good crazy, though, and especially so since Noah had been thrown into the mix. "It's proving a challenge, but we're hoping the kids get bored and forget about it. So they won't notice the difference when we swap them."

He gave me a nudge. "Hey, do you reckon anyone else living in this massive country pile is having sex tonight?"

I snorted. "That question's crazier than having dope growing in the kitchen. Of course they bloody are. Have you seen Lucien and Jay together?"

"Yeah, I guess."

"And your dad was in a very frisky mood when we left

the pub."

He gave me a shove. "Ugh, that's gross."

"What? Calling him your dad, or that he's probably balls deep in Marcel right now?"

I squealed and wriggled away as a sharp poke in my ribs turned into a full-on tickling match. Noah won, of course. Pleased with himself, he grinned down as he pinned me to the bed with his body, holding both my arms above my head. He followed the grin with a kiss.

"I'd like to be balls deep inside you."

Oh, God, could he read my thoughts? I felt my skin turn a hitherto unreached shade of crimson. "I'd...um, yeah," I squeaked.

"Kissing you is pretty good, too, though," he said softly. "I'm fond of kissing."

Relaxing, I kissed him back, heat fading from my face. "I'd noticed." I tipped my head up, surveying his tight grip on my arms. "Are you going to give those back?"

He shrugged. "Maybe. They need tasting first."

Making a biting sound, he sank his teeth into the ticklish fleshy part of my upper right arm. I squirmed with laughter as he licked and soothed it better. He travelled farther down the limb; the sensitive diamond of flesh at my inner elbow received the same rough treatment, and then my forearm and wrist before he sucked and nibbled the tip of every finger. Popping off my thumb with another heart-stopping grin, he turned his attention to my withered arm, and I automatically stiffened.

"You don't have to do it to that one," I mumbled, looking away.

He said nothing, but neither did he release his grip. I braved a glance to find him inspecting it curiously. From shoulder to elbow, my arm looked perfectly normal—not top of the pile if arms were being dished out, but totally normal. Beyond, my forearm was thinner than it should be. The muscle and bone held in Noah's loose fist tapered and faded to nothing, the skin colour gradually turning a purplish unhealthy hue as it puckered unevenly around the stump. Arthur once charmingly described it as cauliflower painted the wrong colour. Even I preferred not to look too often.

"Does me holding it like this hurt?" he asked eventually, and I shook my head, my mouth dry.

He studied it a second longer. "Good."

Dipping his head, he slid his grip farther back towards my elbow and pressed his lips against the ugly skin of my forearm. My heart thudded in my chest as I tried not to squirm.

He did it again, slightly farther along, and once more after that, until his tongue tickled the blunted end of my stump, where my wrist and hand should have been. Rob had always pretended my stump didn't exist, deliberately avoiding looking at it, and I'd been complicit by hiding it behind my back or up the sleeve of my sweater. I'd done the same the few times I'd hooked up with a man in a club. After one guy had recoiled in horror and another had asked to take a photo, I'd purposefully begun buying oversized knitted sweaters with baggy sleeves. My face burned as Noah worked his way along, and I closed my eyes, shrinking inside myself. A second later, when I thought I couldn't bear it for another second, his lips left my stump and landed back on mine. When he'd thoroughly reacquainted himself with those, he pulled off, rearranged me under his arm to his exact liking, and yawned.

"I'm knackered. Your arm tastes good, like the rest of you. Can we do this all over again in the morning?"

CHAPTER EIGHTEEN

NOAH

LIFE CARRIED ON as before, except in between pulling pints and practising my bowling, I now had the vicar's boy to kiss. All three activities were going well, especially the last one, so God knew why my brain burbled with unease. Why couldn't I just be content to ride along on a simple future which seemed to be taking care of itself? I'd scraped a little cash together and had the offer of more steady work—Lizzie-the-landlady told me I could keep my shifts at the pub after

Donna returned, and I promised I'd let her know. The more I kissed the vicar's boy, the more I wanted to stay at Rossingley. And a benevolent man had offered to lend me the money to go to college. So exactly what was my fucking problem?

Pride was my fucking problem. And a masochistic tendency to treat kindness and generosity with an unhealthy dose of suspicion. I might be reluctant to accept Marcel's offer, but love and kisses did not pay for college courses. Nor did they cover the cost of a roof over my head. Toby would say I had one already, here at Rossingley for as long as I needed, so what was I worried about?

The simple truth was, I didn't belong in this vast mansion amongst all its priceless treasures, however much the other permanent residents tried to persuade me otherwise. I scurried around Rossingley like a rat in a palace. Being catered for made me uncomfortable. Lucien's culinary skills extended to making a pot of tea. If Jay felt like cooking, he cooked for everyone. If he didn't, the food appeared anyhow because a very nice lady called Mary miraculously produced it. My clothes were mysteriously laundered within a day of discarding them, and unseen hands tidied my room in my absence. Lucien knew nothing different; Jay indulged it; Toby had grown accustomed to it. Yet my skin prickled even at the thought of it.

So, what to do? How did I keep Toby, but not stay? How did I learn a trade without borrowing money from Marcel? How did I accept my father but forget what he'd done?

*

I FOUND TOBY kneeling on the floor in the playroom, patiently building a tower block out of plastic bricks for a very snotty and irritable Orlando to gleefully knock down. From Orlando's drooly chortling, it was evidently the funniest game ever invented, temporarily distracting him from his heavy cold. Toby wouldn't let me kiss him when he was working, so in the gaps between shifts at the pub, I had to content myself with following him and Orlando around like a weird, sexually frustrated groupie.

"Have you had any more thoughts about enrolling for the course in September?"

A week had gone by since the open day. A week filled with kissing Toby late at night when I came home from work and waking with him tucked under my arm every morning. I touched his cock and brought him off every chance I could get, and he touched mine. We'd become competent at both activities simultaneously. Tonight was my night off from work (not from touching his cock), and we both had a free day tomorrow, which hopefully meant exploring more.

"It's brilliant they would be happy to accept a few of your Level 1 credits from elsewhere," he carried on. "Which will make it a bit cheaper overall. Has Marcel mentioned his loan again?"

He hadn't; he didn't need to. He'd left the ball firmly in my court. "Nah, it's up to me now."

As we created the mother of all plastic brick towers, Toby waited for me to say what I should have said. That, of course, I would take Marcel up on it because, of course, it would mean more of what Toby and I had together. But me being me, I kept my gob shut, and Toby being Toby, bit his lip.

Orlando had recently started treating me like his own private jungle gym, and eventually, I gave up helping Toby with the tower and lay on my back so Orlando could crawl and drool his steaming germs all over me.

"Well, for what it's worth," Toby said finally, "I think you should accept Marcel's offer. I...I want you to stay."

He focused on a precarious outpost of the main tower, balancing four bricks on an improbably narrow base. For an unlovable bloke like me, Toby wanting me to stay should have been more than enough, shouldn't it?

"I dunno. It's like they're trying to buy me into their lives. Bribing me."

I felt slightly foolish. I didn't even know if I believed that any longer. A forcefield of distrust prevented me from accepting people's motives at face value. Anyone else in my position would have bitten Marcel's arm off. Toby paused, a brick in his hand and a puzzled expression on his face.

"No, they're not. They're trying to help you; that's all. And anyway, if that were the case, then surely Marcel would have offered to give you the money outright?"

"Maybe he can't afford to do that."

Toby threw me a look. "Er...it's Marcel. Yes, he very much can."

I had given the course plenty of thought—pretty much every second that wasn't spent thinking about Toby. I'd even filled in the online application form, minus the funding section. As I lay awake, my mind had run away with dreams of working for old Mick-the-mechanic up at the Rossingley garage and coming home each evening to the patient man currently trying to talk sense into my thick skull without losing his rag. Listening to Toby now, saying yes to Marcel seemed such a small thing, so why couldn't I just bloody do it?

"I said I'd chew it over and let them know."

I paused, exasperated I couldn't articulate my mental hurdles to Toby, probably because I struggled to frame them clearly in my own mind. "I don't know why Marcel would make such an offer," I ended up saying. "What's in it for him?"

"Oh my God! Nothing, you idiot!" Toby frowned. "Or everything, depending on how you want to view it."

My skin prickled with annoyance. I didn't appreciate being called an idiot, even if, coming out of Toby's mouth, it sounded close to an endearment. No one except Toby would have got away with it. "Nothing *and* everything? You're not making sense."

Orlando chose that moment to sneeze explosively, and by explosively, I mean all over my face. Surprised by the force of it, he sat back suddenly on my chest, in awe of the baby snot plastered across my cheek. Toby snorted with laughter.

"Oh my, that's absolutely gross."

Swiftly, I handed him back to Toby, who swooped on Orlando's face with a wad of tissues, managing to make nose-wiping fun. Meanwhile, I swiped gingerly at the sticky goo on my cheek.

"Christ, I don't know how you do your job."

Orlando was the sweetest baby ever, but on this occasion, he'd only added to my general irritability.

Toby chuckled. "Because Orlando is adorable. And that sneeze was Orlandish for 'I agree with Toby that Noah is being idiotic'."

He was trying to be funny, to diffuse the situation, yet my annoyance skyrocketed. We needed to end this conversation now before I said something I'd regret. Outwardly, I remained calm, inwardly, I was boiling over. It was all right for Toby, with his cosy nest here at the big house and a slew of relatives down the road. He'd never failed at anything or let anyone down. He could make any decision he liked, even a really poor one, and the Rossingley safety net would always be here to pick up the pieces when everything went tits up. His family would still love him afterwards.

If a delightful baby hadn't been distracting him, perhaps my growing irritation might have been more obvious to Toby. Instead, he chatted on obliviously.

"I'm sure Marcel would gladly pay for the whole course upfront, but he knew you wouldn't accept, so he's offering you a loan instead."

He handed me a clean tissue—part of his job seemed to incorporate having an ever-ready supply of them. I snatched it from him ungraciously.

"He's right, I wouldn't have accepted. But I still don't understand his angle."

"Oh my God. Sneeze on him again, Orlando. He obviously didn't get the message the first time."

"Please don't." I kept my tone light. Cleared of snot and with renewed vigour, Orlando resumed his climbing. I had grown extremely fond of this baby, but right now, I wished more than anything he was with his daddy, who was going through paperwork in the library. The *library*, for fuck's sake.

"It is obviously a new concept to you, Noah. But this is how decent families work. They help one another. They look after one another. It's a good thing!"

"I don't have a bloody family!"

Startled at my raised voice, Orlando's usually merry features began to crumple. Immediately, Toby swept him off my belly and began soothing him and glaring at me. Unhappy whimpers turned to tears, and Toby's face hardened even more. I sat up, straightening my clothes.

"Sorry," I mumbled. "Sorry for shouting and swearing in front of him. I'll go. I'll get out of your hair."

Toby rocked and shushed Orlando in his arms, and the baby began to settle. "These tears aren't *entirely* your fault.

He's been grizzly all morning."

His tone said otherwise. I couldn't believe I'd fallen out with him, and so abruptly too. I wanted to stay and explain that he would never comprehend how I felt, how what he interpreted as a pleasant conversation pondering my future carried so much weight. How it was about so much more than a discussion regarding whether Marcel lent me some bloody money or not. How Toby's own opinion of me mattered, and that already, after only a few days of closeness, he'd exposed cracks in my tough façade and slipped through them. How easily mild upset switched to anger and resentment.

My eyes drifted around the lavish playroom, its ornate moulded ceiling, the plush furniture. How could he ever begin to understand when he had all this?

"You know what? Maybe you should go. We can continue this conversation later," he said stiffly. "I am working, after all. Orlando comes first."

With a loving parent's sixth sense, Jay poked his head around the door, and I hoped, for Toby's sake, he hadn't overheard us arguing. "I'm popping across to the dower house. I'll take Orlando with me if you like, Toby, and give you a break. Hopefully, the fresh air will help him sleep."

Toby leapt to his feet, Orlando snuffling in his arms. "I'm

happy to take him out if you have work to do. I was about to get the pushchair anyhow."

Jay came into the room and carefully took his son from Toby, planting a kiss on top of his curly mop of hair. Love and kindness oozed from the fucking walls of this place.

"Nah," Jay replied looking down at his son. "We're good. I was suffering a slow death by email. We'll go and spread our germs all over Uncle Freddie."

After he left, I expected Toby to make an excuse and disappear off somewhere too, but instead, he rounded on me. Seemed our argument had only just begun. He pointed in the direction Jay had gone.

"See? It's like I said. Jay's demonstrating it perfectly for you! Families look after one another. Marcel's trying to give you that, and you're being too stupid to see it."

"But Marcel's not my family. He scarcely knows me!"

Toby glared angrily and poked a finger at my chest. "I've got news for you, buddy. Yes, he is! He's married to your dad. And if my parents are anything to go by, happily married people usually share stuff, including money. What's mine is yours, and all that?"

"Don't call him my fucking dad."

"Why not?" snapped Toby. "Because that's what he is.

Whether you like it or not. Just get over yourself, Noah. He'd be a bloody good one, too, if you'd stop being such a dick and let him."

And there we had it. The sperm donor. The root of all my problems. "Not quite on a par with a vicar, though, is he?"

Toby slapped his head despairingly. "Jesus, Noah! Just bloody listen to yourself! He's. Your. Dad! You might not want to use that word, but that's what he is! He can't change the past, so he's doing everything he can fucking think of to make it up to you! So you can have a better future than he ever gave himself! And if you can't see that and won't just...just...allow these good people to give you a fucking leg up in life, then you're more bloody stupid than I thought."

I'd punched people for a lot less. Instead, I squeezed my fists into tight balls of fury, nails savagely digging into my palms as if hurting myself would stop me hurting Toby. He squared up to me anyhow, cheeks flaming and blue eyes flashing, a slip of a man, a flyweight who'd never hit anyone in his life. A pacifist. Yet still ballsy enough to tell me precisely what he thought and to hell with the consequences.

We eyed each other dangerously, and despite the rage surging through me, I couldn't bring myself to hit him. Perhaps because somewhere in my bewildered little soul, I knew his words made sense. A bigger man than me would apologise and accept he had a point, but I wasn't that man, so I continued being vile and gave a humourless laugh.

"Who the fuck do you think you are, Toby? Look at you—trotting off to college, having a nice little career, living in this fancy place, going home to mummy's for dinner a couple of times a week. You expect me to stand here and take advice from a guy whose biggest worry is deciding who's going to open the batting at the fucking village cricket match? You haven't got a fucking clue what real life feels like. Because it's all so bloody easy, isn't it?"

He studied me for a second longer as I spewed vitriol, our faces up close, so close we could have kissed. He had more pretty freckles sprinkling his cheeks and nose than I had brain cells, and they were likely a damn sight more useful.

As he stepped back, broadening the distance between us, a rueful hurt replaced the anger in his eyes.

"You're quite right," he said in a tight voice, lifting up his arm. "I know nothing about real life. Spot on, Noah. Well done."

His sleeve slipped back, revealing knobbly purple flesh, and he cast his gaze over it before throwing me a sad smile. "Yep, you're right. My life has been incredibly easy. So fucking easy."

Shit.

"You know what I mean. I meant..."

"Listen. The only thing standing between you and accepting the loan, accepting Guillaume, and accepting fucking *happiness*, is in here." He tapped on his temple as if emphasising each word. "Stupid. Stubborn. Pride. So go on, go and fucking throw it all away."

He shook his sleeve back down over his withered arm. "See if I care. And when you've done telling me how fucking easy I've had it, why don't you fuck off back to your miserable life somewhere else."

CHAPTER NINETEEN

TOBY

"DARLING, YOU'RE NOT yourself. We're worried about you."

Even though Noah and I hadn't known each other that long, a sense of having lost my best friend cloaked me. I desperately missed him. We might still be living under the same roof, but for all that I'd seen him since our argument, he might as well already have moved out.

"My mum and dad are too."

I'd thought Orlando and I were alone when Lucien collared me in the kitchen. Jay was at work, the twins at school, and Noah was hiding somewhere far away from me. I hadn't heard Lucien come home until he'd found me miserably ironing the twin's school uniforms, Orlando sleeping peacefully in his pushchair next to me. I switched off the iron, and Lucien ordered me to sit down, then produced tea and biscuits.

"Why don't you tell me what's gone wrong."

I'd kind of avoided Lucien—I'd avoided everyone, to be honest, which should have been easy in such a large house but was proving more of a challenge than I'd thought. The one person whom I should have struggled to avoid, because he slept in the room next door to mine, had become as elusive as the ghost of Lady Louisa. He hadn't packed his bags and buggered off yet, though, which was something.

"We had a row," I said glumly. "Our first argument, and I have a feeling it might be our last. I told him he should accept Marcel's offer and accept Guillaume too. To swallow his pride and seize the opportunity. But in much stronger terms. As you can see, it didn't go down too well."

I sighed heavily and rubbed my eyes. I'd not been sleeping properly since. "Sorry. It will be my fault if he disappears back up north and Guillaume never sees him again."

Lucien's arm snaked around my shoulder. "Nonsense. You're the only reason he's still here. He'd have upped sticks months ago if it weren't for you. We've been useless in comparison."

I wanted so much for that to be the truth. "Why can't he just accept everyone for who they are and what they're trying to do for him?"

My anger at Noah's stubbornness oscillated with a deep sadness that he'd never known what support from loving, good people felt like, and he was throwing it all away. A whole heap of guilt featured heavily, too, because waving my ugly, useless arm at him had been an inexcusable cheap trick. I couldn't bring myself to admit to Lucien I'd done that.

"I think," Lucien began slowly, "That we accept the love we believe we deserve. And unfortunately, Noah doesn't believe he deserves any."

He took a delicate sip of tea. Having been to work, he was dressed as conservative Dr Avery, and his less playful mood matched his attire. I rarely saw this serious persona at home, but today it suited my unhappiness and the quietness of the late afternoon.

"You know, I pushed absolutely everyone away after my family died," he remarked, taking another sip of tea. "I shut myself up in this vast ivory tower." He tipped his head towards the ceiling as if indicating the rest of the house. "Well, one tiny corner of it. Several times, I seriously contemplated killing myself."

I stared at him, startled, as he calmly put his mug down then wrapped his hands around it. He threw me a wan smile.

"It's true. I don't think even Freddie and Marcel, despite all their efforts to support me, understood how close I came. I felt horribly guilty, you see, that I'd been spared to live, when I wasn't half the person my brother Oliver, or my parents, were. In the year after their deaths, I didn't believe I deserved any love at all."

He swallowed, and his voice, which had started out firmly, faltered a little. "They were such generous, good, and kind people. To everyone. And I was an opinionated, annoying diva." He gave a brittle laugh. "I still am."

One of the slim hands which had been clasped around his mug moved to his throat, to where I knew his string of pearls lay tucked underneath his conservative work shirt. Slipping his elegant fingers between the buttons, he fondled them, almost without realising, and his gaze dropped to where his and Jay's beautiful baby serenely slept.

"And do you know, Toby," he continued, giving Orlando

the fondest of smiles. "Just when I felt I had no hope and absolutely nothing left, a boy came along. A very lovely boy, with gloriously broad shoulders and a heart big enough to carry two of us."

The hand around his pearls gripped a little tighter, the knuckles white. He swallowed again, almost painfully, and a single glittering tear trickled down his flawless pale cheek. I had a feeling Lucien hadn't allowed his emotions about that dreadful period to spill over for a very long time. Witnessing them was a privilege, and as he daintily wiped the tear away with his fingertips, he spoke again in a voice barely above a fluttery whisper.

"That boy—my wonderful husband— didn't see the cold, reserved Dr Avery that rejected everybody else's offers of support. He only saw a lonely man whom the world thought had everything, when, in truth, he had nothing. And Jay showed me that, together, there was a way through."

As he composed himself, I quietly pondered his words. Lucien Avery, the sixteenth earl. As tough as old boots. One hundred percent in control and with a solution for everything, benignly governing the estate and his household with an enviably smooth confidence. Making it all seem so easy. I guessed he hadn't always been that way, and I wished Noah could be here listening to him instead of me. Noah, who had convinced himself he had nothing when, if he only dared open his eyes and trust in us, he could have everything.

Orlando stirred in the ensuing silence as if reminding Lucien how far he'd travelled since those dark, dark days. As his eyes landed on his beloved Papa, a slow smile spread across his chubby face, accompanied by an adorably deep sigh of contentment. Lucien shook his head, blinked a few times, then tutted before attempting a bright smile back.

"Look at me, Orlando. Your silly papa. Like a maudlin old queen sobbing into his teacup. Your daddy would be horrified."

The no nonsense, sixteenth earl had returned. He stood and extracted Orlando carefully from his pushchair. Nuzzling him close, he breathed in the baby's deliciously warm biscuity scent. "I think, Toby, that it's about time Noah's father talked some sense into him, don't you? Just like Orlando's dear daddy talked some sense into me."

*

NOAH CONTINUED TO lay low over the next couple of days, but at least he hadn't vanished. He kept to himself, raiding the fridge whenever the kitchen was empty, putting in some extra shifts at the pub, and spending time in his room or wandering the estate alone. He missed cricket practice, leading to talk of the Second-Best Man being roped in at the last minute, not that anyone had yet dared to float that idea to Lucien. Noah remained polite to Lucien and Jay, by all accounts, but our cosy mornings in the kitchen, bouncing Orlando on his knee, were a thing of the past.

I wondered what he was waiting for. More money saved, perhaps, so he could afford to rent a room somewhere far away from Rossingley. Or perhaps he was hunting for a better paid job for the same reason. If so, he should stop feeling a stupid obligation to give Lucien half of everything he earned; Lucien had bunged the money in an old teapot to give back to him when he'd finally sorted himself out.

Lucien thought Noah was hanging around for an entirely different reason altogether. That he was waiting until he had the courage to face me or until he'd worked his problems through in his head. Jay, not one to normally proffer an opinion, agreed. Orlando missed him dreadfully.

After cricket practice, I trailed the rest of the team to the pub, knowing Noah wouldn't be working, not wanting to go but not wanting to be at home either.

Rob stood at the bar with a couple of friends. I hadn't

seen him around much since the tractor rally, which was no bad thing. His crowd were their usual selves as far as I could tell. They dominated one corner, spread themselves wide, and guffawed at one another's witticisms a little too loudly in the style of heterosexual young men in pubs up and down the country. Usually, I didn't let it get under my skin, but tonight every alpha roar set my nerves jangling. So I left early instead of hanging around for a lift back with Jay.

"Toby. Wait up."

A set of feet crunched on the gravel behind me. My heart quickened, hoping to turn and find Noah. Seeing Rob standing there was a disappointment. My God, how times had changed. What I'd have given a few months ago for Rob Langford to leave his mates and chase me out of the pub.

"We're over, Rob," I said, continuing to trudge up the hill. "Just to make it clear. So don't suggest anything." I made a brittle attempt to laugh. "Not that, you know, there was ever an 'us', but I'd hate you to suddenly have decided the time was right to declare undying love for me. You're too late. I'm no longer interested."

He walked alongside, and I lifted my gaze to see if any evidence remained of Noah's punch to his jaw. There wasn't; the bugger looked as fine as he ever had. And his good looks had no effect on me whatsoever.

He gestured to the drive. "Can I walk you home? And we'll talk on the way?"

I looked up and down the drive. From the way they'd been tucking into the beers, Jay and Reuben would be another hour yet. I could have pointed out that I didn't need walking home; I was a bloke and knew the area like the back of my hand, even without a torch. But he seemed to want to, and curiosity got the better of me. "Sure. But I'm warning you, don't start anything."

"Has this change of heart got anything to do with the new guy?"

It had everything to do with the new guy.

"Maybe. Or maybe I've realised I don't need to be used by you anymore."

"You used to beg me, Tobes."

We'd reached the part of the drive where it swelled and divided—one way to the dower house and the other way up to the imposing front entrance of the big house. I stopped walking, and so did Rob. He threw me a familiar look, one that used to guarantee I'd drop to my knees for him, and he made a move towards me.

"I said no, Rob. Not now, not ever again."

"Come on, you know you want to really." Ignoring me, his hand landed on my hip.

I threw him off, more violently than I ever had before. There was no room in my heart for a man like him anymore. I knew the real thing now, even if I'd only had a brief taste of it. "Fuck off. I said no."

Something in my expression stopped him because, unusually, he didn't persist. His hand withdrew. "Sorry, Tobes,"

"Thank you. Finally, you've got the message."

"So, not even a goodnight kiss?"

His voice was teasing, the threat over. I shook my head, rolling my eyes.

"No. Not even."

"Still friends though?" More teasing. And perhaps still hopeful I might change my mind.

"Yes, I suppose. Still friends. God knows why. And as long as you never try it on with me again." I paused. "Rob, you could...have you ever thought of, you know, finding someone and...accepting how you are?"

Thrusting his hands in his pockets, he stared at the gravel between our feet. I'd never had the nerve to broach the subject with him before, too enamoured of him maybe, too afraid of rocking the boat and losing my place in his limited affections.

"Yeah, I've thought of it."

"And?"

He lifted his head, and his narrowed blue eyes met mine. "And, yeah. Maybe."

We embraced, but not in a sexy way. More of a big brotherly hug, which was fine with me.

"That miserable sod behind the bar is lucky to have you," Rob said in a muffled voice as he squeezed me tight.

"Yeah, er...about that. Let's just say he's a work in progress."

"And he's got an impressive right hook."

I squeezed Rob back; if this was the last time I'd cop a feel of his solid body, I was going to make it a good one. Which reminded me of something. "I can't believe you've actually had your hands and your mouth all over Freddie Avery. You fucking jammy sod."

CHAPTER TWENTY

NOAH

DON'T MENTION IT. Don't mention it. Don't mention it.

"What the hell were you doing with him?"

Toby jumped a mile. Turning from hanging up his coat in the cloakroom, he found me waiting for him, arms folded and breathing fire.

He exhaled loudly and swore. "Christ, Noah. You frightened the life out of me."

"Are you back with him?" I demanded, just in case he

hadn't got it the first time.

He looked me up and down, his expression unreadable. "Hi, nice to see you too. Although I reckon headless Lady Louisa would have given me more of a welcome."

Okay, so I may have let my anxiety get the better of me. He brushed past, and I followed him down the dark passage and into the kitchen. I loved his busy, hip wiggling walk. It was as if he always had somewhere important to be. I loved the way he slowed it down, too, when he took Orlando out to say hello to the cows. There wasn't much I didn't love about him, to be honest.

Thankfully, we were alone. Lucien had disappeared up to his private sitting room hours ago, and Jay wasn't back yet.

"Of course I'm not with him," Toby said irritably. "He wanted to talk; that's all. Not that I have to justify myself to you."

"Does he need to have his big farmer's hands all over you to talk? Can't he talk to you on the phone, from, like, Antarctica? I'm a jealous fucker, remember?"

"Huh. Not so jealous that you haven't been keeping away from me for a week."

He picked up the kettle, walked over to the sink, and filled it with water. Seeing as he was avoiding eye contact, I addressed his narrow back.

"I had some thinking to do. About a lot of things."

"About buggering off again? Those sorts of things?"

"Yes," I conceded. "Amongst others."

He viciously flicked the switch on the kettle. "Take a proper coat with you this time. And a warm hat. It's still quite chilly at night."

I watched as he stretched up for a mug, then clattered around in the cutlery drawer with more force than strictly necessary to retrieve a teaspoon. I sucked in a deep breath.

"Look, Toby. I'm not very good at saying sorry. But I...I apologise."

There, I'd said it, and it hadn't been as hard as I'd imagined. He didn't need to know I'd been practising in front of the bathroom mirror all evening, swallowed pride in one hand and a desperate need to bury my face in his hair balanced in the other. Judging that had gone well, I pushed on with the second half.

"I'm sorry for the horrible words I said and implied. You haven't had things easy; I know that. Even though you make everything you do seem so...so...effortless." I hovered behind him as the kettle chuffed out a thin wisp of steam. His hand gripped the waiting mug tightly, his stump hidden up his sleeve.

"You're um...quite amazing. I think so anyhow."

Almost imperceptibly, his shoulders dropped, so I carried on, wanting more than anything to slide my arms around his narrow waist and feel the weight of him against me.

"So can we be friends again now?" I sounded like a small kid in a playground asking the bigger boys for his ball back. *Please say we are.*

The kettle came to the boil and switched itself off, although Toby made no move to pick it up. With a small shake of his head, he chuckled softly. "You're the second person to apologise to me tonight. And the second to ask me if we are still friends."

Finally, he turned to face me and leaned back against the worktop. With his arms folded defensively, he shook his head again in bemusement. "Although Rob didn't tell me I was amazing. I'm not, by the way, but I'll take it."

I took a step towards him. "Can you be, like, a bit friendlier with me than him? I...I'm going to need you more. I need to be first with you, not second."

That wasn't as hard as I thought it would be either. Before I became too carried away and put my foot in it, I leaned down, grabbed his face, and kissed him. The plush silk softly kissing me back was every bit as glorious as I remembered.

"You are first," he murmured around my insistent tongue. The band of tension wrapped around my head unwound a little. "There is no second. But this isn't going to magically change things. Problems aren't like electrical appliances. You can't just turn them on and off."

"I know." I swept my thumb along the angular line of his jaw. "But kissing you is smoothing the way."

Eventually, I pulled off him; he sounded like he was struggling to breathe. Holding him in my arms, I decided that in a minute, when I'd kissed him a bit more, I'd take him to bed. I'd bought some supplies on my last trip into Allenmouth and planned on making use of them. Up until now, we hadn't done much more than hands and mouths, but I knew what I wanted; Toby could fill me in on the practicalities. As I gazed down at him, his eyes searched mine.

"You need to let me help you, Noah. You need to let me inside. I can't help otherwise—none of us can—if you don't tell me what you're thinking. Or where we're all going wrong."

"You're not going wrong," I answered immediately. "I've got to...I've...I can't explain how I feel. I'm not like you, I'm not used to all these people..." I searched for the right word. "...caring about me, I guess. And I want to let them help, I want to trust them, I really do, but something stops me from just...giving in."

A familiar frustration washed over me. "As I said, I can't explain it very well."

On tip toe, he reached up, sliding his arms around my neck and into my hair, dragging my head down. Soft lips brushed against mine. "Try. I'm here for you. Just throw the words out, Noah—I'll put them together."

Oh, God. This boy. If he could handle me at my worst and still wanted me, then anything seemed possible.

Naturally, Jay chose that precise moment to come home from the pub. Too bound up in the fabulousness of the moment, neither of us heard or noticed him saunter into the kitchen. Not until he switched on the dazzling overhead lights.

"Jesus Christ, Noah! Put him down!"

Shitting hell. I sprang away from Toby as if I'd been electrocuted, and to the sound of Jay pissing himself laughing.

"Finally. You've made friends again!"

He grinned with delight, almost punching the air. "Thank fuck! No excuses not to turn up for cricket now, Noah. I can stand down Second-Best Man. You have no idea how much that will please my husband."

While I was dying of embarrassment, Toby chuckled and

raised his eyebrows. I swore this lot spoke in riddles.

"Are we talking pink-feather-boa level of pleased?" he asked.

Jay was already on his way to the stairs. "Oh, yes, most definitely." He winked at Toby. "Don't let the kids disturb us too early in the morning."

*

EVEN THE KNOWLEDGE that in another part of this vast house, Toby's employers were probably chortling happily at my expense didn't put me off my stride. I dragged Toby urgently by the hand along dark corridors that no longer held the power to terrify me until we reached my room and barrelled through the door. I faced him, standing in the middle of the floor, his hand still gripped in mine.

"I bloody love you, you know."

There. I'd said it. The other thing I'd wanted to say. I hadn't needed to practice this one; the words had been waiting for days on the tip of my tongue. Probably not the most romantic declaration, but it summed up my feelings exactly, so I was going to roll with it. I saved Toby from answering by capturing his perfect lips with my own again. We kissed where we stood, a two-headed mess of tangled limbs and tongues, our echoing breathy sighs turning to frustrated growls for more. As he ground against me, I obliged, almost ripping apart his jeans to release his beautiful cock, then sank to the floor.

"I bloody love doing this too."

I sucked him off as if devouring ice cream on a scorching hot day, lapping at the taste of his sex, where it oozed from his slit, licking up and greedily swallowing his bitter salt. Flattening my tongue, I swallowed him down, fucking his cock with my mouth, every perfect whimper and deepening thrust taking him closer to the edge. I couldn't get enough of his smell, burying my nose in the musky masculine scent of his pubes. When the first hot spray hit the back of my throat, I choked it down, and the next, and every fucking drop after that until I'd wrung him dry, and still I was parched for more.

Afterwards, flushed and relaxed, he looked so fucking perfect. And so fucking dressed. The jeans came off, his sweater followed. My own clothes joined his on the floor.

Still not enough. I needed more. More than hands and mouths. I needed my body inside him. An uncharacteristic wave of shyness rippled through me. What if he didn't want to? What if he wanted it the other way around? What if I buggered it up? Literally.

His hand had been resting on my hip, and it slid down towards my straining cock. He bit on his lip. "What do you want to do about this?"

Curling his palm around it, he gave me a firm rub, and I hissed with pleasure. *No more rubbing like that*, was my immediate response, not if I had designs on following through on plan A. In the end, Toby made it easy for me.

"Gay fuck?" His eyes sparkled, and my old friends, dimple one and dimple two, lit up his face. My cock liked the sound of that idea, too, and I gave the base a warning squeeze.

"Oh God, yes. I've bought some stuff. But I've never done it with a bloke before, so you'll have to lead the way." I flashed him a cocky grin. "Don't worry; I'm a quick learner."

Toby hesitated. "Erm...okay. But I've never done it either."

The violent screeching of brakes in my head was swiftly followed by a comedy U-turn. "What? But I thought...you... Rob...you..."

"No, never," he confirmed. "I've never liked anyone enough or been comfortable enough with someone that it was something I wanted to do. Including Rob and the grubby front seats of his Land Rover. You're the only man I've ever actually lain in a bed with."

So much for being shown the ropes. For a minute, we stared at each other like a right pair of chumps, him still with his hand on my rapidly wilting cock. He shivered; goose-bumps pebbled on his arms.

"And now?" I asked. "Are you sure? I mean, we could do something else; we've never..."

Closing the gap between us, Toby smoothed his hand and his left forearm down my back until both rested on my arse. Both felt equally lovely. "Of course, I'm sure. More than anything. Losing your virginity to a difficult, grumpy north-erner is, like, every gay boy's dream come true. I swear."

The cheeky dimples reappeared; my cock revived. *He'd never liked anyone or been in a comfortable enough relation-ship.* Until me. In one swift movement, accompanied by his squeal of shock, I lifted Toby off the floor and carried him to the bed. Seemed like I was going to have to take charge after all.

They could keep their massive stately homes with freez-ing cold bedrooms. When I had a place of my own, as long as it had a warm, comfy bed with Toby in it, I didn't care what the rest of the house looked like. Pulling the duvet over us, I settled between his legs.

"Better?"

He nodded. "I want it like this," he said. "Facing each other."

I wasn't entirely sure how to get the logistics of that right, but his wish was my command. I began with what I knew—kissing. I started at his mouth, providing a useful distraction from my fumbling with a bottle of lube. What the fuck was I supposed to be doing? Dousing us both in it, I guessed.

I moved from his mouth to his jaw and the scarcely-there stubble covering it. And then to the warm hollow behind his ear—I dipped my tongue into that, causing him to sigh and arch his hips. Or maybe my slick fingers were responsible for his sounds of pleasure and revived cock, perhaps because two of them had slid behind his balls and were at his hole, rubbing gently, pressing more firmly on the inviting bud, then teasing their way in. Another sigh, followed by his thighs falling open, begging for more. Then another roll of his hips onto my fingers. So fucking hot.

"You like that, babe?"

His breath landed in rapid steamy, wet puffs against my neck, quiet moans joining them with every stroke of my fingers. "God, yeah. Yeah."

I pulled the duvet aside, suddenly so much warmer, and looked down at him. His small pretty cock lay proudly on his belly, dripping wet. My wrist had disappeared behind his balls, my fingers hidden in a satin vice. Experimentally, I crooked them in the manner I liked doing to myself. Toby whimpered and thrust up; his stump, all self-consciousness forgotten, exposed on the pillow over his head. The fingers of his right hand dug into my bicep. Even fucking hotter. With every writhe of his hips and jerk of my wrist, the underside of my own cock, engorged, heavy and impatient, brushed against the crease of his thigh and belly. Any longer, and I might not last.

I chanced a glance up at Toby's beautifully flushed face, tilted back, his lush swollen lips belonging only to me, slightly parted. A sheen of sweat coated his brow. Fucking lovely.

With that brief assessment, I concluded I must be doing it right.

"Are you...can I...?"

"Yeah, fuck yeah. Now."

The condom—a familiar step successfully negotiated, then more lube, for him and for me. Which meant the time had come to slip my hands behind his slim thighs, splay him wider, and line myself up with his glistening hole, all ready and open. Bracing for a second, I shot him another glance, at the watercolour-blue of his eyes, now dilated black with need. I looked at his mouth, at his freckles, then once more because

I could, at his fucking joyful scores of freckles.

"I bloody love you so much," I whispered as my tip breached his entrance. At his sharp intake of breath, I paused and ran my hand soothingly down his thigh, my fingers tracing a path along the creamy flesh. His body tensed as I sank a little deeper, tantalisingly caught in a halfway house.

"Are you okay?"

He bit his lip; he winced, and we waited. I closed my eyes and pictured the intricate engine under the bonnet of Jay's Jag in an attempt to ignore the tightness circling my cock and the effect it was having on my balls. Something gave, Toby let out a breath he'd been holding, and his passage opened up around me.

"You sure?" I checked. "We could stop if you're not." *No fucking way could we stop.*

He nodded encouragingly as I inched closer.

"Fuck, Noah, it feels so good. I can't describe it. It hurts, and I'm burning up inside, but it feels so good." His eyes fluttered open, his watery gaze locked onto mine as both his arms came up, and his hand tangled in my hair, pulling me down to slant his mouth over mine.

"I love you, too, by the way," he murmured around our kiss, and I slid all the way in. "And that feels even better."

We were slow and clumsy at working out a rhythm, giggling softly that it took a while to find one, and not caring that we weren't very good. Just the doing was enough, and the knowing that more times would follow, better choreographed times, maybe times when we'd try it the other way around. The future was ours for the taking. Every amateur push and pull still carried me closer to the sun anyhow. To the core of him, his essence, his heat. I did my best to have every part of us touching—mouths, hips, bellies, hearts, my cock buried deep. His arms and legs wrapped around me as he clung on, and I licked and bit him as we fucked, claiming him as mine.

I came way too quickly—before I'd even worked out how to get my hand jerking him at the same time as shagging him, never mind the voice at the back of my head saying he should come first. As my cock hit his sweet spot, his undone cry of shock flung me hurtling towards the end, whether I wanted it or not. Chasing his release with a moan, even as I withdrew, he arched and tightened his whole body, restlessly grabbing my fingers to plug his now gaping hole, to fill that needy gap and rub that needy spot. He came seconds later, pumping his own cock, spraying my face, and painting stripes on his chest, my fingers still filling his hole, my love filling his heart.

CHAPTER TWENTY-ONE

TOBY

I FELL ASLEEP wanting to kiss Noah some more, and the feeling hadn't left when I woke late, pleasantly achy and wrapped in a duvet smelling of sex and us.

Unfortunately, I was alone.

A bolt of panic seized me. I briefly wondered if I'd dreamed the whole thing until Noah wandered back into the bedroom wearing nothing more than a white towel tied around his waist. It set off his skin tones and perfectly outlined his obvious erection. From his arrogant smirk and the sass in his walk, that was old news. OMG. How the hell had I found myself in possession of such a hot boyfriend?

As the towel dropped to the floor, his sinful dark gaze dropped to my mouth. I salivated. So did my dick.

"You're up early." Oh my God, that was the sort of joke my dad would come up with.

He shot me a grin anyhow and palmed his length a couple of times before diving under the covers and crawling up my body. "I've been up for ages."

Ooh, good. Looked like we were going to celebrate last night's sex by having sex again. Not sure I was quite up to the whole shebang just yet, but any time he felt like exploring my—

"I had things to do. Travel plans to sort."

He tweaked my nipple, laughed, and tweaked it again before treating it to a firm lick. *Travel plans.* I wriggled with discomfort, and he stopped. His previous sentence had negated his right to lick my nipples quite so freely.

"I went downstairs to give Lucien my rent money for the week, and to tell Jay I wouldn't be at cricket training. And then I needed to let Lizzie know I wouldn't be available from tomorrow night, and then I..."

I switched off, to be honest, not even feeling or caring

that his tongue and teeth were nibbling their way from one nipple to the other or that his fingers were snaking down to my groin. I'd lost interest. I'd be okay, I guessed. I mean, if he wanted to still see me, we could arrange to meet up. If he'd decided to find a room to rent in Allenmouth, then that might work for a while. But he said *travel plans*. No one made *travel plans* to go to Allenmouth. You just hopped on a bus and went. Bristol was a bit farther and had more rental options. More job and college options too. I had access to a car, so we could meet up when he was settled maybe, although not for an overnight stay. So that would be a couple of buses. Obviously, him going back up north would signal the end of things, but it could be worse, I supposed. At least Noah had proved that some guys didn't mind my...

"Are you even listening? Lucien said four or five days would be fine. He said you never take your holiday leave allowance anyhow. They'll juggle work around with the kids, and Jay's sister said..."

"Sorry, no, I missed that bit."

"And then I phoned the vicar."

"What the fuck?"

He pinched me hard on the fleshy part of my thigh. "You weren't listening, were you? I'm going to France. I heard what you said, even though it made me angry at the time, and I've given it some thought. I've decided I need to spend some time with Guillaume away from everybody else."

Oh, thank God. He wasn't leaving. A heavy sigh of relief whooshed out of me. Nipple sucking was back on.

"What's that got to do with my mum? Have you suddenly got religion? They're on the hunt for a new bell ringer since Alison-the-accountant moved back to London. Is she trying to persuade you to do that?"

"No. Just listen for a second. I'm going to France for a few days, and you're coming with me. I'm going to try to work things through with Guillaume. Like you told me to. It's all booked—flights to La Rochelle, time off work, everything."

I was going with him?

Now my mind raced for a whole slew of different reasons. I never thought of myself as disabled, handicapped, or differently abled, or whatever the correct term was these days. My own disability was relatively minor in comparison to many. Aside from struggling to find a sexual partner happy to overlook my ugly stump, which had proven slightly tricky among the feckless gay youth at college, most of the time, I totally forgot it singled me out as different at all.

That is, until I entered an airport. I hoped Hell had

reserved a special corner exclusively for the people who designed them. And I was one of the lucky ones. It wasn't as if I needed a wheelchair or learning aids or daily living assistants. I had two strong legs, good eyesight, and perfect hearing.

I ran through my mental airport torture checklist. I'd need luggage, but dragging along a suitcase was a big fat no. I'd nip home and dig out my old student rucksack. I'd pick up my passport from my parents' house, too, find a paperclip, and pin it open at the photo section, ready, so I didn't get flustered flipping through the sticky little pages one-handed while everyone tutted behind me in the queue. And I'd wear my ugly old parka with all the pockets so I could easily swap between producing my passport and showing my ticket. I say 'easily'. Someone at the check-in counter once remarked I was 'all fingers and thumbs', a joke which unsurprisingly landed like tumbleweed.

Would I have room for a second pair of shoes? I hated slip-on loafers—maybe it was the name that put me off, but to my mind, they were only one step from slippers designed for elderly people, or kids who hadn't yet mastered tying laces. And the last time I'd fumbled with that stupid, slippery, clanking seat buckle, the air steward had leaned across and snapped the ends together for me, without even asking, as if I was a fucking toddler.

"I wanted to ask your mum a few things first." Noah's voice butted into my thoughts. "She said you'd be anxious. You look anxious."

"What? I'm not anxious." *So fucking anxious.*

"About the travelling and the airport. Especially the airport."

I swore my mum could actually see inside people's heads sometimes.

Noah's lips landed on my cheek with an audible *mwah.* "You don't need to be anxious, you know. About anything at all. Because you'll be with me."

*

ONE OF THE upsides of having a half-French boyfriend was going to be the trips to visit his French father, because his hometown was very pretty. Plus, there was the kissing. An obligation that my half-French boyfriend took extremely seriously. He even kissed me on the plane! In front of, like, people!

He made the whole journey a doddle, to be honest. I don't know why I'd fussed so badly in the hours leading up to it. Basically, Noah ensured my only responsibility was to not lose my passport or phone. At the security scanner, an impatiently sighing guy in the queue behind us benefited from the full glare of Noah's fight-or-fuck expression, while I fumbled to remove my coat. Believe me, the fucking option of that menu most definitely wasn't on offer. And when he asked my permission before crouching to quickly tie my trainers on the other side of the X-ray machine, and then cupped my face in his hands and delivered a fat wet smacker on my lips before telling me *again* that he bloody loved me, well, I could have fucking died of happiness.

Anyhow, Marcel had treated us to a taxi, which dropped us off at the edge of a pedestrianised area near Saint-Martin port, slap bang next to an impressive stone edifice dominating the entrance to the old touristy part of town. The thing looked hundreds of years old; back in the day, it must have been some kind of defensive fortress. This afternoon, however, it served a stark reminder as to why we were here in the first place.

"That's the prison," said Noah needlessly.

Few holidaymakers guessed what lay behind the elaborately carved frontispiece of the citadel, nor at the end of the elegant esplanade. A harsh metal lookout post peeked from the top of one of the original battlements, easily mistaken for a weather monitoring device or some sort of telecommunications apparatus.

The weather had taken a turn for the better over the previous few days, bringing the early-season tourists out of hibernation. I counted around twenty or thirty of them dotted around the grassy park area surrounding the prison. Beyond, on the long sandy beach, dog walkers and joggers went about their day, making the most of the spring sunshine, which cast bright rays on the prison walls, transforming the cold grey stone to a honeycomb golden yellow. Grandparents looked on benignly as toddlers wore themselves out; young couples held hands and smiled at one another. The newly wed and the nearly dead was how my mum would have described the scene, folk escaping to the sun before the school holidays arrived. A toddler's squeal from the colourful play area cut through the sounds of light chatter as an ice-cream fell from her sticky grasp onto the ground. Her young dad hushed his offspring in a rapid burst of French, and I smiled inwardly, wondering how Lucien and Orlando were faring on their own all day.

"It's an amazing building." I gazed up at the sweeping expanse of ornate brickwork. A simple modern sign with the wording *Ministère de la Justice* graced a vast arched entrance-way, otherwise, I suspect the building looked exactly as it had done when it had been built three centuries ago.

"Probably not so swish on the inside," Noah remarked.

We both took a moment to study it before he spoke again.

"Could you imagine walking through that door, right now, and knowing you're not coming out again for at least another fifteen years?"

"God, no."

It was a sombre thought. "And all the time you were inside, you'd know that all this waited on the outside"—he gestured across the park— "and that the sea and the beach lay just a few feet away, but you weren't going to be allowed anywhere near it? Christ, I bet the inmates can see it from a lot of the windows." He took a deep breath in through his nose. "And can certainly smell it."

He picked up our small, shared suitcase—because that's what wonderful half-French boyfriends did, and we strolled towards the port, leaving the prison behind. Interspersed with typically French cafés, stylish boutique shops full of expensive fripperies lined the cobbled street. It was easy to understand why Lucien was so fond of the place; it whispered understated wealth in a way that other holiday destinations of the rich and famous flaunted their bling. Although he joined me in peering through windows and scoffing at the prices, Noah was mostly quiet.

"Are you nervous?" I asked.

We were approaching the marina. A picture-postcard stone archway curved between a cocktail bar and an antiques shop, framed in pink and yellow hollyhocks, and we stopped to admire it. An equally pretty cut-through path lay beyond, leading to a row of green-shuttered fisherman's cottages. Noah scratched his head and frowned, oblivious to our pretty surroundings.

"Yeah, a bit. I'm not sure exactly how I feel. I'm all over the place, to be honest. It's hard to explain."

I took his hand and gave it a squeeze. "Tell me about it?" I suggested. "As best you can?"

He huffed out a sigh and contemplated our joined hands before giving me a wry look. "Well. You'll be pleased to hear that I'm still angry. About all sorts of stuff. About Guillaume shagging a random tourist on the beach, for instance, taking advantage of his flash footballer status. And that such a quick thoughtless thing could ruin my mum's life when she was still a kid herself. Because of it, she resented me, so we've never really got on. I blame him for all of that. I'm angry, too, that he's got this label as a murderer, a label he'll always carry with him because it's true. He *is* a murderer. Even if the guy he murdered wasn't someone fit to be alive anyhow. And that I'll always know I'm the son of a man who murdered someone."

I nodded in what I hoped was a wise, encouraging manner. For a boy who couldn't explain himself very well, he was doing a comprehensive job. "That's...um...quite a lot of anger."

"I haven't finished yet."

His throat worked as he swallowed before starting again. "I have a huge chip on my shoulder about stuff."

"No shit."

"Mostly about the inequality and unfairness of things," he continued, with a glare through excessively thick eyelashes, a glare that had the effect of making me horny, not fearful. I bit my lip, suppressing a smirk.

"I hate that some kids, like Lucien's, will grow up never wanting for anything, but still have to deal with plenty of abuse for having two dads. That kids like me never had a dad at all. That you were born with your hand missing, and blokes like that farmer, Rob, and the guy at the airport think it's okay to give you grief for it. As if missing a hand on its own wasn't bad enough. That some people live in massive stately homes and have more money than they can ever spend, while others are out on the street at night just trying to stay alive."

He paused and huffed out a laugh. "I think you probably get the picture."

That was quite a lot to unpack all at once, too much for someone like me. Instead, I dragged him into the alley; a huge lump had appeared in my throat, and I might have cried otherwise. Not because I was sad, but because my grumpy northern lad had a soul so full of fucking goodness that I needed him to know right now. And if anyone saw us, two men kissing and hugging and clinging to each other in the middle of the street, then I didn't care. Mind you, this was France; emotional incontinence was positively encouraged. Anyone watching probably thought we were just work colleagues greeting each other after a lunch break spent apart.

"You've got me now, Noah. I can't help with much of that, but you don't need to shoulder it on your own any longer. You can share some of it with me."

"Good, because I couldn't do this—I couldn't be here without you."

I thought back to the airport and how easily and unthinkingly Noah heaved our bag into the overhead locker, then pretended he hadn't noticed how long it took me to click together the two ends of my seatbelt. "I couldn't do this without you either."

He smiled at me then, and not the difficult to interpret smile that sometimes preceded the fight-or-fuck look. Merely a relieved one, as if he'd stumbled through the front door like my mum did sometimes with too many bags of shopping and managed to offload a couple onto me.

"My mum always tells me not to worry too much about the things we can't change," I said because bringing one's mother into a tender romantic moment was always a good thing to do. I plunged on anyhow. "Acknowledge them, but then park them. And concentrate on the stuff you can change."

I scrolled back through his list. His relationship with Guillaume—he could work on that. Perhaps with his mum, too, although I had a feeling that was a fight for another day. My missing hand was a lost cause; he didn't need to be angry on my behalf about that, although knowing I had him in my corner, battling the starers and the whisperers and the damn fucking ignorant, was sexy as fuck.

Noah stroked his fingers through my hair. "That's solid advice. Is your mum, like, a vicar or something?"

"We could always try and find someone for you to talk things through with," I began hesitantly. Hesitantly because this conversation could go one of two ways. "You know, maybe a counsellor or someone?"

He picked up our bag again and planted a kiss on my nose. "Yes. You might be right. But I still hadn't quite finished. Because you'll also be pleased to hear that since I've been at Rossingley, I can now see the good too. Coming here to this island—seeing how beautiful it is and wanting to try to understand Guillaume better. I can see the good in Lucien and Jay and everyone else who has made me feel like I could belong somewhere. Like Lizzie behind the bar. I like drinking milk, so I can even see the good in the fucking cows. Not in that bloody bull though. But definitely in the cute manny looking at me as if I've grown three heads."

Chapter Twenty-Two

Noah

THE TALL IMPOSING house overlooking the far end of the port wasn't as austere as I recollected from the dank film of January. Warm afternoon sunshine dappled the grey bricks, rendering them several shades lighter. And as we mounted the wide steps, I decided Marcel was exactly the sort of person who deserved to have plant pots full to bursting either side of his front door. A riot of colourful geraniums had replaced the winter pansies. He deserved a lover who bought fresh yellow and red flowers for his desk too. The man himself flung wide the grass-green front door before I even had a chance to lift the heavy iron knocker.

"*Bonjour, bonjour! Entrez!*"

At Rossingley, it was easy to forget Marcel was French. Having been educated and spent time working in England, he spoke English flawlessly. Under his own roof however, he fully embraced his origins. Getting beyond the front door took around ten minutes, what with the kissing, the kissing, and, oh yeah, the kissing. Not to forget the inquisition about the flight, the taxi, the short walk across the port. He was dressed chaotically, like someone chairing a very important business meeting but also planning on a spot of weeding during the coffee break.

In summary, he was delighted to see us.

Guillaume, my father, was more reserved. He politely asked Toby if he'd ever visited the island before, trying to conceal his anxiety with a firm handshake. I recognised it in the way he slightly rocked on his heels, stealing quick glances over towards Marcel, as if for reassurance. His mannerisms matched my own. Determined to avoid a single awkward lull in conversation, Marcel ushered us upstairs.

"Come, I'll show you to your rooms; you can put that bag

down. Can you manage? Guillaume, carry it for Noah...no, he's managing...it's okay. The rooms are just up here...mind the turn...the step can catch you out...aah...here we are..."

Seemed we were all a little anxious. Breathlessly, Marcel paused at the top of the stairs, and Guillaume laid a gentle hand at the small of his back.

"Relax, *mon cœur*," he said. "There is no rush."

Nodding rapidly, Marcel answered him in French, a flush of colour rising to his pale cheeks. Guillaume gave a low chuckle and rolled his eyes. "My husband has prepared two rooms for you." He threw me an amused look. "I said you would probably only require one. They are the two at the end of that corridor."

He pointed. "But the choice is yours. The bathroom is opposite."

With his breathing back under control, Marcel added, "The yellow room has a lovely view of the port. The blue room is marginally bigger. And farther from...um...our room. Very...aah...private. And the bed is firmer."

The blue room it was, then. The only view I'd be admiring for the next few nights stood right next to me.

Marcel grew increasingly flustered. "But you can decide, and...yes...as Guillaume said. We...what I mean to say is don't let us being here...aah curtail your activities."

Heat radiated from Toby, and I didn't dare look any-where other than at the bedroom doors, as if the room in-structions had been terribly complicated. My father also bit his lip, clearly wrestling with a snort of laughter. For the rec-ord, I had no plans to curtail any of my activities, not where Toby was concerned.

"Marcel," said Guillaume gently. "Why don't we let the boys get settled?" He turned to me. "Come down when you're ready. Take your time; Marcel and I usually enjoy a little siesta around this hour anyhow."

"Oh my God." Toby laughed as he closed the door of the blue room behind us. "Marcel is cute beyond words."

I dumped the bag and wound my arms around his neck. As I reacquainted myself with Toby's mouth, I happened to agree. My father and I shared the same taste in quirky men; both Toby and Marcel needed a little protecting from life's harsh realities every now and again, a role my father and I were made for. Marcel's strength lay in his gentleness and his sweet naivety, and I saw that in Toby too. Miraculously, both of them saw the good in men like me and my father.

The centre piece of the room was an old-fashioned four-poster decorated with a faded embroidered eiderdown and topped with what looked like a single enormous pillow. Shaped like a fat sausage, it stretched from one side of the dark wood headboard to the other. Toby informed me it was called a bolster. Two square pillows lay on top of it. Layers of linen and woollen blankets made up the bedding. And then there was a throw too. Typical French, making everything complicated. I was reluctant to disturb it. A spindly ornate desk with about a thousand little drawers caught my eye. Much simpler.

"What are you smiling at?" Toby asked.

I looked down at my favourite person in the whole world and brushed my lips against his freckly forehead. "You. The *bolster*. That desk. Everything."

"If you'd lived in a stately home for as long as I have, you'd know that isn't a desk, it's an *escritoire*. No gentleman's residence is complete without one."

I kissed his forehead again and rubbed myself against him. "Fancy enjoying a siesta over the *escritoire*?"

*

WE ATE OUT that night. Whoever said cookery was the French national sport had not peeked inside Marcel and Guillaume's cupboards. Until Guillaume had moved in, Marcel had been so immersed in his own brilliant mind, he'd relied on his sister to provide most of his meals, or he forgot to eat altogether. But then, when you lived next door to a row of sophisticated bistro-style restaurants and had plenty of money, why cook?

We sat at an outside table under a heated lamp, amongst well-mannered, well-heeled tourists. Marcel and Guillaume, clearly regulars, did the kissy thing with the restaurant owner and chatted endlessly in French before ordering for all of us without glancing at the menu. Toby and I weren't fussy—we'd eat anything, and I'd never been anywhere even near as smart. As I was so obviously related to Guillaume, the owner shook my hand vigorously, then spouted a torrent of French. Guillaume looked on as if proudly presenting his Olympic medal-winning son and not...me. I knocked back my tiny glass of lager—seemed the French didn't serve pints—relieved when another one replaced it.

Marcel shared stories about Lucien that made my skin burn and Toby roll around with laughter. The one about a gap year trip to Morocco, that under no circumstances should we ever divulge to Jay, had my eyes popping out of their sockets. I wasn't sure I'd ever be able to look Lucien in the eye again.

Seemed Guillaume and I were both content to let our respective partners carry the evening; Guillaume ate quietly and steadily, letting his gaze fall fondly on his husband, much in the way I watched Toby, knowing he'd be back in my arms later. We would be hands and mouths only tonight. As much as I wanted more, we were new to this, and Toby needed to recover after our adventures over the *escritoire* this afternoon. I'd been deep inside him for only the second time, bent over a piece of antique furniture much less fragile than it pretended to be, even if all those little drawers had rattled like letterboxes with every gloriously urgent thrust. I'd announced the state of our relationship much more explicitly than rucking up the sheets on only one of the beds. This time, I'd held off until Toby had come first, with my hand around his shaft, my breath in his ear, and my cock buried.

With the subtlety of a brick, Marcel dragged Toby away after dessert. Taking his arm, he insisted they visit a splendid secondhand bookshop hidden down one of the side streets, to purchase a book he wanted us to take back for Lucien. We watched them disappear amongst the other evening strollers, taking not just themselves, but the free-flowing conversation too. Which obviously left me alone with my father, who, thankfully, immediately signalled for two drinks.

"Digestifs," he explained with a small smile. I'd never encountered a digestif in my life, but from its name, I guessed it was a sophisticated alcoholic equivalent of the mint imperials that came with the bill at my old local curry house back up north.

"*Pastis.* A Marseille speciality. Although in Marseille, some insist it should only ever be drunk as an aperitif." He shrugged in the loose French way. "*Tant pis.* I prefer it as a digestif. And I haven't been back to Marseille for many years."

Two tumblers were placed before us, containing an inch or so of dark-yellow liquid, not dissimilar to concentrated piss, along with a fresh jug of water. Now truly alone for the first time ever with my father, I became unaccountably nervy. Any alcohol would be welcome.

"My Marcel is one of a kind, *non?*"

"Yeah."

"He was very excited about you coming to stay with us."

"What about you?" I asked boldly. We might as well get down to it.

Guillaume considered his answer. "Hopeful that it would be better than your last visit."

Even the few hours since our arrival had already superseded that. He poured a hefty glug from the water jug into his digestif, and I watched with increasing fascination as the clear yellow liquid turned an innocuous milkshake white. He chuckled at my expression.

"Like a chemistry experiment, *non*? Marcel once explained the science of the molecules to me."

He lifted the tumbler to his lips and took a healthy swig. "I don't care about the molecules. It's the drink of kings."

"Oh fuck! That's fucking disgusting." I spat my first mouthful back into the glass, my English genes rebelling. On a scale of zero to ten, it ranked a solid fifteen, right up there with its reckless cousin, Campari, Lucien Avery's favourite tipple.

Warily, I sniffed the glass—a mix of aniseed, liquorice, and pungent herbs better suited to sprinkling on pizzas, not for mixing with enough alcohol to dissolve your tongue. Guillaume found my watering eyes and lunge for the water jug highly entertaining.

"Christ, I'm not French enough for a drink like that," I spluttered, so glad Toby hadn't been there to witness. Guillaume merely laughed again, more relaxed, and took another swallow as if battery acid was his drink of choice.

"When I was in there—" He jerked his head in the direction of the prison. The ramparts weren't visible over the roofs of the portside houses and restaurants, but there was no mistaking where he meant. "—I dreamed of this drink. My uncles and grandfather, my older cousins—all the men would sit around after dinner sharing a bottle of it. Long into the night. Drinking, gossiping, smoking, while us children ran around, playing. We have hot nights down there, in Marseille. Much hotter than here. Those were the nights I missed the most. And now—" He held up his glass with a sad smile, his dark eyes that mirrored my own, examining its contents. "—this drink reminds me of everything I lost. And at the same time, everything I now have."

He'd painted a pretty scene. I fleetingly imagined how different things might have been between us. How my life might have turned out if I'd grown up in the family he'd described.

"We walked past the prison on the way here," I offered.

"It's a handsome building, *non*?"

I nodded my agreement.

"Not on the inside."

I didn't offer the stock reply, "I can imagine," because I couldn't at all. I hated whenever anyone gave me that answer. I'd never walked in his shoes, just as he'd never stepped into mine. And just as I'd never walked in Toby's.

I studied him, totally at ease in the smart surroundings, dressed in his nice clothes. The geographical distance between the restaurant and the prison walls was around three hundred yards, the metaphorical gap immeasurable. A few women had studied him, too, I'd noticed, as we sat down, not that he'd ever have eyes for anyone other than Marcel. The softening of his mouth whenever he looked at his husband, his every word and every gesture, told me that.

"I had a very happy childhood," he continued. "No father in my house, like you, but a big family. Lots of uncles and cousins. My older cousin took me to football practice, and all the men in my family took it in turns to be in goal while I practiced free kicks until it became too dark to see the ball."

Guillaume ordered me another lager, then ordered himself a second pastis. We regarded each other warily. We could talk about his cousins, the island, and the price of bread and never be any closer than now, two acquaintances sharing drinks across a red-and-white chequered tablecloth. Or take the plunge; a better understanding of each other now might shift the direction of our lives forever. Who knew? One day, we could become like the old men he talked about on hot evenings in Marseille. That easy familiarity, that sense of belonging that he once had, lost, then rediscovered with Marcel.

That Toby had at Rossingley. That I'd sought when I'd set out, back in January, to track down my father, even if I hadn't realised at the time.

"But you haven't been back?"

He shook his head, swirling the liquid in his glass. "No." That French shrug again. "I'm not welcome. Maybe one day, who knows?"

"Don't you hate seeing the prison every day?" The question had bugged me since the first time I'd come to the island. If it had been me, I'd have wanted to run as far from it as possible and never return.

He shook his head. "No, I don't mind. Like this *pastis*, it reminds me of how far I've come. Of everything I now have. Like a son."

He grinned, almost boyishly. "And whenever I dare to disagree with him, Marcel points to its high walls and threatens he is going to have me locked up inside again."

We sat in silence for a minute or two. Guillaume settled the bill, and while he chatted with the waiter, I thought about my extended French family all going about their business, oblivious to my existence.

"Marcel is not going to pay for your college course," he said abruptly after the waiter left. "It is generous of him, but it isn't happening."

"Okay." Whatever. At least his change of heart took the conundrum out of my hands.

"Because I am paying for it. All of it, and you will not pay me back. A gift, not a loan. It will be my money we use, not Marcel's. And you will say yes."

"Er...what if I don't want you to?"

He laughed, then drained his glass. "I'm not asking you, Noah. I'm telling you. I could spend hours explaining how it is the minimum I can do after not being a parent during your childhood, or you can work that out for yourself."

"What, so you're using money to offload your guilt, is that it? Because if so, I'm not bloody interested."

I'd raised my voice and several diners turned to stare haughtily at the uncouth Englishman interrupting the sophisticated tranquillity of the restaurant. Frankly, they could fuck right off. Guillaume, however, appeared unperturbed.

"Marcel mentioned you might say that. Listen to me; I will explain."

He sipped his drink. "I had a lucky, happy childhood. And the beginning of a wonderful sporting career. Ruining the first half of my adult life was all on me, no one else is to blame."

"And? Your point is?"

He leaned forward in his chair and steepled his hands. Not in a threatening fashion exactly, more an invitation not to disagree with him. "You, Noah, are going to enjoy a version of my life, but in reverse. The bad part has already been and gone. Your difficult childhood happened—I'm sorry, but I can't turn back time. However, I can make sure the first half of your adult life is everything you would like it to be. And that is all we will say about it."

He stood and shouldered on his jacket. "Come. Marcel will think one of us will have lost their temper and thrown the other into the port if we don't get home soon."

Neither of us spoke on the short walk. Guillaume was a complex, complicated individual. Hardened, difficult perhaps. But not the man I'd thought he was when we first met. Contrite but not apologetic. Wise, but knew he didn't have all the answers. He was thrilled he had a son; I understood that now, but neither of us was naive enough to think we'd slip overnight into the easy familiarity of someone like Toby and his dad, for example. Because I could be fucking complicated and difficult too. Maybe one day, but for now, this was enough.

"Thank you," I said as he let us into the house. "For the

dinner and...for...for the other thing. And for inviting us here to stay."

"The first of many successful visits, I hope."

"I'd like that."

At the top of the stairs, Guillaume gave me a manly hug before parting ways. We were both a little tiddly, so it didn't feel too awkward. Almost natural. Maybe next time, we'd manage it sober.

Toby was already tucked up in bed, and I quickly stripped and climbed in, literally—I'd never been in a bed so high.

"I hope we don't fall out in the night," I observed, settling onto my back. "It's quite a drop."

Toby rolled on top of me, delightfully naked. I walked my hands down to his peachy arse, barely two handfuls, and he sighed contentedly. With my lips, I traced his nose, his eyelids, and each cheek, like the soppy lovesick fool I'd become.

"I love you."

"I know," he replied. "I'm exceedingly lovable. How did it go?"

"Really well. A good start." Which about summed it up.

"Did he ask you about the college course?"

I recalled the stubborn set of Guillaume's features and how I'd known immediately that disagreeing with him would have been pointless. Because it was like looking in a mirror. I grinned to myself. "No. He *told me* about the college course. I'm going, he's paying. End of chat."

"Wow." Toby chuckled. "As Lucien would say, *how virile.*"

I gave his arse a sharp pinch, and he squealed into my neck. "How was Marcel?"

"Oh my god. Himself. Sweet, charming, eccentric, and fucking embarrassing. If you look inside the drawer to your left, you will find that he's thoughtfully filled it with 'supplies'."

Snorting with laughter, I leaned across and opened the drawer. "Jesus! How much sex does he think we're gonna have?"

"Oh, that's nothing. It gets much worse," continued Toby. "He attempted the safe sex chat. With an enormous amount of mortification on both sides and a lot of stammering on his. Oh my God, I'd have taken a deep and meaningful discussion with a long-lost, ex-convict dad any day over that five minute of my life. I had a speech impediment myself by the end of it."

I rifled through the contents. "What do we do? There

are, like, fifty condoms in here! If we only use three or four, they'll be questioning our stamina. If we pretend we've used most of them, they'll think we're at it like fucking rabbits." A sudden thought struck me. "Do you think this is how much my dad would get through in an average weekend?"

"They'll have stopped using condoms years ago." He snuggled up to me. "Lucky for them."

"We could stop using them," I ventured. "I mean, only if you want to. We should get tested and stuff first, obviously. We could go together next week. There's a place next to the hospital in Allenmouth."

He lifted his head and gave me raised eyebrow.

"Yeah, so I might have googled it." I rifled through the drawer again. "But in the meantime, we need to pocket some of these, so they think we're near the rabbit end of the spectrum. I don't want my dad to think I can't keep up."

Yes, I was officially now competing with my dad. The guy had a few years on me, but I'd seen those women checking him out. He was an exceedingly good-looking man.

"God, I can't believe Marcel did that. It's kind of sweet, to be honest."

Toby sniggered into my armpit. "Welcome to having a set of caring parents, Noah. This is what they do. Just be grateful he hasn't got a photograph album of your childhood that he's waiting to show your first serious boyfriend. And yes, I did have a lazy eye when I was four that required a patch over it for six months. And no, it was not cute."

CHAPTER TWENTY-THREE

TOBY

"DO YOU THINK I should ask him before the cricket or after the cricket? Or even during the cricket? During match tea?"

Our few days on Île de Ré had passed in the blink of an eye, a whirl of meals, romantic strolls in the evening sunshine, cycle rides along the coastal path, and lots and lots of glorious sex. And that was just Marcel and Guillaume—Noah and I quite enjoyed ourselves too. Parting at the end had been a happy non-event seeing as we would be visiting again at the end of summer and then probably at Christmas too; Noah and his dad had many years to make up.

"Yes," I decided. "I'll ask him during match tea. I think that's the best idea, don't you?"

Orlando sucked noisily on his dummy, fathomless brown eyes regarding me impassively. I handed him a plastic pouch full of stale bread, which he clutched to his chest like a sack of gold bullion, then kicked his feet impatiently to remind me those ducks wouldn't feed themselves.

"Well, you're not much use," I fussed, tucking the cottonwool-soft pushchair blanket cosily around him. Lucien and his bloody Mongolian cashmere. "Maybe I'll ask him tomorrow when it's all over."

"Ask me what?"

A warm hand caressed the curve of my spine then slipped easily inside the back pocket of my jeans like it belonged there. I swore Orlando rolled his eyes. Since our trip to France, I'd been fairly sickeningly in love. Arthur and Eliza had begun making retching noises whenever Noah and I came within ten feet of each other, and even Jay confessed my doe eyes made him a little queasy. My mother had the family photo album poised on the coffee table and opened at photos of my christening for whenever I next invited him over.

"Um...nothing really."

"Tell me." Softly urging, his voice was a warm rustle of leaves against my ear. Noah had been sickeningly in love, too, since our return. I kind of liked this version of him, although the sultry grumpy version was pretty hot too.

"Orlando and I have had an idea," I began carefully as I clicked off the brake.

"He's gonna blame this on you, buddy." Noah laughed, ruffling Orlando's hair. He fell in alongside me on the way down towards the lake. "It must be bad."

"No," I said hastily. "It's not bad. Well, no, it's just...big."

"Okay. I'm ready."

"Um...you know how you've struggled to find anywhere decent to live?"

He nodded. Yesterday had been a depressing circuit of viewing spare rooms available for rent in Allenmouth. The good ones had already been snapped up or were out of Noah's budget; the rest remained vacant for reasons that became immediately obvious on entering the premises.

"Anyhow," I continued, quickly glancing up at him. My idea had come too soon, way too soon, but who knew when the next opportunity might arise?

"Orlando pointed out that the tiny cottage Reuben once

rented is currently empty. I know you wouldn't be able to afford the rent on your own because even though it's small and Lucien keeps rents low, it's still too much for you. But Orlando suggested that if we rented it together, then I could pay half, and actually, your half would be about the same amount as a room in Allenmouth, or maybe a bit more, so it would still be expensive, but we could share food bills and all the other bills, which would make things cheaper, and I have enough for the deposit even though you don't, and if you let me pay that, then that's a thing we could do, and I'd still be close to work, and sometimes I'd stay in the big house if Lucien and Jay were away, which would give you your own space, and it's furnished and there is a regular bus service to Allenmouth now, that stops really near the college, and you can get a season ticket which is cheaper than..."

He shushed me with a kiss. In front of Orlando, which broke all my rules. Orlando, however, had spied the bright green head of a mallard duck, so he wouldn't have noticed if all four Teletubbies *and* the hideous creepy baby with his face in the sun came dancing across the lawn. More importantly, the mallard had spied Orlando's bag of bread and given all his ducky friends the head's up.

Noah's teeth tugged gently on my bottom lip as he pulled

away. Swoon. His own lips quirked in amusement. "Did Orlando come up with that idea all on his own?"

"Yes, but I pointed out to him that maybe it was too soon, and you wouldn't want to live with me because, well, it is too soon, and also you might not want to be stuck in the countryside because it's a bit boring, and nothing much happens here, aside from cricket training and ferrets that eat pork scratchings and tractor rallies and growing cress on bathroom windowsills and..."

Noah swallowed my babbling in another heart-stopping kiss. "Not just a pretty face, is he?" Another tender kiss. "Neither are you. Does the cottage have a view of the cows?"

"No. It overlooks the stables."

"Is it haunted by a headless woman?"

"Not that I'm aware, no."

He planted a final lingering kiss on my mouth, carrying with it the promise of many, many more. "Then tell Orlando he's a genius. And I said yes."

EPILOGUE

LUCIEN, SIXTEENTH EARL OF ROSSINGLEY

"WHAT? GREATER THAN the Ashes? Lucien, are you seriously suggesting England versus Australia is *not* the most hotly contested rivalry in cricket? Because Wisden's Almanack, otherwise known as the cricketing bible, no less, begs to differ."

I harrumphed inelegantly. "Wisden's, Marcel, is penned each year by a grubby hack who has never set foot on the Rossingley estate. Darling, *this* is the greatest rivalry in the history of *any* sport. Not only cricket."

"And our trophy's bigger," chimed in Toby.

"Thank you, poppet." Finally, an ally. "As Toby knows all too well, and you should, too, size absolutely matters. The Rossingley trophy is practically visible from space, whereas the Ashes is a ghastly dull terracotta urn, no bigger than an *average* man's cock. Not that any of us have seen one of those for a while, have we, my darlings?"

Marcel rolled his eyes, Toby blushed madly, and Noah sank deeper into his deckchair, his face a delightfully pretty picture.

"And our contest boasts a longer history than the Ashes—the first recorded match was keenly fought in June 1839."

"Who won?" asked Marcel innocently. Honestly, why I considered him my best friend was utterly beyond me.

"You know damn well who won. The farmers were a virile and macho bunch even in those days. All that impeccable white linen, gosh, can you imagine? Utterly divine. But they shan't win today." I took a deep breath, filling my lungs with pure Rossingley air. "I have a gut instinct. And I always trust my gut instincts. You should too."

"Lucien, your gut can't even cope with full-fat milk—why on earth should I trust it to predict the outcome of a cricket match?"

Some things change, some stay the same. Back in 1839, sheep grazed the outfield most of the year round, and it wasn't until my great-great grandfather, in 1922, limited grazing to wintertime only, to keep the grass down. Then followed the thirteenth earl, who, after a hattrick of shocking defeats to the farmers, blamed his bad form with the bat on the pitch quality being so much poorer than the lawns at Eton and thus permanently sectioned off the ground, altogether, that was still in use today.

My father, and my grandfather before him, had loved to brag that it never rained on cricket match day as if the Duchamps-Averys could command the weather. I don't know if I believed them or not, but as Marcel, in his mathematical element, made himself comfy in the scorer's chair and I plonked myself next to him, we prepared to venture into bat under a blue sky as flawless as a bolt of mulberry silk. I invoked the royal 'we'—I personally had no intention of grass-stains coming anywhere near my burnt-sienna trouser suit.

"What the devil are you wearing today anyhow?" queried Marcel. "Have you been raiding the twin's dressing-up box again?"

Toby snorted.

"Marc Jacobs *leisurewear*, you poor philistines, from last year's collection. Jay says the colour accentuates and contrasts beautifully with my eyes, and the style highlights my youthful, boyish shape."

His actual words had been "Christ, Luce, your arse is bloody fantastic in that orange thingy," but Marcel certainly didn't need to know that.

"You look like Mr Tickle."

The young farmers trotted out onto the pitch and began lobbing the ball to one another. My estate team were, as usual, dressed in cream couture, while the farmers—men of all shapes and sizes—looked as if they had salvaged their kit from the school lost property bins. If that was intended to make us drop our guard, they would be sorely mistaken. Their rag-tag exterior hadn't fooled us for a minute.

The annual Rossingley cricket match fell on what should have been my brother Oliver's forty-second birthday. Not many people knew that—Jay did, of course, and Freddie would check up on me at some point. My Uncle Charlie, busy umpiring, probably remembered too. I used to hide myself away on the lead up to it, but I was much stronger these days. Oliver adored his cricket—he'd have even given Jay a run for his money—and so the whole village coming together was as good a way as any to remember him.

I liked to imagine he'd have approved of what I've done to the place. Not the chartreuse flock wallpaper in the dining room—he'd have loathed that, reminding me Rossingley was a six-hundred-year-old stately home, not a tart's boudoir. The scatter cushions, dotted with mini embroidered penises (masquerading as candles unless very closely inspected), he'd have scattered somewhere else, and my ridiculous collection of concrete elephants, collected from random trips to B&Q with Jay, would have been tossed into a skip years ago.

But I didn't mean the décor—that was just stuff. Filling the house with my rainbow family, however? Yes, he'd have wholeheartedly approved of that.

Gandalf and Uncle Charlie, dapper in their umpire's white coats, wandered over to check Marcel was ready to begin scoring. Which meant it was time to issue Uncle Charlie a stern warning.

"Darling, please see if you can refrain from pinching Gandalf's bottom between overs this year. Or at least not in front of the facing batsman; it tends to put them off."

Honestly, anyone would think those two had invented sex, the way they pawed each other. No need to question how they occupied their retirement days. By occupying each other as far as I could tell. Uncle Charlie chuckled heartily, a joyous sound I'd never have associated with him five or six years ago.

"Match day isn't just for you youngsters to gad about and enjoy yourselves, you know. I may be old, but I think you'll find there is still plenty of snap in my celery."

Marcel and I shuddered in unison, and Toby gasped audibly. Noah's head had dropped below the level of his shoulders.

"Goodness me, is that the time? Let the games begin, shall we?"

Winning the toss—a phrase which always brought to mind a delightful visual—the estate team elected to bat first. With Freddie and Jay opening, the rest of the team lined up in deckchairs and settled down for a spot of sunbathing. Noah and Toby shuffled along the line to keep Guillaume company and to escape our teasing. Joe passed around a tin of his sister's lemon drizzle cake; Reuben followed it up with Freddie's ornate silver hipflask of sloe gin, and my husband readied himself for the first ball of the match.

"Toby and Noah look very cosy waiting to go into bat," I remarked to Marcel. "Although that look Noah is giving Toby is positively *carnivorous*. Reminds me of a look someone else gives *you*."

Marcel glanced up and smiled at the two boys, who were lost in conversation with each other and oblivious to my husband's excellent opening shot to the boundary.

"If Noah's anything like his father when we first began dating, then I'm surprised Toby's mustered the strength to play cricket today," he remarked. "And Noah's twenty years younger. Sport would have been the last thing on my mind."

"Sport is always the last thing on your mind, darling."

Marcel chose to ignore me. "By now, my celery would be positively *limp.* I'd be sequestered in a darkened room with my testicles bathed in organic almond milk and with only the *Bloomberg Business Week* podcast for company."

I shuddered. "Gosh, Marcel, I didn't believe it possible for anyone to succeed in putting me off sex, but you and my uncle Charlie are having a damned good try. And may I say, that's quite a *specific* kink, darling. Oh, jolly good shot, Freddie. Bravo."

My eyes drifted from the cricket over to the shaded far side of the pitch. Jay's parents were earning their supper tonight by keeping a close eye on Eliza and Arthur, who were using their plastic cricket bats as swords, just as Oliver and I used to do. Perilously close to the battle zone, Orlando snoozed beatifically in his pushchair.

With my heart stuffed full of something almost too big to be labelled love, I turned my attention back to the remaining batsmen awaiting their turn. Then nudged Marcel to follow the direction of my gaze. Noah rested a hand briefly on Toby's knee as they laughed together over something.

"Aah." Marcel beamed. "The fiercely burning flame of young love. So sweet together, aren't they?"

"They are, yet they still have a way to go," I mused. "Noah can be awfully tricky, but on balance, I think they'll make it, don't you?"

"He's his father's son. Of course, he'll be tricky. But Toby's made of strong stuff. All the time Noah was busy making the same points over and over, and busy building the same wall, young Toby was busy knocking it down again. I think they'll be fine. Now, stop talking; you're messing up my score sheet. Was that the fifth or the sixth ball of the over? Sixth, and so Jay is facing again."

Gosh, my oldest friend almost sounded wise for a moment. Observing Toby and Noah made me feel decrepit, but fortunately, tracking my husband lope between the wickets, scoring yet another couple of runs, made me feel about eighteen. Jay was unconsciously beautiful loitering around the kitchen, drinking tea, and spoon-feeding Orlando, but in rumpled cricket whites, holding aloft his bat to acknowledge his half-century, he transcended sublime. With a blessed sigh of contentment, I crossed my legs so Marcel wouldn't notice—burnt sienna wasn't terribly forgiving.

"You're drooling, Lucien. From two orifices."

"No, I'm not! Just appreciating good line and length, darling; that's all."

Jay added a further couple of runs to the scoreboard, and then once more, it was Freddie's turn to face the bowler. The disadvantage of having an old Etonian in your team, particularly a wealthy and extremely handsome one, was that the opposing side relished the opportunity to take him down a peg or two.

"It's red, it's round, and you hit it, mate," hooted a farming outfielder after a nervy Freddie swung and missed the first ball of the new over. Rob Langford, one of his former paramours, bowled against him, not that that would make him go easier. At least Freddie hadn't gone out for a golden duck like last year, so we'd take that as a win. Hopefully now he'd got his eye in, he'd post a decent score.

"They're bullying him again," grumbled Marcel.

"They always bully him. And 'sledging', darling, is the cricketing term. You've been scoring matches for yonks;

surely, you know the lingo by now. Sledging makes it sound friendlier. And our Freddie can handle himself."

He certainly could. The *advantage* of having old Etonians on one's cricketing side was that they had been mercilessly bullied at school about absolutely anything that singled them out from the crowd, from having a too-new shiny trunk to a father in parliament. Which meant Freddie didn't give two hoots about a spot of sledging. Cool as a cucumber, the next ball, he tapped almost to the boundary. The one after that sailed straight over it, disappearing into the rough for six.

"Seeing as you know what the ball looks like, *mate*"—his cut-glass tones reached the ears of the spectators as he addressed his outfield tormentor— "you might like to go and join in the hunt for it."

And so the afternoon trundled pleasantly on. Oliver would have been in his element and joined in the sledging with the best of them, a tradition as old as the game of cricket itself. Freddie put in a respectable thirty-two runs, and Jay pushed his half-century up to seventy-six, finally getting out with an easy ball but setting them up with a decent target to chase.

"Ooh, look, Guillaume's turn to bat," Marcel remarked carelessly. "Now is the moment to make your third wicket comment—it's been an hour and a half already. You're slipping, Lucien."

"Maturing, darling, not slipping."

As a village outsider and French to boot, Guillaume could expect the farmers to verbally hammer him, and he wasn't disappointed. If they'd known his chequered history, they might have been a little more circumspect.

"Bowl a wheel of brie at him next time; he's got more chance of hitting it."

"Bowl him an accordion—let's see if he can play that."

Guillaume shut them up by knocking them about the park for a while before an easy catch in the slips had his son taking his place on the pitch. Joe and Lee followed each other in partnering Noah with a remarkably respectful forty between them. It was then Will and Toby's dad's turn, and once they were seen off, in a relatively straightforward fashion, only Toby remained.

"How cute is that? Toby striding out to partner your stepson."

"Aah, my stepson. I'll never become tired of hearing that word." Marcel jotted down Toby's name on the score sheet. Rather pointlessly, as even Toby himself joked he only ever made two runs—the one onto the pitch and the one off.

"Did you hear they're moving in together?" Marcel added excitedly. We both watched Toby adjust his helmet before striding out to the middle. Not even our arch-rivals would mock the efforts of a one-handed cricketer. In fact, they clapped him onto the pitch, the round of applause led by Rob, who maybe wasn't such a bad sort after all. Merely lacking the right man.

"Darling, I'm their landlord," I murmured as I joined in the clapping. "Of course I heard. I'm thrilled for them both. Ooh, look! Match teas are coming out."

International cricket has been described as baseball on Valium; village cricket was the same but with a hefty slug of food and drink thrown into the mix too. What other sporting competition paused for an hour at lunchtime for the players to indulge in afternoon tea and cake?

"We have some rather splendid sandwiches prepared for the farmers this year—egg and cress—all home grown on the estate. Eliza and Arthur have been frantic with excitement at sharing their carefully cultivated produce."

Marcel eyed me suspiciously. "Since when did you express an interest in sandwiches? And how does one grow an egg?"

"One's hens grow one's eggs, darling. Don't be so literal.

And we have an abundance of cress this year. A rather unusual variety. I'd hate it all to go to waste. Hopefully, the young farmers will stuff themselves with so many sandwiches it will make them rather sluggish for their own innings after tea."

"I wasn't aware egg and cress had that effect on a man," replied Marcel. "But I'm prepared to be proved wrong."

Marcel and I stood and applauded as the players walked off the pitch. And then he joined me in shedding a tear as Noah placed a solid arm around Toby and pressed his lips against his temple as if they were taking a stroll alone together through the estate, not declaring their happiness in front of the entire village. Noah had put in a respectable score; Toby had scored his usual duck and cared not a jot. When one was winning at life, who cared about a stupid game of cricket?

As long as we actually won that stupid game, naturally.

*

SUMMER EVENINGS AT this time of year stretched out for miles. Jay joined me on our usual bench to witness the finale of this memorable one. Behind us, in the ballroom of my ridiculously large house, the estate cricket team were raucously celebrating our triumphant win over the village, our first victory in far too long. My presence wouldn't be missed for an hour or so.

The Rossingley estate spread out before us, the land warmed and soporific after a day of unrelenting sunshine as if it had also enjoyed a splendid match tea and now desired nothing more than a soft pillow on which to lie down and rest.

My head found its usual comfy home in Jay's lap. He stroked an affectionate thumb across my brow, and a sun-blessed palm caressed my cheek before soft lips landed on mine, delivering the sweetest of kisses, each one as exquisite a joy as the very first. I dreamily gazed up at him. My darling Jay, my dear husband, my very, very best of men. The generous sweeping bow of his wide mouth, so familiar to me, curled into the most tender and most loving of smiles.

"We've done all right, haven't we, Luce?"

As the curtain of night dropped, the garden birds were always the last to fall silent. They were a talkative bunch. A bossy nuthatch usually insisted on having the last word unless the barn owls were on the prowl, softly reminding the others to exit the stage. Soon, Jay and I would also slip away to return to our children and guests. Boisterous celebrations would continue well into the night and well into next year too if the estate cricketers had anything to do with it. But for now, we stole a precious moment alone, and with an imaginary glass, I raised a silent toast. *This one is for you, dear brother.*

"Yes," I replied. I reached up for another kiss. "Yes, my darling. We most certainly have."

Acknowledgements

Thank you to so many of you who have read and enjoyed the Rossingley series, and I hope you enjoy this instalment just as much. In addition, I'd like to thank my publisher, NineStar Press, and above all, my editor, Elizabetta, for her endless patience and encouragement.

About Fearne Hill

Fearne Hill lives deep in the southern British countryside, a stone's throw away from the private country estate providing her inspiration for Rossingley. She looks after varying numbers of hens, a few tortoises, and a beautiful cocker spaniel.

When she is not overseeing her small menagerie, she enjoys writing contemporary romantic fiction. And when she is not doing either of those things, she works as an anaesthesiologist.

Email

fearne.hill@fearnehill.com

Facebook

www.facebook.com/fearne.hill.50

Facebook Group

Fearne Hill's House

www.facebook.com/groups/1172459269938382

Twitter

@FearneHill

Instagram

www.instagram.com/fearnehill_author

OTHER NINESTAR BOOKS BY THIS AUTHOR

The Last of the Moussakas

Rossingley Series

To Hold a Hidden Pearl

To Catch a Fallen Leaf

To Take a Quiet Breath

To Melt a Frozen Heart

Connect with NineStar Press

WWW.NINESTARPRESS.COM

WWW.FACEBOOK.COM/NINESTARPRESS

WWW.FACEBOOK.COM/GROUPS/NINESTARNICHE

WWW.TWITTER.COM/NINESTARPRESS

WWW.INSTAGRAM.COM/NINESTARPRESS

Printed in Great Britain
by Amazon

22460001R00219